of cou...
in English.
she actually pu... ...ded a job in Amazon.com's Books edit...al department. She spent over five years reading for a living before retiring to concentrate on her own stories. Stefanie currently resides with her family in Seattle. You can find out more about Stefanie and her books at www.stefaniesloane.com and www.facebook.com/stefaniesloane, or by following her on Twitter @stefaniesloane.

Praise for Stefanie Sloane and her intoxicating novels:

'Smart, sensuous, and sparkling with wit' Julia Quinn

'Sloane cements her reputation with a powerfully emotional, sexually charged story that will keep you up all night' *Romantic Times*

'Stefanie Sloane writes utterly delectable and seductive Regency romance!' Teresa Medeiros

'Captivating . . . With her fresh, original voice, Stefanie Sloane will charm her way into readers' hearts' Susan Wiggs, *New York Times* bestselling author

'Fabulous . . . everything readers of Regency romance crave' Amanda Quick, *New York Times* bestselling author

'Perfect blend of tender romance and heart stopping adventure!' *Fresh Fiction*

By Stefanie Sloane

STEFANIE SLOANE

The Devil in Disguise

headline
ETERNAL

Published by arrangement with Ballantine Books,
an imprint of The Random House Publishing Group,
a division of Random House LLC.

First published in paperback in Great Britain in 2015
by HEADLINE ETERNAL
An imprint of HEADLINE PUBLISHING GROUP

1

Cataloguing in Publication Data is available from the British Library

ISBN 978 1 4722 2845 1

Offset in Sabon by Avon DataSet Ltd, Bidford-on-Avon, Warwickshire

Printed and bound by CPI Group (UK) Ltd, Croydon, CR0 4YY

Headline's policy is to use papers that are natural, renewable and
recyclable products and made from wood grown in well-managed forests and
other controlled sources. The logging and manufacturing processes are expected
to conform to the environmental regulations of the country of origin.

HEADLINE PUBLISHING GROUP
An Hachette UK Company
338 Euston Road
London NW1 3BH

www.headlineeternal.com
www.headline.co.uk
www.hachette.co.uk

For my mom, Lois Faye Dyer.
I never would have managed to finish this book—
any book, honestly—without your belief that I could.
You are amazing, selfless, strong, and true.
In short, you're my hero.

Lady Lucinda Grey had not precisely decided what she would do if the overly eager Matthew Redding, Lord Cuthbert, compared her eyes to the Aegean Sea. Or the most brilliant of sapphires. It had all been said before and—Lucinda admitted with a stab of regret—in much more creative ways than poor Lord Cuthbert could ever dare dream.

"I shall faint, I believe," she said succinctly, straightening the Alençon lace fichu neatly tucked into her jonquil gown.

Lord Cuthbert stopped ogling Lucinda's bosom abruptly, a look of confusion clouding his round face. "I beg your pardon?"

Lucinda realized her earnest suitor clearly felt he'd reached the point in his seduction where she should have been dizzy with anticipation and too caught up in the moment to speak.

"Lord Cuthbert, I do apologize," she offered, taking advantage of the moment to discreetly reclaim her hand from his damp gloved grasp. She slid to the end of the settee, putting two feet of gold damask cushion between them. "Pray continue."

Lucinda felt compelled to see this thing through, despite the temptation to feign what would surely be a spectacular fainting spell. Lord Cuthbert's fumbling attempt at romance was, she realized, not unlike happening upon a carriage accident; be it concern or distasteful fascination, one simply could not look away.

Nor faint away, she acknowledged with a frustrated sigh.

Over the last few weeks, Lucinda had acquired far more experience with this sort of thing than she could have ever imagined or wished to endure. The endless parade of suitors who had found themselves on her doorstep this season had been uninspiring, to say the least.

This was all her dear friend Amelia's fault, of course, Lucinda reflected as Lord Cuthbert droned on. If Amelia hadn't married the Earl of Northrop last year and if the couple had not displayed a love so wide and vast that those observing wondered if they might very well be lost forever . . . well, Lucinda would not be in this predicament.

A fellow ape leader for the last several seasons, Amelia had, until the altogether unexpected appearance of the earl, been a staunch supporter of a woman's right to peace. And quiet. And sanity. In other terms, a woman's right *not* to marry.

"If only Lord Northrop had not worn Amelia down," Lucinda muttered under her breath, causing not even the slightest pause from the windbag before her.

Lord Cuthbert was completely absorbed in his rehearsed speech, which left her free to return to her contemplation of the events that had led to his presence in her parlor.

Discreetly counting the winged cherubs that inhabited the plaster ceiling in force, Lucinda begrudgingly admitted that Lord Northrup had not precisely worn Amelia down. Not exactly. That was to say, not at all. On the day the two met it was as if the heavens echoed with the cries of angels—and Cupid himself nearly collapsed from the joy of uniting such a pair.

Uncharitable and unkind, Lucinda mentally chided herself. She adored Amelia as though she were her own sister. To be unhappy over her newfound marital bliss would be inexcusable. And in all honesty, Lucinda *was* pleased for her friend. It was just that they had both been so convinced that love was a ruse, invented to keep the poets out of trouble. And now one had only to look upon Amelia and her new husband to know that they'd been utterly wrong.

But the real difficulty was that—London being London—Amelia's blissful state meant that the entirety of polite society assumed Lucinda would follow suit and be felled by love as well.

Frankly, Lucinda found the whole thing somewhat alarming.

And Amelia was no help. Utterly smitten and convinced Lucinda should share her happiness, she had done nothing to defend her friend and dispel the ton's false assumption. On the contrary, she'd worked feverishly to provide every opportunity for Lucinda to achieve an equally sublime level of bliss. And after countless prospects, all of which had been met with what could be politely called mild disappointment on Lucinda's part, Amelia had grown desperate.

Which was how Lucinda had arrived at this moment with Lord Cuthbert, forced by good manners to endure his declaration of undying affection.

Cuthbert's patting of his mud brown hair into place pulled Lucinda from her thoughts. Clearing his throat with theatrical emphasis, he continued his attempts at poetic flattery. "Lady Lucinda, your eyes are, to be sure, the bluest of blues that I've ever encountered. Truly, without a doubt."

She stared at him. She did not know what to say.

He blinked. "Quite blue. Really, truly very blue."

And in that moment, Lucinda realized that there was only so much a lady of reasonable intelligence could be expected to endure.

"My lord," she began, rising from the settee and smoothing the fine lawn skirt of her morning gown, "I fear our time together is at an end."

Cuthbert practically jumped from his seat. He stepped clumsily toward Lucinda, stopping mere inches from her. "Lady Lucinda, are you well?"

It was just the cue she needed. She'd faced much worse from importunate suitors over the last three weeks and hadn't a doubt her dramatic flair would serve her well in this instance. "I seem to . . . that is to say . . ." She hesitated, swaying ever so slightly while raising her hand to her temple. "I must retire. Immediately, if not sooner."

Cuthbert seemed to take this latest development as an opportunity, moving to stand unbearably close. He placed his hand at the small of her back. "My dear lady, you must tell me what you need and I will fetch it at once."

He was determinedly solicitous; Lucinda had to commend him for that. She was going to have to skip to the coup de grâce.

"Lord Cuthbert," she said, pausing to give what she hoped was a convulsive swallow. "I feel obligated to inform you that I fear I shall cast up my accounts at any moment. And I would so hate to ruin your extremely unique puce waistcoat."

Cuthbert nearly shoved Lucinda to the settee in his eagerness to escape the baptism. He bounded across the room to reach a small armchair where Lucinda's maid, Mary, was seated. "Attend to your mistress," he barked. "At once."

"My lady," Mary said quickly, shaking herself from

what clearly had been a pleasant daydream and standing.

Lucinda bit back a smile and focused her gaze on Cuthbert. "Thank you, my lord, you're most kind."

Clearly his fondness for the puce brocade far outweighed his affection for Lucinda. He backed quickly toward the doorway. "Of course, of course. I'll call again at a more convenient time."

Lucinda's butler, Stanford, appeared with such alacrity it was apparent he'd been waiting just outside in the hall.

"My lord," the stony-faced butler intoned, his emotionless gaze focused on the gilded mirror just beyond Cuthbert's large head.

Lord Cuthbert bowed before falling into step behind Stanford.

Mary closed the door quietly.

"He was the worst by far. What on earth could Amelia have been thinking?" Lucinda said, exasperation clear in her voice as she stood.

"That you've refused every eligible man in London under the age of seventy?" Mary answered, her years of service to Lucinda evident in her impertinent answer.

Lucinda laughed, Mary's blunt observance easing the annoyance of the last half hour.

"I do believe Lord Mayborn is actually three-and-seventy." Lucinda said. "And I highly doubt I've made the acquaintance of 'every eligible man' in the entire city. Surely there are at least one or two more for Amelia to proffer up in her quest for my everlasting happiness."

"I've heard Lord Thorp's son is available," Mary answered, peering into the now silent hall before holding the door wide for Lucinda.

Amused, Lucinda arched an eyebrow at her maid's too

innocent expression. "I prefer my men properly attired, which does not include apron strings. And while I do like a good challenge," she added dryly as she crossed the threshold, "I fear the twenty-year gap in our ages would prove to be an obstacle even I could not overcome.

"Hmph," Mary said with unshakable calm as she followed her mistress out of the room. "You've no romance in you, Lady Lucinda. Not at all."

"Well, when it comes to infants, I'd have to agree with you," Lucinda answered over her shoulder as she walked toward the staircase.

Mary hmphed again. "Don't play coy with me, miss."

Lucinda stifled a grin at Mary's curt tone. "Oh, Mary. It's just not true and you know it."

"Really, now?" the servant answered, the sarcasm somewhat lost in her rough Liverpool accent.

Lucinda mounted the carpeted stairs. "*Really,*" she confirmed. And it was the truth. She believed in romance as it pertained to the likes of Antony and Cleopatra, Henry VIII and Anne Boleyn, Arthur and Guinevere, Amelia and John—though the tragic ending of all but her dear friend's relationship were unsettling, to say the least.

I really must remember to mention this to Amelia, she mentally took note, reaching out to skim the smooth marble balustrade.

The point was, romance was all well and good for others. It simply was not for Lucinda. She did not need a man to make her life complete. Nor did she particularly want one; the emotional upheaval and mercurial behavior that seemed to accompany love was something that she neither understood nor desired.

"I'll have to take your word for it, I suppose," Mary answered unconvincingly, then gestured for her lady to continue up the stairs, swatting at her derriere when she did so and eliciting a hoot of laughter from Lucinda.

William Randall, the Duke of Clairemont, bent to nip his mistress's breast and licked upward to the vulnerable spot where her pulse pounded at the base of her throat. The woman beneath him twisted, panting, her lush curves slick with sweat where their bodies pressed and slid, bare skin against bare skin.

"Harder, Will." The throaty gasp was half plea, half demand. "Now."

He could see it in her eyes—the heady mixture of heat, passion, and urgent need that told him that a woman was about to come. Never one to deny a lady, he thrust deeply, ruthlessly holding back his own rising need for release.

"Your Grace. If you please . . ."

"No need to be so polite, Beatrice," Will muttered before he realized she hadn't spoken. He bit off a curse and went still, looking over his shoulder.

The ducal bedchamber was cast in gloom, the heavy silken curtains drawn against the afternoon sunshine. Nevertheless, Will instantly recognized his valet's stiffly erect figure, standing just inside the closed door. "What is it, Smithers?"

Lady Beatrice Winn's fingers tightened on Will's forearms, her body stiffening beneath his, and he glanced down at her. Her eyes widened with alarm, chasing away the raging passion of only seconds earlier. Will soothed her concern with a brief, hard kiss. "If you'll excuse me for one moment," he began, lifting off of her, "I'll deliver the sound thrashing that most certainly is in order and return to continue our . . ." he paused, dropping his bare feet to the floor and standing, "discussion of charitable endeavors."

Beatrice discreetly pulled the sheet up to her shoulders, her mouth sulky with frustration. "Think nothing of it, Your Grace. My charity can wait—though do keep in mind that the longer one is kept waiting, the more needy one becomes."

He fully understood Beatrice's warning. She'd proven to be well nigh insatiable in past encounters. "Not to worry. Try to remember where we left off, won't you?"

Satisfied that she was as comfortable as a mistress might be when interrupted by her lover's servant, Will reached for his dressing gown and shrugged into it with quick jerks. He roughly knotted the silk tie and turned to his valet. "Smithers, you have my full attention for precisely two minutes. Shall we?"

Will stalked from the room, waiting until Smithers joined him in the hall and pulled the door closed behind them. "Bloody hell, man, do you have any idea how near I was—"

Smithers quickly gestured toward the stairs. "Lord Carmichael awaits you in your study, Your Grace."

For precisely three seconds, Will held himself silent. And then: "Again you prove yourself unimpeachable, Smithers."

Will quickened his pace and descended the steps two at a time. "Though you could work on your timing, man. One, two minutes, perhaps, could have been spent in quiet contemplation outside my door, if you understand me?"

"Of course, Your Grace, though Lord Carmichael led me to believe his business with you is of some importance," Smithers replied from several lengths behind. "Might I bring you a coat, or perhaps breeches?"

Will couldn't help but grin at Smithers's undying devotion to propriety, even after many years in his employ. "Not necessary, Smithers. But see to Beatrice. Some tea, perhaps?"

"Of course, Your Grace," Smithers said instantly.

Barefooted, Will strode down the hall on the second floor and turned left into his study, slamming the heavy wooden door behind him. Much to his frustration, the sound failed to elicit even the slightest arching of an eyebrow from the man sitting behind his desk.

"You really should have taken Smithers up on the breeches, Clairemont," Henry Prescott, Viscount Carmichael, said dryly, his eyes never straying from Will's.

Damnation, the man can't be surprised. Will sat down and carefully arranged his dressing gown. "Come now, Carmichael. Clothing can be an impediment in certain situations. If I had known to expect you, then perhaps other arrangements could have been made."

"It's three o'clock in the afternoon. Surely 'other arrangements' could have, and should have, been made with regard to your games above-stairs. Won't her husband wonder where she's gone off to?"

Will returned Carmichael's halfhearted reproach with a smile. "You know very well Winn is likely as not foxed by now. And even if he wasn't, he couldn't care less about Beatrice. Which is why she's the ideal woman for me. I really should be thanking the fellow, come to think of it."

Carmichael quirked a brow and said nothing, which Will found highly annoying. "Are we done making comment upon my personal exploits?"

Carmichael looked as if he might smile. "Quite."

"Excellent." Will shifted his position, careful to keep a hand on the disobedient gown. "Now, old man, tell me, are you here on Corinthian business or were you simply anxious to see me?"

Will was a member of the Young Corinthians, a clandestine spy organization that operated deep within the British government. Carmichael led the elite force with an iron fist, managing the many lords in service with skilled precision.

Carmichael smiled at the reference to his age, no more

than half a dozen years separating the two. "Very well, on to business." He stood, his wiry frame taking little time to unfold. "We've received intelligence from several reliable resources in France regarding a kidnapping plot about to be put in play."

"And the target?" Will leaned forward, instantly focused on the threat, their conversation about his mistress forgotten. "Princess Caroline, perhaps?"

"No," Carmichael answered as he started to pace. "No, the goal is money, but this time the target is a wealthy young woman. More specifically, the wealthiest woman in England."

Will frowned as he began a mental check of who that might be. Despite his own family's social significance, he paid little attention to such things, and identifying the chit presented a challenge. "You'll have to give me a clue, here, old man. I'm afraid my years spent cultivating a rake's reputation have hardly left me on intimate terms with the ton's wealthiest debutantes."

"Lady Lucinda Grey," Carmichael answered, stopping just in front of the mullioned window. "Daughter of the late Earl of Sinclair. Of course, the title now belongs to a great uncle. But Lady Lucinda inherited a fortune in unentailed property from her father. Not to mention a town house and other bits and baubles from her mother."

Will let out a low whistle of appreciation.

"Do you know her?" Carmichael inquired.

Will relaxed into his chair, stretching his long legs out in front of him and crossing them at the ankles while still managing to remain decently covered by the gown. "Lady Lucinda Grey? Only by reputation. Good Lord, from what I've heard of her, the kidnappers should be fearful. Beautiful, charming, and intelligent enough to deny thousands of men the honor of her hand for nearly a decade. Lady Lucinda will have her captors enthralled in no time."

"Perhaps. But I'm afraid we can't count on her charms and ability alone," Carmichael began. "Fortunately for our purposes, she's apparently looking for a husband this season."

Carmichael paused, and he looked at Will as if he ought to know what the hell he was talking about.

"This is where you come in," he finally added.

Will straightened and tried to look into Carmichael's face. But the old man was standing with his back to the window, and his face had been cast into shadow, making it difficult to read his expression.

Will cleared his throat and began carefully, choosing each word with the same precision he reserved for his work. "I'm not sure I understand, especially in light of our conversation a few moments ago. I've spent years cultivating a reputation guaranteed to make the ton believe I'm an irredeemable rake. It's been an excellent cover. I'm the last man anyone would believe to be looking for a wife, never mind the richest, most sought-after woman in all of England."

"Your reputation is an impediment in this instance, I'll admit. But you are, after all, the best actor among all the Corinthians, are you not?"

Will leaned a bit to the right but, much to his frustration, still couldn't see Carmichael's face clearly. "Flattery will get you nowhere, old man. Besides, why not hedge your bets and use someone who actually has a prayer of breathing the same air as Lady Lucinda? Talbot or Wharton would be perfect. They're such, such . . ." He waved a hand, searching for the appropriate term.

"'Gentlemen' is the word I believe you're looking for."

Will shifted to the left but still could not see Carmichael well. "Yes, gentlemen, or in other words, men who would be allowed within ten paces of the woman. Unless it is your intention to terrify the chit.

One look at me and she'd succumb to a fit of the vapors."

"Oh, but you have something that no other man in England has," Carmichael said with calm conviction. "And it's something she desperately wants."

Will stood and walked to the fireplace, where he leaned his forearm on the mantel. "What could I possibly have that Lady Lucinda Grey would desire?"

He had a clear view of Carmichael now and easily read the satisfaction on the man's face.

"King Solomon's Mine."

Will was confused. "Why would the richest woman in all of England want my horse? She could buy a stableful of champions."

Carmichael moved around the desk to stand in front of Will. "King Solomon's Mine, as you well know, was bred in Oxfordshire on the Whytham estate, which borders Lady Lucinda's Bampton Manor."

"But why would a woman want a horse merely because he was bred next door?"

"You know women. They're softhearted creatures with minds of steel. And once those minds are made up . . . well," Carmichael shrugged, "there's little that can be done to change them. Our intelligence tells us Lady Lucinda was present at King Solomon's Mine's birth and she spent much time thereafter with him. Apparently, she developed a fondness for the colt and considered him her special project. That is, until you won him."

Will had a brief, swift flash of memory. The look of sheer disbelief on Whytham's face when he realized he'd lost the son of Triton's Tyranny had made it a truly unforgettable hand of cards.

"That's all well and good, but what does my owning the horse have to do with Lady Lucinda allowing me into her company?"

"Rumor has it she enjoys a challenge," Carmichael answered. He glanced at his engraved watch and frowned before abruptly tucking it back into his waist-coat pocket. "You're a resourceful man. I'm sure you'll think of something."

Carmichael's tone worried Will. He'd known the man too long to be fooled by his seemingly casual words. "Surely you don't expect me to offer her Sol in a wager of some sort?" He didn't add he'd rather lose a limb than the stallion. The comment would only serve to confirm Carmichael's suspicion that Will had a much softer heart than he would ever admit.

"As I said, you're a resourceful young man."

Will would have pressed further, but the look on Carmichael's face stopped him cold. "There's something you're not telling me. Come now, old man, what is it?"

"It's Garenne."

Will froze. "What do you mean?"

"He's involved."

"No." Will shook his head, refusing to believe it. "That's impossible. He's dead. I saw the body with my own eyes." The night the Corinthians had taken the French assassin down on a nondescript Parisian street was seared into his memory. The organization had breathed a collective sigh of relief with the death of Garenne.

Carmichael cleared his throat. "What was it you called him—the Chameleon?"

"He had a gift for disguises, that much is true," Will said brusquely. "But the man's size, his clothing . . ." He wanted to convince Carmichael, wanted to convince himself. "We received intelligence. It guaranteed that we had the right man."

"We've confirmed sightings of him in Paris," Carmichael said quietly. "And two recent killings of Corinthians involved his calling card."

Will felt his stomach roil at the thought of Garenne's signature. The sadist left each of his victims with a fanciful letter "G" carved into his left breast, the knife strokes revealing the victim's heart, exposed by the crude cuttings of a madman.

Will flexed his hands before curling them into fists, slamming one and then the other onto the polished top of the massive oak desk.

"He's rumored to be working for Fouché," Carmichael added.

"Napoleon must be trying to stick his bloody fingers in every pie on the Continent," Will said tersely.

"I'm afraid keeping up with Joseph Fouché's political loyalties is an exhausting task indeed," Carmichael answered. "No, it seems the man now supports the House of Bourbon. They'll stop at nothing to secure control of the Continent—perhaps England as well."

Will looked up at Carmichael, whose brows were knit together in concern. "I suppose you've a starting point for me, then?" he said, carefully resuming his air of insouciance.

Carmichael took a pasteboard card from his breast pocket. "I suggest turning yourself over to Smithers. The Mansfield ball is this evening and we've confirmed that Lady Lucinda will be in attendance." He offered the invitation to Will and walked to the door, pausing to look back. A wry smile tilted his mouth as his gaze flicked to Will's bare toes and back up to his face. "A shave might be in order. She likes her suitors properly turned out. And breeches. Do not forget the breeches."

Will moved to the window and looked out at the garden. The sight of hyacinths, pansies, and a whole host of other flowers that he could not name did little to soothe the growing doubts in his mind. Corinthian business was never a neat and tidy affair. Subterfuge demanded an often skewed view of right and wrong—something that had heretofore suited Will's less-than-traditional view of life.

It's not as if I've never lied to a woman before, he thought as he turned from the window and rested his shoulder against the heavy velvet curtain. It wasn't something he was proud of, but to live as he did and to be an effective agent for Carmichael often made the truth more dangerous than any lie ever could be.

No, it wasn't the lie that bothered him, but perhaps the intent. To court a woman for the entire ton to see— Will paused mid-thought, nearly shuddering as he steadied himself before crossing to his desk. For a man to engage in a series of activities with the believed goal to be matrimony . . . Well, that was a different animal altogether.

Carmichael had spoken the truth when he reminded Will of his expert acting skills. He picked up a cut-crystal paperweight and addressed it in Hamlet-like fashion. "The woman doesn't stand a chance."

Will knew it. Carmichael knew it. The only individual involved in their scheme who was ignorant of this fact would be Lady Lucinda.

Gently replacing the weight to its proper place, Will straightened his dressing gown and reknotted the silk sash. Could he win the heart of an honorable woman? Could he do so with the knowledge that he would, in the end, break it?

Of course he could. A man in his position couldn't afford a conscience. Why his conscience had chosen this particular moment to come to life, he didn't know.

In truth, to leave the woman to the likes of Garenne

was unthinkable. He'd rather slit his own throat than allow the madman another chance to kill.

"Bloody hell," Will swore, padding across the thick Turkish rug with a newfound resolution. "It's the horse that has me worried," he said to no one in particular as he opened the door. "He really is a fine horse."

2

"Bloody hell, Carmichael."

Will eyed the elegantly dressed throng from his coach window. The crowd ebbed and flowed, moving at an imperceptible pace toward the Mansfield mansion. Traffic slowed to a crawl and then a halt. Horses whinnied and stamped, gentlemen offered their arms to twittering ladies, who—if the overheard snippets of their inane conversations were any indication—had lost their heads over the excitement of the evening ahead.

"And I'm not even in the door yet," he grumbled, pressing his weight against the carriage door and releasing the latch.

His footman leapt down from the back of the coach and scrambled to hold the door. He gave Will a quizzical look. "I beg your pardon, Your Grace?"

Will straightened his coat and took a deep breath. "Nothing, Hugh. Nothing at all."

Stepping over a steaming pile of horse dung, he crossed the street and joined the crowd. Almost at once he felt the stares. Then came the whispers, and after that, the urgent conversations clearly concerning him. The crowd parted before him, too stunned to utter a greeting.

"I am apparently Moses," he said under his breath, thinking it was a damned shame he hadn't been able to precede his visit with locusts and flies.

He would, however, draw the line at the death of the firstborn sons. Even he had standards.

With cynical amusement, he made his way into the foyer, eyeing the cluster of ladies and gentlemen climbing the wide marble stairs. With each moment the din from the ballroom seemed to grow in volume, and his annoyance peaked again. Carmichael knew full well what Will thought of polite society—and what they thought of him. His reputation as a hot-tempered man with little interest in propriety was well established. It had served his cover well, as it had his personal life, if he was completely honest. No one bothered to look beneath his gruff exterior, a fact Will acknowledged with both satisfaction and an occasional, but rare, twinge of regret.

And if tonight he actually convinced the fashionable set of his sincere desire to take his rightful place in their midst, what then?

He'd have to live with the ton's smugly satisfied belief that he'd acquiesced to his dead father's wishes and returned, tail between his legs, to assume the mantle of familial responsibility.

Realizing fortification was in order, he abruptly stopped a footman scurrying past with a tray of empty punch cups. "Brandy. Now. I'll wait there." He pointed at the anteroom opening off the foyer.

The young man promptly jumped to the task, tipping the tray as he went, the sound of clanking cups punctuating his progress.

Will had just enough time to enter the room and prop himself against the cream damask wall before the footman returned. He drank the brandy in one swallow and returned the glass to the tray with a decisive click.

"Thank you, my good man."

The liveried servant bowed and departed.

Savoring the slow burn as the brandy snaked its way

to his belly, Will forced himself up the stairs and reached the receiving line.

Lord Mansfield, a portly man whose circumference nearly matched his height, smiled broadly and offered his hand. "Clairemont, welcome. It's been some time since I've had the pleasure of lightening your pockets at Brooks," he said with a wink.

"If memory serves, Mansfield," Will drawled, "I believe I won the last time we played a hand."

"Indeed," Mansfield chuckled wryly.

"Your Grace," Lady Mansfield interrupted, nearly elbowing her husband aside as she inserted herself into the conversation. "You honor us with your presence," she gushed.

"Lady Mansfield." Will inclined his head in an appropriate ducal acknowledgment. "Thank you for your gracious invitation."

"Oh, but no, Your Grace, it is we who are honored that you have joined us this evening," she answered, offering her hand and curtsying to Will before shooting a look of elated satisfaction at the nearby members of the ton.

"Clairemont, my wife, Lady Mansfield." Lord Mansfield met Will's gaze in silent apology. "Priscilla," he muttered, turning to the woman while carefully avoiding the exuberant lavender plumage protruding from her purple turban. "Do behave."

Will tamped down his initial urge, which was to silence her with a cold stare. He thought better of it—for both Mansfield's sake and his own. If ever there was a moment to establish himself as a changed man, this was it.

He took Lady Mansfield's plump, bejeweled fingers in his hand and bowed perfunctorily. "My pleasure, I assure you. In truth, I've been absent far too long from an assembly such as—"

She gripped his hand and gave him a sympathetic look. "Yes, yes, far too long, my dear boy. Why, only last month I happened upon Her Grace while in Bath. She is such a dear woman, your mother. And when I asked after you in passing, I must say that she hastily skirted the subject, offering very little information." She paused for effect, raising an eyebrow at Will and leaning in to murmur conspiratorially, "It was clear she worries after you."

Will froze, hating that he had to remind himself he was playing a part. Hell, hating that he *was* playing a part.

The woman interrupts you when speaking, calls you "dear boy" as though she were your doting aunt from Aberdeen, and has the audacity to assume she knows the private thoughts of your mother. Dear God, he thought, *she's a walking trial by fire. Live through this introduction and the remainder of the evening will be a breeze.*

What was it Carmichael was constantly prattling on about, he wondered? Ah, yes, counting. Count to ten and breathe. Will began his slow ascent to the double digits, his chest expanding and contracting in time.

"Yes, well," he said, finding his equilibrium somewhere around thirteen. Smoothly, he pulled his hand from her fingers. "My mother is an exemplary parent." Will's voice held only a hint of sarcasm as he nodded and stepped back, determined to extricate himself from Lady Mansfield's too sympathetic clutches and make his way into the ballroom.

Laying a restraining hand on his arm, Lady Mansfield began, "Oh, my dear boy, you can be assured that I'll convey your words to her upon our very next meeting and I'm certain . . ."

"My dear, let the poor man go." Lord Mansfield pulled his wife to his side, removing her hand from

Will's sleeve and clearing his way to escape. "Save me a spot at the faro table, will you?" he asked Will.

Will gave Mansfield a look of thanks and nodded. "A glutton for punishment, I see. Just as well," he continued, smoothly stepping out of Lady Mansfield's reach. "I always enjoy a sound thrashing at the card table—not mine, of course."

He heard Mansfield chuckle behind him as the crowd cleared a path for him. He moved toward the ballroom, the din growing louder as he neared, then paused in the doorway.

The noise hit him first, exaggerated and grating, bits of laughter and feigned interest, colorful gossip and tart reproaches all competing against one another.

The heat was next. The combination of hundreds of candles and even more swirling and animated bodies left little fresh air beneath the glittering chandeliers. The sights were as he had remembered from every other ball he'd attended as a younger man, newly on the town. Jewel-toned dresses interspersed throughout the milder tones of pinks, yellows, and blues. Blondes and brunettes, milky-skinned misses and eager young bucks, aged dowagers and graying lords, some dancing, others conversing, while the wallflowers lined the periphery, valiantly trying not to look desperate.

It was all a gigantic waste of time, as far as he was concerned: too loud to converse on anything of meaning, too hot to do more than wish your clothes were off, and too polite. Far too polite. These people knew nothing of real fun. Wild, free, unadulterated fun was more to Will's liking and often included far more fights and much more drinking. Thank God he'd had the foresight to stop the footman earlier.

"You're glowering."

Years of training meant Will was not caught off guard by the whispered statement just to the left and behind him. "And how would you know, Northrop, considering your inability at the moment to view anything but my posterior?"

John Fitzharding, the Earl of Northrop, came around to stand by Will's side. "I don't need to see your face. It's written all over theirs." He motioned to the crowd beyond, many of whom, judging from their looks of anxious surprise, had taken note of Will's unexpected presence.

"It's your fault, you know. I couldn't possibly come off as anything but terrifying standing next to you." Will raked his friend with an assessing stare. The difference between the two was stark. Will knew his tall, broad frame was all hard angles and rugged features, with coal black hair and deep hazel eyes. He was the dark Devil to Northrop's leaner body, angelic golden hair, blue eyes, and gentlemanly appearance.

They'd joined the Young Corinthians around the same time, becoming fast friends despite being different in practically every way. Northrop's calm-and-collected nature complemented Will's wilder tendencies—a fact that had saved Will on more than one occasion in those early years.

"It's more than your muscles and famously short temper that fascinates them," Northrop said, just a hint of amused sarcasm accompanying his smile. "They don't know why you're here. And not knowing something is unacceptable to this set. Knowledge is power, after all."

Will met Northrop's half grin with his own. "Bloody hell, can't a man go looking for a bit of entertainment without the entire world wondering what he's up to?"

"Is that it, then?" Northrop asked, one eyebrow lifting in patent disbelief. "You're here for a bit of entertainment?"

Corinthian law forbade discussing a case with fellow members who weren't directly involved. It kept things less complicated. And while Northrop might hint at his suspicions over the reason for Will's appearance, Will could not, would not, reveal his true purpose.

"More than simply entertainment, I suppose," he began. "If you must know," he said, adopting the role of liar as easily as he would throw back his brandy, "my mother has finally succeeded in making me consider the future. It's time I found a wife."

Will watched Northrop take the information in, knowing full well he'd not be able to tell if his friend believed him. As one of the most valuable members of the Corinthians, Northrop would, of course, expertly mask his true thoughts.

The man merely adjusted a cuff. "Well, it's about bloody time we made a gentleman out of you."

Did Northrop believe him? Will couldn't let the thought linger. Besides, it didn't matter much either way. Northrop would help when Will asked, without questions. Slipping a finger between his cravat and neck, Will feigned discomfort. "Let's not get ahead of ourselves. First, the lady. Any suggestions?"

The two looked about the room, Will with one particular woman in mind. He immediately spotted Lady Northrop, John's wife and reputedly Lady Lucinda's inseparable companion. A circle of men surrounded Lady Northrop; she stood next to another woman who was partially hidden from Will's view by the group. The men appeared to be enthralled by the lady's every word, Will noticed with some cynicism.

"Let's see. There's Madeline Haywood," Northrop began. "Her intellect rivals that of a sack of potatoes, but she's fairly attractive."

The group around Lady Northrop shifted, allowing Will a clearer view of the woman at the center.

Bloody hell. Lady Lucinda Grey was beautiful. Not just pleasing. Not just pretty. Beautiful.

Will felt heat rising from his belly to his chest. A mass of honeyed yellow curls artfully framed her face—and *that face*. The bluest eyes Will had ever seen shone like, well, he wasn't quite sure, not being poetically inclined, but even from his distant vantage point the brilliance of them could not be denied. Her lips, slightly pink, delicately shifted from question to statement and back again, surely hypnotizing the lot of fools around her.

Don't look down, man. Whatever you do, do not look any farther.

But his eyes seemed to act of their own accord. His gaze lowered from her pert, ridiculously charming chin, and he found himself in forbidden territory. The creamy, milk white expanse of skin that showed above her pale pink evening attire begged to be caressed. As for what came next, even Will felt embarrassed over his reaction. The lady's breasts were, in a word, perfection. Nicely rounded and set high, they appeared to be the ideal size for Will's hands. His palms itched to feel the weight of them.

"If you prefer a touch more intelligence," Northrop said, clearly unaware of Will's distraction, "perhaps Honoria Willett. She's the one in blue, next to her man-of-war-sized and exceptionally opinionated mother, Lady Dandridge." Northrop paused for just a moment, then added, "Come to think of it, I fear your newly reformed temper may not be ready for Lady Dandridge. What do you think?"

Will couldn't respond. If anyone had told him before tonight that he'd be dumbstruck at the mere sight of a woman, he would have ridiculed them as lackwits.

"Clairemont?" Northrop said. "Clairemont? Are you quite all right?"

Will pulled his gaze from Lady Lucinda and attempted to focus on his friend. "What was that about ships?"

"Keep up, man." Northrop frowned, his sharp gaze

searching Will's face. "Your title and wealth aside, the truth is, you scare the hell out of most men, never mind these naïve misses. You'll need your wits about you to accomplish the task at hand." He looked to the crowd and back. "Now, back to Madeline—"

"And Lady Lucinda Grey. Do I frighten her?"

Northrop looked into Will's eyes more sternly. "You can't be serious. Lady Lucinda Grey? Will, she's not . . . that is to say—"

"The richest woman in all of England. Prim, proper, intelligent, and notoriously particular when it comes to men?" Will interrupted, returning Northrop's look with a seriousness all his own.

"Yes," Northrop countered, lowering his voice before continuing. "But that's not the point, Clairemont. She's a particular friend of Amelia's and because of this I've had the opportunity to further my acquaintance with her. She's a lovely woman. Yes, she's prim and proper and quick-witted. But beyond that, she's loyal and kind and—"

"You sound as though you're describing a favored dog, Northrop. Come now, why, exactly, are you concerned over my possible interest in this woman?" Will pressed, growing slightly irritated.

Northrop blew out a breath and broke his gaze, looking instead at his wife, standing next to Lady Lucinda. "Listen. This is a woman who has refused every eligible bachelor in England. I'm only trying to save you a wasted effort."

"Will you present me or not?" Will asked, his tone and directness telling Northrop what he couldn't put into words.

Northrop flinched slightly, a sign he had some understanding that this touched on Corinthian business. "All right, then, but, Clairemont," he said, placing his hand on Will's shoulder, "have a care, won't you?"

"Have all the rumors about me finally convinced you of my black heart, then?"

"You know I don't give a deuce about what people say. I trust you. It's Lady Lucinda I'm concerned for. She'll not recognize the game you're playing. You're too good at it."

"I need an introduction," Will said simply.

Northrop closed his eyes for a fraction of a second longer than was normal. "I don't want to see her come to harm. However dire the consequences of your assignment, in the end she'll not understand."

Will's eyes met his friend's. "If you do not wish for her to come to harm," he said softly, "you'll make the introduction."

It was the closest he'd ever come to divulging Corinthian business. But Northrop's concern and obvious affection for his wife's friend deserved something more from the situation.

Northrop dropped his arm to his side and motioned Will to follow him across the ballroom.

Will felt the eyes of the entire room on him as he walked toward the women. *Am I that monstrous?* he wondered, nearly tempted to curl his lips and growl at the whole lot. As his father before him, and as far back as anyone cared to remember, the Clairemont men had always possessed a remarkable resemblance to one another. Of course, he'd failed to inherit his father's cold countenance, having been born instead with the McClaine family temper, or so his mother had always told him.

No matter how hard he'd tried to please his father by pretending to be more like him, he always fell short.

Until one day when his father delivered a particularly vile set-down. Will had been only ten, but something in his father's tone and demeanor made him understand full well that the duke loathed not only his son's temperament, but everything else about him.

Northrop made his way to his wife's side and pressed a light kiss to her cheek. "Lady Northrop, have I told you how lovely you look tonight?"

"Only twice in the last hour," she answered, her violet eyes filled with amusement.

The gaggle of young men acknowledged Northrop's presence with brief nods before returning their full attention to Lady Lucinda, who stood transfixed by something behind them.

Confused, all of them turned, then flinched in unison upon seeing the duke.

"Gentlemen," he said, giving each an intense look of warning before returning his gaze to Lady Lucinda.

Mumbling various and assorted excuses, the men hastily said their good-byes to the ladies before scattering to the four corners of the room.

Will stepped closer to the trio and waited for Northrop to make the introduction. He couldn't take his eyes off Lady Lucinda. The low buzz and whirr of the room all but stopped for Will as he recovered his poise.

"Your Grace, it's been some time since we've had the pleasure of conversing," Lady Northrop said.

It took a moment for Will's addled brain to resume functioning. He looked at Lady Northrop, noticing too late the hint of confusion playing across her features.

Snap out of it, man.

"Lady Northrop, it's been far too long," Will replied, even though he knew full well that, for Lady Northrop, it hadn't been long enough. She'd never been unkind to him, but it had been clear from the beginning of Northrop's courtship she'd been less than ecstatic over her husband's friendship with him. He couldn't blame her. Really, what upstanding young wife would look to encourage her husband in spending time with a reprobate?

He bowed over Lady Northrop's hand, catching sight of Lady Lucinda's curious look as he did so. She smiled at being caught and a dimple flashed at the corner of her mouth. *For the love of all that's holy,* he thought with bemusement, *how was a man expected to concentrate with such a creature about?*

He looked at Northrop, who'd been taking in the interaction with keen interest. Leveling a final warning look, his friend began the introduction. "Lady Lucinda, may I present to you His Grace, the Duke of Clairemont."

For a moment Will felt time begin to slow again. He shook off the spell as best he could and forced his lips to move. "Lady Lucinda, it is indeed a pleasure to make your acquaintance." He accepted her offered hand and bowed, covertly taking in the length of her as he did so.

She curtsied low, the graceful movement placing her breasts directly in his line of sight.

Will fought the urge to linger and looked at her face, catching an arched eyebrow and, perhaps, the merest hint of a satisfied smile.

She rose slowly. "Your Grace, it is a great honor to meet the infamous Iron Will."

It was his face—more specifically, his smile—that caused Lucinda's heart to skip a beat for the third time that evening. A young boy caught doing something he should not, that smile said. Utterly charming and devoid of any lechery, unlike the myriad men before him, who'd failed her test.

Amelia had scolded her on a multitude of occasions for shamelessly using her physical attributes in an attempt to separate out the men looking for more than a pretty face from the men looking for . . . well, looking.

And, while the Duke of Clairemont was clearly admiring her for something other than her brain, Lucinda couldn't quite muster the indignation to be offended.

Perhaps it was more than his smile. Perhaps it was his fierce stare, which she'd noticed almost immediately from across the crowded ballroom. She'd turned, and her heart had skipped a beat. The man had called to her with that piercing, focused stare; his eyes, as she could now clearly see, were a deep hazel.

She'd tried to ignore him, tried to pretend that her heart had not quickened the moment he'd walked into the room. She had to maintain her composure, converse with her companions with something that at least approximated intelligence.

But it was no use. She kept glancing about, trying to find him again despite her best intentions. She was utterly distracted, a complete ninny. No fewer than three gentlemen had asked if she was overheated.

And then she'd spotted him again, speaking with Lord Northrop in what appeared to be a serious conversation.

Suddenly, without warning, the duke stalked toward her. He moved like a force majeure. Was it his size that made him command such attention, or his demeanor—his gaze never leaving hers, a determined set to his brow that could not be mistaken for anything but purpose?

And then, right next to her, Amelia said with a sigh, "How odd that His Grace would choose to attend Lady Mansfield's ball. Truly, there must be a full moon."

Lucinda took a deep breath, then hastily drank her lemonade. She wasn't a mere miss with little or no experience with men. She was, in fact, six-and-twenty and, if one cared to ask any of the grande dames in attendance, painfully past ready for the shelf. No, the ton acknowledged that Lady Lucinda Grey had never, ever been laid low by a man.

Which was why it was particularly frustrating for Lucinda when her heart missed a beat yet again. *Blast,* she thought to herself as the man in question stopped mere feet from her.

She couldn't look away.

Or was it that she wouldn't?

"Lady Lucinda, may I present to you His Grace, the Duke of Clairemont."

Lucinda had started at the sound of Lord Northrop's voice, his words snapping the spell that held her.

The duke made a polite remark and then it was Lucinda's turn to respond. "Your Grace, it is a great honor to meet the infamous Iron Will."

She could hardly believe she'd dared use the man's questionable sobriquet, a sentiment shared by all three of her companions, if their looks of astonishment were any indication.

But slowly, the duke's surprised expression turned to delight, his full lips curving in an amused smile. "Lady Lucinda, I believe I like you already."

A small laugh escaped Lucinda's lips. She considered giving him a vaguely polite response, but the obvious enjoyment in his eyes made her reconsider. "You are something altogether different, Your Grace, aren't you?"

He moved ever so slightly closer. "You've no idea, Lady Lucinda. No idea."

Lucinda had to force herself to remain still, hold her ground, and not close the small space that separated her from the duke. What was it about this man that made her act differently? Feel differently? *Want* differently?

Staring into his bottomless eyes, full of mischief before, and now—well, only Lucifer himself could say. Lucinda wondered what made her want to find out. "Is that a challenge, Your Grace?" she asked with light curiosity, her tone matching his.

It was the duke's turn to laugh. "I believe it is, Lady Lucinda. The question is, are you inclined to accept?"

Lucinda's mouth went dry and her mind raced. Surely such questionable banter was beyond acceptable behavior, even for a lady of six-and-twenty.

This was Iron Will. A man with a rake's reputation. A man polite society had deemed wild and unruly. Were it not for his title as the Duke of Clairemont, he might very well have been banned from tonight's ball.

To further the acquaintance would be impossible.

Unthinkable. Madness.

She threw caution to the wind.

"Let the games begin," she answered, her mouth curving into a wicked grin before she offered her hand to the duke.

"Indeed."

Antoine Garenne was careful to keep his distance, all too aware his failure in this endeavor would mean his death. Not that death itself was a concern. No, not when one lived an existence such as his. But dying would be so inconvenient and, to be quite honest, terribly dull when compared to spending the coin he'd been promised if he succeeded in capturing the wealthy Englishwoman.

The possibilities for purchases were endless. Whores. The best wine. An exquisite wig made of real human hair that would make the perfect addition to his exhaustive collection of disguises. More whores.

The ballroom was crowded but he adroitly slipped between chattering groups, avoiding collisions. But an inebriated pig of a man staggered, lurching into him and bumping his arm, nearly sending the tray of champagne he carried crashing to the floor.

"*Imbécile,*" he muttered under his breath, cursing his need to masquerade as a servant. Still, the disguise had afforded him entry into the Mansfields' palatial town house and provided access to the target. He'd been unprepared for the complication presented by the bear of a man conversing with her, however. He'd recognized the man on sight, a familiar foe who'd made appearances in his life unscathed up until this point.

The Duke of Clairemont could well prove a problem if Garenne did not adjust his plans accordingly.

He was a creature of habit with a nearly psychotic need for exactitude. The thought of altering his well-thought-out mission caused Garrene's throat to constrict, the heat of the room doing little to ease him. Pain stabbed just behind his right eye, only once, but it was followed by the inexorable tightening of an invisible band at his temples. The warning was explicit. He needed to leave the ballroom. Now.

Shortening the time line is of no consequence, he assured himself, impatiently stopping to allow a whale of a woman to pass by. *In fact, it will only mean I may return home that much sooner.*

His throat relaxed slowly as he absorbed the improved plan. The invisible iron band around his head eased and the pain slowly lessened. *Yes, I'll take the woman soon and be done with this filthy country forever.*

He snaked nimbly through the crowd as he made his way to the kitchens to refill his tray of champagne glasses.

3

"May I have this dance?" Will asked, bowing before Lady Lucinda with every ounce of gentlemanly grace he could summon.

She slowly extended a gloved hand, her eyes fixed firmly on his.

"Lucinda, dear, I believe your dance card is completely full," Lady Northrop began, the tension in her voice causing the entire party to turn.

"Amelia . . ." Northrop wrapped his arm around his wife's waist and pulled her close. "Let Lucinda be. Surely one dance will not overset the entire evening?"

"No, of course not," Lady Northrop answered quickly. "One dance couldn't possibly be of any consequence. I'll hold back the tide of your suitors," she said, looking directly at Lady Lucinda with an earnest glance, "but do hurry back."

Lucinda released Will's hand and patted Lady Northrop on the arm. "One dance, then, and I'm certain there will be no need for a queue on my behalf. However, I trust you will ask Lady Mansfield to clear the front hall if the need arises, won't you?" she teased, squeezing Lady Northrop's arm with affectionate reassurance.

Lady Northrop gave Lucinda a small private smile. "Of course."

Will turned Lucinda toward the dance floor, surprised by his determination to have her to himself.

"Is there a reason we must make haste, Your Grace?" she asked.

He stepped onto the marble floor and gently pulled Lady Lucinda with him. "Only that I cannot resist the waltz," he said, glancing at the musicians as they readied for the next dance.

She followed his gaze, taking note of their preparations before looking back at him. She arched an eyebrow. "Of course," she answered.

Will settled his free hand at her waist, vividly aware that the gently rounded slope of her bottom curved just beyond his fingertips. Without conscious intent, his grip firmed and his fingers moved lightly over the soft silk of her gown, testing the supple warmth beneath.

A faint shiver rippled through the woman in his arms and Lady Lucinda eased away from his touch in one swift small step.

Her gaze met his, and in the brief moment before her lowered lashes shielded her expression from him, Will thought he glimpsed the same heat and surprise that raced through his veins.

Had she too felt the attraction sparking between them? Did she want to explore the unknown feeling as much as he did?

If she'd only raise her lashes, he could search for answers.

"And you, Lady Lucinda, do you enjoy waltzing?" he asked, after a frustrating moment when she appeared enthralled by his cravat.

His ploy worked. Lucinda's thick lashes swept up and she met his gaze. "It depends upon my partner, I suppose."

Her poise was once more intact. But there was a glimmer of something, though Will could not be sure precisely what it was.

The music began and she followed him gracefully as he swung her into the steps. "Yes, indeed, a skilled partner is truly a necessity," he murmured, rewarded by the barely perceptible tensing of her slim fingers against his palm as he urged her slightly closer.

Satisfied that she wasn't immune to the strange spell he felt binding them together, Will easily led Lady Lucinda in the simple pattern of whirls and twirls.

Will knew the loftier ladies of the ton had termed the waltz the "forbidden dance" due to the proximity required of partners. Privately, he could only wonder at the naïvety of anyone who considered something of such a tame nature "forbidden."

Though, he had to admit, he was finding it hard to focus on his duty with this particular woman in his arms.

Lady Lucinda was the perfect partner—all lightness and grace as the two revolved around the room. The delicate scent of her perfume teased his nostrils with each movement. Although they only touched where her hand lay on his and his hand rested at her waist, the supple flex and sway of her body was pure temptation. Her diamond earbobs caught the candlelight, glittering as the dance pattern repeated and he swung her in smooth turns.

He could have watched her all night. The swift turns and pure enjoyment of the dance heightened her color. Would she turn that same shade of pink in his bed? he wondered. His groin tightened at the swift mental image of Lady Lucinda stripped of her evening wear and lying underneath him.

"Your Grace?"

He forced the picture from his head and looked down at Lady Lucinda. "Yes?"

"You appear to be woolgathering. Am I that poor a conversationalist?"

Her question made Will realize just how much valuable time he'd spent admiring her. The level of distraction was a startling testament to how unusual his reaction to her had been.

Sparkling diamonds and pink-hued skin be damned. He had to introduce the courtship before the dance ended. Once she was back in Lady Northrop's company, it was unlikely he would have a second chance.

Will gave her a small smile, the one countless women had told him could melt the coldest of hearts, and deftly steered them around another couple. "On the contrary," he said as they completed the turn. "I was just considering the necessity of having a suitable partner. Such a need goes beyond the dance floor, wouldn't you agree?"

Lady Lucinda stiffened slightly but completed the turn without consequence. "Exactly how far beyond the dance floor were you considering, Your Grace?"

She was direct, he'd give her that. And though the time he'd spent with her was relatively short, he instinctively knew that all the pretty words in the whole of England would only serve to weaken his position.

"The dining room, the library, Lady Lucinda," he murmured, his gaze holding hers. "And, for that matter, every other room to be found under the ridiculously expansive roof of Clairemont Hall."

She followed his lead as they completed the final turn and the music ended. Then she sank into a low curtsy, rising gracefully to survey him.

"Clairemont Hall—your family seat?"

It was clearly a request for clarification. Will nodded abruptly.

"Am I to understand that it is your intent to court me, Your Grace?" She sounded neither disdainful nor dismayed, only slightly puzzled.

He set her hand on his bent arm and led her to the edge of the crowded room. "Yes," he answered simply.

She stopped abruptly, forcing Will to halt mid-stride.

"Your Grace, though we—that is to say, while *I* may have given the impression this evening that we . . ." she began, her voice low, her tone apologetic but resolute. "I cannot allow you to court me. You know this as well as I."

The orchestra began another song, the music blending with the laughter and conversation of the throng that surrounded them.

"Are you afraid of me, then, like all the others?" Will asked, looking at the crowd, then back at Lady Lucinda, surprised that her answer mattered.

She stood a bit straighter, clearly relying on all five feet and four inches of her slender frame to underscore her words. "I am *not* afraid, but I *am* practical. You've no desire to live in my world, nor do I possess an interest in joining yours. Compatibility on the dance floor is hardly a foundation for a lifelong commitment, Your Grace."

Will realized that Lady Lucinda would not be wooed by his questionable charm alone. Dangling King Solomon's Mine as a lure to entice her had to be done. He had to succeed, as he always did. Still, it took a moment to reconcile himself to the task.

He realized that reluctant as he was to lose his favorite horse, betraying a woman of Lady Lucinda's substantial character was another matter entirely. It didn't sit well.

This bloody well better win me a medal of some sort, he thought, a sharp pang of regret appearing in his heart.

He pushed open the set of French windows leading to the veranda and side garden before responding. "If I cannot convince you with our compatibility in the waltz, Lady Lucinda, then how might you feel about our mutual interest in a horse?"

*   *   *

In truth, Lucinda was far more intrigued at the mention of a horse than she was worried about the duke's having pulled her into the garden. "I'm sorry, I don't quite understand, Your Grace," she answered, allowing him to lead her to a stone bench neatly tucked between two flowering jasmine. "What could a horse possibly have to do with your need of a wife?"

He seated her with inherent politeness before joining her. The bench may have been sufficiently wide for an ordinary man and a lady, but the duke was not an average-sized man. The muscular bulk of his body crowded the seat, his knee brushing hers as he stretched his long legs out in front of him. His shoulder nudged against hers, the powerful muscles of his thigh a scant inch, if that, from her own silk-covered flesh. She felt surrounded by him, the heat of his body enveloping her.

"Do you recall a colt by the name of King Solomon's Mine?"

Shocked, Lucinda's heart leapt, her breath catching on a silent gasp, but she endeavored to mask her surprise. "Yes, I believe so," she managed to say with creditable nonchalance. "He was foaled some four years ago on the Whytham estate. I understood he was lost in a gambling wager—to you, Your Grace."

"Very good, Lady Lucinda. I won King Solomon's Mine from Whytham and have owned him ever since." His Grace drew in his legs and turned toward her, the already questionable amount of space between them narrowing with his movement.

A shimmer of sensation began in Lucinda's toes, slowly working its way up through her calves and knees, then her thighs and belly, settling in her breasts, where the tattoo of her pounding heart accelerated ever so slightly. Whether it was caused by news of King

Solomon's Mine or her close proximity to the duke, Lucinda couldn't quite discern. Nor could she bring herself to put more, safer distance between them.

"How fortunate for you, Your Grace. He has grown to be a most singular horse, I am sure," Lucinda said, hoping her ridiculously swiftly beating heart would not betray her. "But I still fail to see how your horse has anything to do with me."

The duke placed one hand on the bench, his fingertips nearly touching the silk gown covering her thigh. "I was led to believe King Solomon's Mine held a special place in your heart. Perhaps I was misinformed?"

"No, not entirely," Lucinda said, distracted as she fought the unacceptable urge to close the distance separating her from His Grace. "That is to say, I *was* present at his birth and he truly is a remarkable horse—or so I assume, having not seen him for some time."

The bench where they sat was in full view of other couples strolling along the garden paths in search of respite from the ballroom's crowds and heat. Nevertheless, Lucinda knew she mustn't lose sight of the potential danger to her reputation by simply being seen with the notorious duke. Her need to appear disinterested in King Solomon's Mine, however, was consuming all her attention. She would simply have to rely on her position in the ton to protect her, she decided. At the moment, it was far more important to deal with the duke's unexpected and intriguing insertion of King Solomon's Mine in their conversation.

Did he know about her and her aunts' plans and the importance of the stallion to their success? How could he?

He couldn't, she told herself, because all four women had sworn a vow of secrecy.

"Yes, he is a remarkable horse," the duke agreed, his

words interrupting her frantic thoughts. "And he could be yours."

"Am I to believe that you're offering King Solomon's Mine as inducement to allow you to court me?" she asked, with no attempt to disguise her disbelief. She stared at him, searching his eyes for a clue. Surely this was a game he played, but to what end, she couldn't discern.

"A wager—a priceless horse for the honor of your company." There was a gruffness to his voice that had not been present only a few moments before, and his hazel eyes darkened with unnamed emotion. "If I can't convince you to wed me after, say, three months of courtship, then King Solomon's Mine is yours. And if you consent to be my wife . . ." He shrugged, a wry smile lifting one corner of his mouth. "Then King Solomon's Mine is yours on the day we make our vows. Either way, you win."

"You're mad," she whispered in response. And perhaps she was as well, she thought, for she was sorely tempted.

He rose, inclining his head in a brief, polite bow just short of curt. "You're not the first to make such a claim, nor will you be the last," he said. "But I require an answer, one way or the other."

Lucinda stood, her legs unsteady as she stepped just beyond the duke's reach and turned to face him.

She couldn't possibly allow him to court her. Could she?

She narrowed her eyes at him, forcing her thoughts to move beyond his handsome face and the prized stallion he dangled before her.

The Duke of Clairemont's family possessed all the right connections. And he was wealthy enough.

He was neither as old as Methuselah nor as young as Lord Thorp's boy, whom her maid firmly believed to be next on Amelia's list. No, he measured up in nearly every single category, save for his reputation.

Black.

No, blacker than black, Lucinda thought, eyeing him as he tapped his boot. His conquests were legendary and too numerous to count. From women to fights, drinking to—well, Lucinda could only imagine—the gossips proclaimed Iron Will's appetite for life was voracious, terrifyingly so.

"Have you come to a decision?" the duke pressed, shifting impatiently.

"A moment more, if you please," Lucinda temporized, plucking a flower from the jasmine before returning to her thoughts.

Of course, she supposed it only made sense that a man of the duke's experience would seek out the one woman in all of England whose reputation could counteract the effect of his own questionable choices.

Really, it made perfect sense, as anyone who bothered to think on it for more than four seconds would see.

And the horse. Well, her aunts could not object to three months spent in the man's company in exchange for King Solomon's Mine.

Surely she would prevail—and her success would change their lives forever.

All Lucinda had to do was allow the man into her presence.

To court her.

It couldn't be too difficult.

Resisting him wouldn't be too difficult, she told herself firmly, absently brushing the velvety soft blossom across her lower lip.

He watched her unblinkingly. In desperation, she looked at the heavens, concentrated, and accurately identified Orion, the Hunter. Ironic though it was, Lucinda congratulated herself for completing a task that required her wits. Given that Lord Clairemont's presence appeared to elicit a physical response she'd never before experienced, she was relieved to learn that the duke held no power over her when held at arm's length.

Which is where he would remain for the entirety of their courtship, she vowed. *If* she agreed to his proposition. She needed more time to consider whether she should do so.

"I will take your proposal under advisement," Lucinda answered, pointing the jasmine at him to underline her decision.

He reached for the flower and took hold of Lucinda's hand. "Of course. Though you should know, I'm not a patient man."

"Patience is a virtue, Your Grace," she said, tugging her hand from his. "And one you'd do well to practice should you wish to go forward with this . . . this . . ." She halted, unwilling to use the word that even now seemed implausible when applied to herself and the man known as Iron Will.

"Courtship, Lady Lucinda," His Grace finished for her with amusement.

Clearly, she thought with annoyance, the idea of such a connection held no trepidation for him.

And God help me, Lucinda thought as she gave him a curt nod, tilted her chin, and turned toward the ballroom. *God help us all.*

4

A gentle breeze stirred the crimson silk curtain concealing the half-open window in Lucinda's bedroom. Her town house in Grosvenor Square was an elegant, beautifully appointed home, and usually Lucinda found it wonderfully comfortable.

Not so tonight.

Unfortunately, the air did little to cool her. She stripped off her diamond earbobs, bracelet, and long gloves, waiting impatiently as Mary freed the clasp of her glittering necklace. The maid deftly unfastened the pale pink gown, retrieving it when Lucinda stepped out of the crumpled silk. Minutes later, Lucinda was free of her undergarments and dressed in a favorite nightgown of pale blue silk, inset with matching lace.

Mary swiftly plucked the pins from Lucinda's coiffure. Lucinda shook her hair free and took the brush, pulling it through the long strands herself as Mary left the room. Normally, she found the rhythmic strokes of brushing soothing, but tonight her nerves wouldn't be calmed. Restless, she quickly braided the thick mane and paced across the room.

Walking didn't ease her.

She still felt overly warm.

She crawled onto her bed and drew up her legs, wrapping her arms around them and resting her chin on her bent knees.

Thoughts of the duke's proposal—and, frustratingly

enough, of the duke himself—sent diminutive flames flickering across her too sensitive skin. One touch from him had done more to wreak havoc in her meticulously ordered life than the fumbling, bumbling, fervent pleadings of eligible bachelors from London to Scotland.

And he barely touched me. What have I done?

She vividly remembered the warm weight of his hand at her waist and wondered whether her vow to keep him at arm's length was sheer bravado on her part.

"Well, my girl, what news have you of the ton?"

Lucinda started at the sound of her aunt's voice and turned, hand pressed to the silk covering her pounding heart. "Aunt Bessie, you nearly frightened me to death!"

Elizabeth Bradshaw, the Marchioness of Mowbray, sauntered barefoot across the plush cream and scarlet Persian rug toward Lucinda, a delicate Wedgwood plate piled high with macaroons balanced carefully in her right hand. She wore a dressing gown of deep rose, the silk clinging to her curves. It emphasized what Bessie was perhaps most proud of at fifty-and-some-years of age—a shapely figure that had inspired awe in the male gender from the day she'd come out.

"Hmmm, I suspect that whatever is occupying your mind at the moment has far more to do with your excitable nerves than my sudden appearance," Bessie answered with her usual shrewd perception, setting the plate on the bedside table before joining Lucinda.

Lucinda avoided her aunt's gaze and instead concentrated on tracing her fingertip over the scarlet floral pattern embroidered on her coverlet. "Whatever would make you think such a thing?"

The closed door of her bedchamber burst open with a clatter.

"Utter one more word without us and we shall never speak to either of you again!"

Lucinda smiled as her two other aunts—Bessie's sisters, Victoria and Charlotte—hurried toward the bed.

Encased in yards of white muslin and wrapped in fine cashmere bed shawls, the middle and youngest of the Grey sisters managed to exude an excruciating level of primness that made Bessie's eyes roll nearly to the back of her skull.

"Really, girls," Bessie said, shaking her head. "Are you at such an advanced age that you must cover yourselves from head to toe?" she asked.

Lucinda hid a smile as Bessie, in an automatic move, leaned back slightly so that even Charlotte, whose eyesight was poor at best, could not fail to notice her sister's impressive bosom.

"Once a lady, my dear Bessie, always a lady," Victoria St. Ainsbury, the Duchess of Highbury, answered emphatically with only a touch of sarcasm. She nudged her elder sister aside with her bony hip to make room for herself next to Lucinda.

Lady Charlotte Grey patted Bessie on the shoulder, took a place at the end of the bed, and eyed Lucinda expectantly. "All right, dear, proceed."

Lucinda took in the sight of her three aunts, "the Furies," as they were known to all. As unlike from one another as anyone could be, the sisters shared one trait: sheer, single-minded willfulness. Their differences could always be resolved by their agreement that absolutely nothing should stand in the way of what they wanted. Not men, not society, and certainly not one another.

"It's King Solomon's Mine," Lucinda began, taking note of the immediate reaction that each sister had to the prized stallion's name. "I've been offered the chance to win him."

"How utterly glorious!" Bessie shrieked. "Rufus will be green with envy. A stallion with the bloodlines of

King Solomon's Mine practically guarantees success. Ours will be the superlative breeding program in all of Britain."

Victoria halted Bessie's rhapsodizing by gently covering her sister's mouth with her palm. "Yes, Bessie, we're all aware of what King Solomon's Mine has to offer," she said before Bessie could interrupt her. She huffed to a halt, drawing a deep breath before continuing. "But do not torture your son with the news just yet. How, exactly, Lucinda, will you go about winning him?"

Lucinda tugged at her long, thick braid. "It's rather simple, really. I've only to allow someone to court me for a specific amount of time. At the end of that time, if I've managed to avoid losing my heart, the horse is mine."

Bessie pulled Victoria's hand away from her mouth and sat up straight. "Considering that you've refused most of the eligible male population of England, this will not be a problem. Now," she continued, reaching for the plate of macaroons. "let us celebrate with a tiny midnight morsel, shall we?"

Charlotte took a treat from the plate and settled back into her cozy spot at the foot of the bed. "Lucinda, dear, I've only one question: Who is he?"

"Yes, who is this man?" Victoria asked, speaking between bites. "I'm afraid I lost track of King Solomon's Mine after that idiot Whytham gambled him away to that infamous Iron Will."

Lucinda discreetly wiped at a bead of perspiration at her temple. "Well," she began, "that is to say . . ." She hesitated and took a hasty bite of her macaroon.

Charlotte gasped, moving closer to the circle of women. "It's him, then, isn't it? The Duke of Clairemont." She looked at her sisters, then back at Lucinda. "It's Iron Will."

Victoria slowly lowered the remainder of her macaroon onto the plate and stared owl-eyed at Lucinda. "Of course not. Lucinda would never entertain the idea—"

"I knew it!" Bessie interrupted. "The open window, your jangled nerves, the telltale perspiration . . . He's captured your fancy! It is Iron Will."

Victoria's eyes were growing wider by the second. "What do you know of such young men? Do act your age, Bessie."

"Really, Victoria, looking at you is more than enough to underscore our advanced years, thank you very much," Bessie interrupted, tossing her head to shake her glossy, dove gray mass of hair over her shoulder for effect.

Lucinda took advantage of her aunts' sparring to stand and cross the room. She fanned herself with her hand before sitting down at her writing desk, the breeze tickling a tendril of hair at the nape of her neck.

"Ladies, I believe we were speaking of the appropriateness of His Grace as a suitor for Lucinda. Do keep to the subject, won't you?" Charlotte chided gently, pushing her robust frame from the bed. "I knew his parents, of course, but I'm afraid I'm not familiar with the boy. Lucinda, dear, is he a gentleman worthy of your attentions?"

Victoria rose from the bed and marched across the room to where Lucinda sat. "A rake of the first order!" she answered in a severe tone.

"A man of experience, to be sure," Bessie chimed in, rolling over on the soft mattress to lie on her side and smile at Lucinda. "But why that should be seen as an impediment is beyond me."

Victoria frowned and wagged her finger at Lucinda, who had not been able to hide an amused grin. "This is hardly a laughing matter, my dear."

"Yes, quite. Of course, Aunt," Lucinda responded,

forcing her lips into a serious line. "Though I would think the news would be cause for some celebration—on your part, in particular, considering your passion for horses."

Lucinda had touched a nerve when she mentioned the one thing in life that had yet to disappoint Victoria. Her marriage at age eighteen to the Duke of Highbury had been a disaster, the duke being far more interested in his many mistresses than he ever was in his wife. Victoria's inability to bear children had broken her heart and driven her further away from her friends and acquaintances, until all she had left were her sisters and Highbury's vast stables.

While the duke understood little about Victoria, he discerned even less about his prized equines. His absence from the day-to-day stable operations left Victoria with free rein to learn all she could. To love as she would, to set free all the passion and caring forbidden her in her marriage.

And she did. Soon every follower of horse racing who ever visited Tattersalls could not get enough of the Highbury horses, their impressive races *the* event to attend.

At first, it was fulfilling for Victoria. But the duke's arrogance over his "influence and guiding hand" caused her mild annoyance with her husband to grow to outright hostility, until Victoria could hardly bear to be in the same room as the man.

And then he was killed in a riding accident, his stubborn insistence that his inexperienced mount take a high fence ending tragically for the horse, deservedly for the duke. The lack of an heir meant the estate passed to her nephew, leaving Victoria a very wealthy woman, thanks to her settlement, but without a home.

Her sisters immediately implored Victoria to join them at Bampton Manor, where they'd resided since the death of Lucinda's parents, the magnificent unentailed estate having been willed to young Lucinda.

Once settled at Bampton Manor, Victoria had enlisted Bessie, Charlotte, and Lucinda's help and began to build her own breeding program. They created a fictitious male farm manager and, using their ample income, began buying colts and fillies, stallions and mares, and housing them on the estate.

King Solomon's Mine was to be the crown jewel of the stables, a stallion with just the right lineage to guarantee the superiority of their bloodstock for generations to come.

And then Whytham, an irredeemable dolt of a man, had gambled away the key to all of Victoria's dreams.

Charlotte, having watched the play of emotions cross Victoria's face as she considered the situation, cleared her throat.

"To my way of thinking," Charlotte said when she had their attention, "we must ask ourselves two questions. First, is the Grey name sufficiently influential to survive the gossip that will likely ensue if Lucinda allows this 'Iron Will' to court her?"

Bessie rolled over and sat up, tucking her legs beneath her. "Despite his rather questionable qualifications," she began, arching an eyebrow for emphasis, "I would not hesitate to say that the Grey name would weather such a trial in grand fashion."

The women looked at Victoria, whose pinched face and heightened color revealed the struggle between her strict adherence to her moral code and her passionate desire for success.

"Yes, of course," she said finally. "No one would dare question Lucinda's good name should she choose to allow this man the honor of her company."

"We are in agreement, then," Charlotte concurred,

moving closer to Lucinda. Gently, she pushed back a stray curl that had fallen over Lucinda's brow. "Now, dear girl, the second question. I assume you will make your intentions clear to this young man, namely that the horse is your desire, not him."

Lucinda nodded in agreement. "Yes, Aunt, I will."

Bessie left the comfort of the bed and with Victoria joined Charlotte. All three of Lucinda's aunts faced her, concern clearly written across each of their solemn faces.

"Human nature being what it is," Bessie began, "we are somewhat hesitant to release you into the hands of such a formidable foe as this Iron Will appears to be."

"Really, Aunts," Lucinda responded, hoping the instant warmth that flooded her veins at the mere mention of the duke's name wasn't visible on her features, "you've never doubted my resolute will to remain unmarried before. Why now?"

"He clearly made an impression this evening," Bessie began.

"Too true. Her color is heightened, it cannot be denied," Victoria observed.

"Do not forget the perspiration," Bessie hastily added.

Lucinda stood, the heat of the room seeming to grow by the second. "I'm that easily swayed, then? Countless suitors have come before and, may I remind you, been denied. But this one, with a wink and a smile will steal my heart silly?"

It was a question posed to all, including herself.

In a matter of mere minutes the man had somehow appealed to Lucinda's basic needs. Despite all that owning King Solomon's Mine would bring, dare she accept his wager? Could she trust herself with His Grace?

The gentleness of Charlotte's voice calmed Lucinda's

shaken nerves. "My dear, you've only to answer the question and we'll never speak of it again."

"Then do ask, Aunt. Now."

"Are you capable of dealing with the likes of Iron Will?"

Lucinda's mind began to race as images assaulted her senses. The duke's voice, soft as silk, when he repeated her name upon meeting. The feel of his hand at the small of her back when they danced. The look in his eyes when he spoke of the courtship. His fingers tracing the length of hers, branding her with a fire that she swore lingered even to this hour.

But she wanted King Solomon's Mine. And what's more, she realized as she looked at each of her aunts, she wanted what they wanted—the happiness and complete satisfaction to be found in doing something well, doing something that would mean so much for so many.

Lucinda squeezed her eyes shut for a moment and forced from her mind all thoughts of the unsettling effect the duke had on her too susceptible body. "Yes."

The note was delivered just after dawn. The merest hint of citrus escaped when Will tore open the seal— Lady Lucinda's scent. His training in the Young Corinthians had ensured he could discern a staggering number of details about an individual in a relatively short period of time. Along with her height and approximate size, he'd already committed to memory her voice and any number of physical characteristics that might be useful during the course of keeping her safe. Or bedding her, though he was fairly sure that both Carmichael and Northrop would have him castrated on the spot.

Another agent had guarded Lady Lucinda when she'd left the ball, and then yet another agent, this one masquerading as a footman, had been installed in her household. Assured she was well protected, Will had gone straight from the glitter of the Mansfields' ballroom to Carmichael's office. The exclusive group of men gathered there was committed to capturing Garenne. Will joined them, spending the next hours poring over documents and maps, discussing and hammering out a detailed plan. When they dispersed to their homes, he was satisfied that their scheme to protect Lady Lucinda was seamless.

He'd managed perhaps an hour of sleep before receiving her note, and there'd been little point in trying for more after reading her reply. Smithers had been too enthusiastic for Will's taste at such an ungodly hour, but he couldn't have done without his valet's help. Arranging his wardrobe fell just below learning to play the pianoforte on Will's list of things one must master before dying, though he had to admit that Smithers's choice for the day was quite . . . well, gentlemanly. Snug, fawn-colored breeches were tucked into his Hessians, which were polished to a high shine. A pale green waistcoat beneath a dark blue coat of superfine cloth was completed with an intricately tied cravat.

The damn neckcloth was the one thing Will could barely tolerate. Brummell should have been hung by a length of his own neckcloth, as far as Will was concerned. The strips of starched linen would see far better use in bandaging a wound or tying a woman to the bed-post.

Depending on one's situation, of course.

Will had endured Smithers's fussing for a good hour before the valet pronounced him fit to leave the house. For his part, Will had thought himself remarkably patient, but he couldn't help but wonder if Lady Lucinda would be suitably appreciative.

With expert maneuvering and a firm hand on the reins of his matched bays, he threaded his high-perch through traffic. He nodded at an acquaintance who hailed him from the walk but did not slow for a more substantive greeting.

He couldn't shake memories of Lady Lucinda.

The blasted woman dancing, smiling as she turned so easily in his arms, nearly coming undone at his touch. His imagination took flight. He wondered if she dabbed the faint citrus scent on her slender wrists, the soft skin just behind her knees, and lastly, between her breasts.

Will grimaced, frowning. Height, weight—these were familiar factors to remember in his line of work. But the feel of her as they danced, conjuring up a vision of her unclothed? Will couldn't quite convince himself as to the relevance of such things.

This was not beginning well. He needed emotional distance from his charge—anything less could result in a slip in his concentration and thus danger to Lady Lucinda.

True, he thought, narrowing his eyes against the midmorning sun, never before had a woman been so intimately involved in Corinthian business, at least not to his knowledge.

Also true, his fondness for the fairer sex was no secret. News of his liaisons had found its way into the gossip rags, the legend of Iron Will growing with each report.

But this was different. Lady Lucinda was different. And it had to stop. It was distracting and, even worse, dangerous.

Will slowed the bays and brought them to a dancing stop, noting the movement of the sun behind the stone façade of de Bohun House. Carmichael had mentioned on more than one occasion that Will's mental strength was rivaled only by his physical prowess. He would test that theory thoroughly with this mission, his wits sure to be put to the test by both Garenne and Lady Lucinda.

He would perform his duty to the best of his ability.

But his fascination with this woman would end at her doorstep.

It would not be simple, but it would be done.

His tiger leapt down from his perch and ran to the bays, grasping halter straps with small hands.

Will stepped down, handed the reins to a waiting groom, and strode up the steps to the front door.

"Where the devil did he disappear to?" Bessie asked, attempting to discreetly poke her head around the gold damask curtains and peer out the spotless windowpane at the street below.

"Remove yourself from view at once," Victoria hissed. She rapped her sister's arm with her fan, the audible thwack earning a startled squeak from Bessie.

Charlotte tsked gently, sighing as Victoria nearly toppled over as she leaned toward Bessie in an attempt to peer outside. "Really, ladies, do you think your curiosity will hasten the gentleman to our door?"

"He has lovely dark hair, that much I saw before he disappeared," Bessie continued dramatically, ignoring Charlotte's mild chastening.

"Are you speaking of the horse or the man?" Victoria asked. And she was so utterly serious that the rest of them could not help but giggle.

"His Grace, the Duke of Clairemont, is in the foyer and wishes to join you, my lady," Stanford interrupted in a flat voice.

The aunts immediately ceased their laughter, but not Lucinda. She couldn't stop giggling, no matter how long she looked at Stanford's morose visage.

"Lucinda, dear, are you quite all right?" Charlotte asked.

She nodded at her aunt and smoothed the skirt of her manila brown morning dress. In truth, she'd been asking herself that same question since waking. A night spent tossing and turning was never a good thing, but when the restlessness was caused by dreams the likes of Lucinda's, well, it was a wonder she'd managed to appear for breakfast. The dreams had started out respectably enough, with Lucinda and the duke finalizing out the details of their courtship. But it had ended with his mouth seeking hers in a breathtaking kiss, then an embrace and the loss of clothing and . . . Lucinda would not think on what came next.

Knowing she would see him today had done little to calm her nerves over breakfast. If the man had invaded her dreams and sent her into such a state, what would happen once he was within arm's reach?

"Enough!" Lucinda ground out, belatedly realizing that all three of her aunts and Stanford were staring at her, confusion clearly written upon each of their faces.

These women were the reason she'd agreed to the courtship, she reminded herself. Her aunts meant the world to her. All three had happily stepped in to care for her upon her parents' death—to teach her, love her, nurture her in a way that only family could. So really, allowing His Grace to court her was nothing in comparison. Easy. Beyond easy.

Or at least it should be.

Lucinda steeled herself with newfound resolution. "Enough," she repeated firmly, anxious to show all that she was perfectly in control. "Aunts, do choose a seat. And Stanford, please show the duke in."

"Yes, my lady." The butler bowed and departed.

Lucinda tucked an errant curl into place, pinched her cheeks for color, and sat in a patterned armchair.

"A chair? Really, Lucinda, after your years of experience in society and dealing with men, surely you know better!" Bessie exclaimed in a hushed tone, rising from the window seat. She pattered quickly across the room and tugged Lucinda to her feet.

"The settee, at once," she demanded, pointing to the cream silk sofa that, in theory, fit two full-grown individuals.

In reality, Lucinda had always thought it was best suited to duos of considerably smaller stature than the average couple.

"Aunt Bessie, the man is a giant," she protested. "I'm not sure that he alone would fit on that particular piece of furniture, and certainly not the two of us."

Victoria plied her fan in a most vigorous manner. "What, exactly, is wrong with the chair?"

"This is a courtship, not a trial. I'm sure even you remember the purpose of such meetings—to converse, to flirt, to establish a connection of a physical—"

Victoria's fan moved faster, her grip threatening to snap the delicate, hand-painted sticks. "This is not at all about conversing or flirting or . . . or . . ."

"I believe her words were 'establishing a physical—'" Charlotte offered with the merest hint of a smile quirking her lips.

"Stop!" Victoria hissed vehemently, clearly not enjoying the joke at her expense. "A horse," she reminded them sternly. "We are here to gain a horse. Now, do sit down before Stanford returns."

Bessie pulled a chair nearer and quickly sat, adjusting her skirts.

Heavy footsteps sounded in the hallway just outside the room. Lucinda could not allow the duke to see her ill at ease. The courtship must begin on her terms, and must remain entirely within her control.

In a decidedly unladylike but necessary move, Lucinda gained a few precious moments by nimbly hopping over the footstool in her path and throwing herself onto the nearest seat—the slight settee.

"Brava," Bessie whispered loudly.

"Hush, he'll hear you," Charlotte warned from her

corner of the room, giving Lucinda a small smile of reassurance before schooling her features into a proper expression of serenity.

Lucinda smoothed her skirts and took a deep breath just as the door opened.

"His Grace, the Duke of Clairemont."

5

Will had lied, cheated, stolen, maimed, and killed in the line of duty. In turn, he'd been shot at, pummeled within an inch of his life, stabbed repeatedly, and nearly drowned—all for King and Country.

One look at the women ensconced within the beautifully appointed sitting room and Will knew, beyond a shadow of a doubt, that it had all been child's play up to this point.

By the time the introductions were made, he had shrewdly assessed and identified which sister would most willingly be finessed (the brazen one), which one would prefer to see him run down by wild horses rather than extend him one ounce of graciousness (the sour one), and finally, which one was clearly undecided, her quiet demeanor showing nothing of her leanings (the reasonable one).

"Do sit down, over there," the brazen one had urged, pointing to the ridiculously tiny settee where Lady Lucinda was seated.

He'd complied, having to practically fold himself in half to fit. Being so near Lady Lucinda was hardly in keeping with his plan to remain cool and detached, but Will knew better than to argue with a determined aunt.

"I hope the morning finds you well," Will said to Lady Lucinda, aware her aunts were listening to each word. He had to twist his neck in a wholly unnatural way to look at her, due to the damned doll-sized seat.

"Where are the flowers?"

Will turned to the sour one. Her pinched mouth looked as if the effort of speaking to him was leaving a vile taste on her tongue.

"Flowers?"

She rolled her eyes, obviously finding him lacking, and pressed on. "Yes, the flowers. Perhaps you're unaware of the workings of a respectable courtship, Your Grace. It is customary to bring a bouquet when calling upon a young woman."

"Aunt Victoria," Lady Lucinda protested, clearly uncomfortable with the woman's bluntness.

Will had never cared a farthing for what people thought of his actions, and he wasn't about to start now. Nevertheless, the woman was Lady Lucinda's aunt. "My apologies. I had forgotten."

"If I find myself in need of flowers all I've to do is walk into the back garden," Lady Lucinda answered with calm practicality. "And there I'll find more than twenty varieties—"

Will pried himself from the settee and strode toward the door. "A moment," he said, then exited the room, finding his way quickly to the rear of the town house. He walked the length of it, peering into each room before finding a set of doors that led to the small garden.

He let himself out onto the neat flagstone terrace, the surrounding flower beds fragrant in the sunshine.

And he began to pick one of each flower he could find, until there were an even twenty blooms with long stems neatly tucked into the crook of his arm.

He returned to the drawing room, and the ladies gasped in unison.

"With my sincere apologies, Lady Lucinda," he said, offering the flowers to her with a deep bow.

Her smile nearly had Will searching for a seat on the far side of the room. Her blue eyes glowed with delight.

She was clearly surprised, which was charming enough, but also pleased, which made Will's chest tighten with . . . with what? Pride? Joy? He couldn't quite name it, but whatever the emotion was, it wasn't good.

The sour aunt who had brought up his lack of flowers apparently thought he'd acted to mock her. Her fan beat an annoyed tattoo on the arm of the Windsor chair where she sat.

In truth, he'd forgotten the custom. His last visit to a woman that could have in any way been considered proper had been too long ago. The women he associated with wanted neither flowers nor ridiculous little gifts. They wanted an occasional very expensive gift—but mostly, they wanted him.

This would take some getting used to, this gentleman business, he realized. The problem was, he didn't have time to relearn his manners. Garenne was somewhere out there, close at hand, and he wasn't a patient man.

Will made a mental note to question Smithers regarding the requirements of a gentleman before turning to sit.

He'd only just settled himself on the settee when the sour one barked at him yet again.

"And the horse, Your Grace. Just where *is* King Solomon's Mine?"

Will was inclined to answer "In my pocket, my dear, along with a suit of armor and the crown jewels, of course," but thought better of it. "He should be taking a mid-morning rest in preparation for our afternoon ride."

"A mid-morning rest? Really, Your Grace, what sort of training regimen do you have for this horse that allows a mid-morning—"

"I assure you that he is—"

"An afternoon ride, how delightful!" the brazen one

said with a gleam in her eye, successfully cutting off both her sister and Will.

"Yes, I prefer an afternoon ride, though—"

"I believe it's time for tea," the reasonable one interrupted Will, crossing to tug the bellpull.

Will didn't bother to address her concerning the tea. He felt a headache coming on. He hated tea. And he'd yet to get a word in edgewise, so best to sit back and plan at this point. He'd be damned if he'd let three unruly women get the best of him, even ones referred to as "the Furies"—though now that he'd spent some time in their company, the title made much more sense.

Lady Lucinda leaned toward him. "I suppose I should have warned you to gird your loins prior to dancing attendance on me," she whispered, a wry smile accompanying her comment.

Will suppressed a laugh but returned the smile, her dimple wreaking havoc on his concentration. "I'm not a regular at Gentleman John Jackson's boxing academy for the masculine company alone. Your aunts may think they have the upper hand, but just you wait."

Lady Lucinda arched an eyebrow, her eyes twinkling. "Now this I must see," she said conspiratorially.

A footman appeared with the tea, placing it on the table, then disappearing.

"Milk, Your Grace?" the reasonable one asked.

"No, thank you."

"Sugar?"

"No, thank you. The blacker, the better," Will answered.

He stretched to take the cup and saucer from her and his thigh brushed Lady Lucinda's. He murmured a polite thank you for the tea and tried to remember what they'd been discussing before he'd been distracted. *Ah, yes— King Solomon's Mine.*

"Despite his prowess, Sol is a sensitive soul, which is

why he's allowed the luxury of a mid-morning rest," he said before downing his tea.

The sour one's lips pursed as if she'd just bitten into something tart. "Really, Your Grace, a horse of his lineage, sensitive?"

"How kind of you, Your Grace," the reasonable one interrupted. "Your attentiveness is truly inspiring."

"Oh, now really, Charlotte. 'Inspiring'? Do you take the man—"

"I was just pondering a walk in the park," the brazen one began in a completely different direction. "Though walking by oneself is lonely, wouldn't you agree?" she finished, batting her eyelashes at Will.

"Why, yes, as a matter of fact I'm in complete agreement," Will answered, still not quite sure what the aging coquette was playing at.

"Excellent. Lucinda, do don your pelisse, my dear."

"But—" the sour one began.

The brazen one rose from her chair and walked toward the pair. "Oh, did I fail to mention that I'd been thinking on a walk not for myself, but for Lucinda? Silly me."

"But—" the sour one said more loudly.

"A bit of fresh air would be most welcome," Lady Lucinda swiftly responded, taking Will's hand and standing.

"Well, I . . . that is to say . . ." the sour one protested, her fan at the ready.

"Dearest Victoria, we'll send Mary along with her cape and gloves to chaperone," the brazen one said soothingly.

Will didn't dare look in "dearest" Victoria's direction. Instead, he stood aside to let Lady Lucinda walk ahead of him, then, bowing to the remaining ladies, hastily gave his thanks, and followed her out of the room.

He attempted to shut the door but encountered resistance.

The brazen one stuck her head out and eyed Will with a hawklike stare. "I believe I see in you what others do not, Your Grace. Please, do not prove me wrong."

And with that, she disappeared behind the door and firmly shut it.

Lucinda was rather proud of herself. She'd made it nearly across the street before letting out the laugh that had been bubbling in her throat for the last five minutes.

The duke had no more handled her aunts than had anyone else in the history of the world.

His smug smile of success all but melted away at the sound of Lucinda's laughter. "Lady Lucinda, I can't imagine what you find so amusing," he said with mock affront, the flash of amusement in his eyes belying his tone.

Lucinda couldn't help but find him charming. He was so large, yet so like an adorable little boy at times. She very nearly reached out to caress his cheek, but thought better of it.

"Come now, Your Grace. It really wasn't that bad." Despite her best efforts to remain solemn, she couldn't prevent a smile from curving her lips. "It was your first meeting with them, after all, and there were three of them and only one of you. Perhaps a few more sessions at Gentleman John Jackson's and you'll be ready for another round?"

"Impertinent chit," the duke said under his breath, taking care to escort Lucinda into the central garden area of Grosvener Square.

Lucinda glanced over her shoulder. Mary had settled into a leisurely pace behind them, slow enough to allow a comfortable conversation, yet fast enough to ensure that the duke would not pull Lucinda into the bushes and have his way with her. Or dash behind a tree with her in tow and steal a kiss. Or anything of the kind. Which Lucinda most certainly did not want to happen. Ever. At least not today.

Well, she was fairly certain anyway.

Why had she not refused when Bessie had suggested a stroll? Because she'd been caught up in his charm, in his smile, in his eyes, which changed from cool hazel to heated green depending upon what he was thinking. What he was feeling.

And just what *was* he feeling, Lucinda found herself wondering, not for the first time.

Drat! This was not like her at all. If this were any other man—Lord Cuthbert, for example—she would not be strolling with him. Nor would she have spent one moment wondering whether he'd enjoyed his tea, never mind suffering curiosity as to his thoughts about her.

This was ludicrous. This was madness.

"Lady Lucinda," the duke said for what was clearly the second or perhaps even third time.

"Hmmm," Lucinda said belatedly, still struggling to marshal her thoughts.

"I've commented on the weather," he said. "Twice."

Lucinda abruptly stopped and stepped to one side of the path. She beckoned him closer. "Your Grace."

"Yes?"

"I've something to ask you."

He leaned in a bit, his broad shoulders blocking her. "In relation to the weather?"

Lucinda huffed out a breath. "No, not exactly. That is to say, not at all."

"I see. Well, let me gather my wits first," he responded, squeezing his eyes shut, visibly bracing himself before opening them. "All right, I believe I am ready."

Annoyed, Lucinda frowned at him. "This is a serious matter."

"I can see that," he said. "I apologize. Now, the question," he finished, the twinkle in his eyes nearly stopping Lucinda from speaking.

"What are your intentions?" she asked plainly.

She could see that she'd taken him by surprise, all of the humor disappearing from his face.

"With regards to?"

"Me. That is to say," Lucinda began, somewhat nervously, "us. You and me, and this, this . . ."

The duke looked amused. "'Courtship,' I believe is the word you're searching for."

"Yes, precisely," she said, somewhat relieved by his bluntness. "I understand that you've nothing to lose—"

"What of King Solomon's Mine?" he interrupted.

"Oh, well, of course. But I mean of a more personal nature, such as your reputation or, well, your heart, if I may be so bold," she answered, vaguely shocked by her honesty. Though at this point, she thought, really—what was the point in speaking in circles when she'd broached such a forbidden topic?

He didn't respond, only stared, his eyes deepening in hue as they searched hers.

"I've offended you, haven't I?" she asked, feeling oddly shy. She looked at the ground, unable to meet the intensity of his gaze as he appeared to consider her question.

"No, not in the least," he said at last, his deep voice strangely soft. His hand was warm when he cupped her chin, tipping her face up so that she was looking at him once more. "I prefer honesty, but I've found it to be a rare quality in a woman."

She exhaled, unaware that she'd been holding her breath, awaiting his reply.

That his opinion should matter so much made her uncomfortable. It was also unsettling that his disregard for society's rules governing male behavior seemed to coax her into behaving in ways she could only term improper.

Before this, only Amelia had been aware of Lucinda's occasionally unruly nature. Even as a child, Lucinda had instinctively hidden that part of herself from the world. And though she enjoyed much of her life as Lady Lucinda Grey, she was always aware that beneath the silks, satins, and jewels she wore, there smoldered a hidden desire to be more than the proper lady the world expected.

Amelia would turn pale and quite possibly faint if she were privy to the conversation taking place between Lucinda and Iron Will.

The proper gentlemen of her acquaintance expected her to be above reproach, the perfect lady. What was she to do with a man who expected her to be only herself?

"Now, to answer your question, my intentions are entirely honorable," he said, lowering his hand and taking her arm.

The duke tucked her hand into the crook of his arm, lessening the distance between their bodies as they walked. "It's no secret that every eldest Clairemont male throughout history has been expected to marry and continue the ducal line."

He looked out over the well-groomed park, his profile turned to her as he took in the shrubs that lined the walkways, the expanse of clipped grass, the strolling couples and nursemaids with their charges.

"And I like you, Lady Lucinda," he continued after a long moment. "You have a mind and you use it. You make me laugh, which I enjoy immensely. And though I feel sure that you've heard it a thousand times before, you are beautiful."

He turned his head to look down at her, pinning her with an intense glance. Lucinda couldn't look away. Tension spun between them, heightening with each moment. The unfamiliar feeling of vulnerability surfaced yet again.

"I've no intent to court you for sport," he resumed, pulling her from her thoughts. "I may be voracious and varied in my many appetites, Lady Lucinda, but in this I am single-minded and focused. You have my word."

She knew to the core of her being that she trusted him. After all, his line of reasoning did make perfect sense; a duke must marry, must have a son to carry on the family line. But beyond that, she sensed that William Randall, the Duke of Clairemont, meant what he said.

And though her intent was to walk away with only King Solomon's Mine after their time together, somehow knowing that he liked her—truly liked her, despite her candor and intelligence—made all the difference.

Lucinda relaxed and allowed herself to enjoy the fine spring day. It was early yet, too early, really, for the more sophisticated set to be out and about, which made their walk even more enjoyable. In truth, when in residence at her country estate, Lucinda often walked for miles in the morning, the stillness of a world that had yet to completely awaken providing a stark contrast to her usual routine of social events and obligations.

Though she'd never admitted it to anyone but Amelia, at times Lucinda chafed from all that went with her place in society. She was far too practical a person to suppose that she would be happy as a squire's wife, but the lure of somehow being free of all of society's expectations that accompanied being titled, rich, and well-bred could be oh so intoxicating.

Perhaps this, in part, was what she liked so well in the duke. His utter disdain for the ton's stricture and society in general was—well, to be quite honest, most refreshing. It was something Lucinda secretly admired.

Regardless, she knew that if even a modicum of

proper behavior was to be maintained, it clearly would be her place to set the standards.

If she could.

She eased away from His Grace, putting several more inches of space between them—and instantly missed his warmth.

"Now I've offended you," he said in a low tone before tipping his hat and rumbling a greeting to Lady Foxbury as her carriage rolled by in the street. The matron's eyes widened with shock as she returned the polite gesture.

Lucinda nodded to Lady Foxbury, quickening her pace when her polite greeting was returned. "Not precisely, no," she answered. "You've surprised me, certainly. But this way of speaking one's mind plainly is something I'm beginning to enjoy."

And something I could easily become accustomed to, she thought.

"In that case," the duke returned, pulling her closer yet again, "let me be perfectly frank and tell you that I much prefer you by my side rather than several steps distant."

Lucinda laughed, knowing her rebellious body also enjoyed the nearness of his much taller, broader frame. "Your Grace, though I understand you've been out of polite society for some time, I suspect you recall what is considered appropriate behavior while courting a lady. This," she said, motioning to the distance she was currently putting between them, "is acceptable. I will not have my reputation sullied for the sake of a horse."

His disgruntled growl should have frightened Lucinda, but she found herself amused and charmed, even when he frowned at her.

"So it's the horse alone that convinced you to allow me to court you?" he asked.

Lucinda chided herself for the delight she seemed to be finding in every tiny detail about this very large man.

Why on earth was she amused when he voiced his displeasure? Why did she not feel threatened by his obvious irritation instead of noticing that his eyes appeared more green than hazel when he wore a green waistcoat?

She shrugged mentally. Surely what she was feeling was a normal reaction to a very handsome man.

"It is King Solomon's Mine that holds my heart, Your Grace," she answered, then added, "he is, after all, quite a horse."

6

"Quite a horse indeed," Will muttered, landing a punishing blow on his sparring partner's jaw and sending him to the mat.

"My apologies, Dinsford." He pulled the man to his feet and propped him up in the corner.

The young man massaged his jaw and grinned at Will. "It's me own fault. Shouldn't'a taught ya the right hook."

Will smiled, taking a towel hanging on a peg in the wall. He wiped the sweat from his arms and bare chest, the pounding exchange of the last hour beginning to make itself felt.

"Something on your mind?"

Will turned slowly and saw Carmichael seated in the shadows against the wall. "I was just about to ask you the same question, old man." He bent to shake his wet hair before rubbing his head with the damp towel. "You've been sitting there for nearly an hour without a word. That's quite an accomplishment for you," he finished, grinning.

Carmichael merely wiped at a bead of moisture that had somehow made its way to his immaculate breeches and stood. "Buy me a drink and I'll tell you."

"I hope the ale is to your liking." Will motioned for his superior to follow him.

Carmichael sidestepped a burly man lifting what

looked to be two sacks full of grain tied to a long pole, before answering, "I suppose it will have to be."

The two men moved toward the edge of the shadowy room, where a table was simply laid with pitchers of ale and tin tankards.

"I see the aristocracy has invaded your pugilistic paradise," Carmichael began, filling a tankard for himself.

Will let out a growl of disgust. "Every ham-fisted idiot with all his teeth wants to lose a few of them here. What was wrong with a bucket and ladle, I'll never know."

He filled his tankard and took a swig, swishing it about in his mouth, then spitting into the empty pitcher, the ale tinged with his blood.

"You might want to hold on to some of that."

Will joined Carmichael on the raised planked seating built to afford an unobstructed view of where the men boxed. "Didn't you know? I've an endless supply of blood."

Carmichael quirked a brow, then unobtrusively took in their surroundings, his gaze sharp. Apparently satisfied that they wouldn't be overheard, he looked at Will. "I understand congratulations are in order."

"Does anything happen in London that you are not instantly aware of?" Will asked sarcastically.

"No. That's the whole point. Now brief me on Lady Lucinda."

Will waited until the pugilists resumed their match. The cheers of the men seated on the benches farther down the room, combined with the thuds from fists hitting muscle and grunts of pain, provided cover for his answer. "Against her better judgment, she's agreed to let me court her."

"I told you she'd fall for your brawny charm."

Will gave Carmichael a piercing look before taking a drink. "Think again, old man. I had to offer King Solomon's Mine."

Will could swear he heard Carmichael chortle, though not a hint of a smile spoiled his solemn demeanor.

"I am sorry for that."

"No more sorry than I." It was true that Will prized the stallion, but he'd been a Corinthian long enough to know that no horse was worth the life of a lady. He'd done his job to the fullest, securing a legitimate reason to spend time with Lady Lucinda so he could protect her. But he'd done vastly more than was necessary. He'd shamelessly flirted with the woman. He'd gone out of his way to impress her.

And the aunts. He'd held his tongue and smiled and did the pretty when he'd wanted to run from the room and break as many items in his wake as possible.

"Bloody hell," Will growled. "I don't know that I'm the right man for this."

Carmichael watched the fighters, their rough dance gaining speed. "Clairemont, you know as well as I that there is no going back now. If it's the horse—"

"It's not the horse, it's the woman. I want to—"

Carmichael applauded a particularly skillful blow. "Bed her? That's nothing to be concerned about."

"Of course I want to bed her," Will said impatiently. "A man would have to be dead and buried not to. No," he said, his frustration growing, "I want to talk to her. I like talking to her. Dammit, the bedding part is natural. Wanting to spend time with her outside the bedchamber is not."

Carmichael turned to look at Will, understanding written across his face. "I see."

"Then you'll find someone else—"

"Just because I understand the situation does not mean that I've any more options than before. You're the man for this assignment." Carmichael turned back to the sparring match. "You've already made the initial contact. To send in another agent at this point would cause suspicion."

Will suppressed the desire to slam his fist through the planked seating and instead unleashed his anger on the tankard, nearly denting the tin. "You don't understand; I fear that my preoccupation may put the mission at risk."

"I trained you myself. I know what you're capable of," Carmichael answered, his tone slightly altered, the earlier understanding replaced with steel. "Are we in agreement?"

Will carefully set the tankard on the wooden bench. He knew better than to press Carmichael further. The man had the temperament of a bulldog, no matter how elegantly he dressed. Once his mind was made up, he was unswerving in his determination. Besides, Will knew that Carmichael was right; to bring in another agent at this stage of the game would be dangerous. In truth, his feelings for Lady Lucinda would only strengthen his resolve to keep her safe from Garenne.

Perhaps that was the answer, then: focus on his hatred for Garenne and let all other emotions go.

"Yes, we're in agreement," he finally responded, settling his elbows on his knees and massaging his temples.

"Good. Now, about Lady Lucinda. It seems she enjoys early morning rides—alone."

Will dropped his hands and turned to Carmichael. "You mean accompanied only by servants, yes?"

"No, by 'alone' I mean just that. She's adamantly opposed to having an escort, despite the best efforts of the Furies."

"Good God, man, you must have been misinformed. Those women control all they survey. Not even Lady Lucinda would dare cross them."

Carmichael rose. "As you've said, she's a most remarkable woman."

* * *

Lucinda wanted to scream with joy. The wind had pulled the pins from her hair, and the thick braid blew free, whipping like a banner as she raced Tristan, her dapple gray gelding, through Hyde Park. The sun had only just come up, setting the birds to singing on what promised to be a fine day.

She slowed the gelding with a gentle tug on the reins and crossed to follow her favorite path. Lucinda lived for her morning rides, free of everyone, even the servants, and the expectations that normally followed her wherever she went.

It hadn't been easy, but she'd managed to convince her aunts of the need for such a thing. Actually, in truth she'd blackmailed each of them into submission. And while reading to Charlotte each evening from the Bible, writing Bessie's frightfully colorful dictation to her many admirers, and sneaking Victoria's favorite brandy past the entire household on a monthly basis was not how Lucinda would ideally spend her time, it was worth it all the same.

She suspected that somewhere, among the groves of oak trees, near the eastern gate by which Lucinda arrived and left, a groom lingered for what must have been, at times, a miserably cold and dreary two hours.

Halting the gelding next to a large rock she'd used to dismount many times in the past, she gathered the skirt of her green riding habit and slid from the saddle. Tristan turned his head, ears pricking forward with interest at the sight of the lush, green grass. Lucinda drew the reins over the gray's head then allowed him to graze.

She gratefully sat down near him, dropping the reins to rest in the spring grass. She'd tossed and turned most of the night, nervous energy coursing through her veins and keeping her from soundly sleeping. Even with a pillow over her head. "Even with two," she solemnly told

Tristan, who simply paused for a moment, then continued to chew the flavorful grass.

The conversation with the duke plagued Lucinda's conscience. "He is, after all, quite a horse," she scoffed, wondering at the boldness with which she'd so easily responded. Really, the entire conversation had been altogether too bold, as Amelia would undoubtedly point out had she known of it.

But she didn't. Not yet anyway. A twinge of guilt flickered. She'd not sought out her dearest friend's company since the ball—or, if she were completely honest, since meeting the duke.

Lucinda pulled a daisy free and began to tear the white petals from the flower, one by one. She knew what Amelia would say of the scheme—even worse, what she would think of Lucinda's obvious attraction to him.

And worst of all? Amelia would be right. Lucinda was treading on dangerous ground, which only made it all the more exciting. Actually, it rather shook the earth, if the current vibration of the ground beneath her was any indication.

Puzzled, Lucinda looked up. A massive, coal black horse and its equally large rider were quickly approaching.

She jumped to her feet, holding tightly to Tristan's reins. For his part, the gray thought little of their impending guests, affording them only a slow glance before setting his sights on a patch of succulent overgrown blades.

The black horse was eating up the earth with his powerful strides, the rider sitting easily in the saddle despite the speed. Lucinda didn't know whether to be thrilled or terrified by the sight and wondered for a moment at the curious relationship between the two emotions.

She couldn't identify the horse and rider, for the morning sun hazed their figures. Her eyes narrowed in an attempt to make out the man.

With nary a second to spare, the rider reined in the big black, and the horse immediately responded, slowing to a canter, then a trot, and finally a walk.

Lucinda gathered her wits about her and prepared to unleash a particularly pungent verbal set-down. She shaded her eyes from the sun in order to see the pair more closely.

"Fancy meeting you here."

Despite having met him only mere days before, Lucinda would have known that voice anywhere. The husky tone sent a shiver down her spine and all the way to the tips of her riding boots. She relished the sensation for a moment then remembered what she had been about to do. "Your Grace, how nice of you to join me. Oh, and I do thank you for refraining from running your overgrown mount over the top of—"

Her reference to the horse had been smartly punctuated with a sweeping gesture and sarcastic look in the horse's direction. That was the moment Lucinda realized the identity of the horse.

"King Solomon's Mine," she breathed, dropping Tristan's reins to rush to his side.

She stroked his head, pressing her own cheek to his before kissing his velvety nose. "It's been so long since I last saw him," she said, tears misting her eyes.

The duke dismounted and joined her. "Has Sol grown that much, then?" he asked playfully.

Lucinda rolled her eyes at him before turning back to the horse. "Oh, no, not at all. It's the forelock," she began, reaching for the long, glossy length of hair that fell just between King Solomon's ears. "He used to wear it to the side much like the other young bucks about town. This is far superior, though, I must say," she finished, giving him a loving pat on the neck before stepping back to reclaim Tristan.

The duke led the stallion past Lucinda to where Tristan was happily grazing. He gestured toward a bench neatly tucked into a copse of trees nearby. "May I join you, or would sharing a seat be too scandalous an act for the proper Lady Lucinda?"

Lucinda knew from the amused half smile accompanying his question that the duke was simply quizzing her, but she desperately wanted to prove the blasted man wrong. "By all means," she replied, failing to add that they were, in fact, not alone, if her suspicion was correct that a groom followed close behind.

She strode to the bench and primly sat down, taking care to arrange her riding habit and reaching to adjust her black beaver hat. She felt the loose braid at her neck and nearly yelped. What must he think? She was unaccompanied, in the middle of Hyde Park, and with her hair nearly falling in her face.

She looked up just in time to catch the duke tossing his crop, hat, and gloves on the ground before pulling at his somewhat wrinkled neckcloth. His hair had been tousled by the wind, the long dark locks escaping what looked to have at some point been a neatly combed style. The once severely pressed wool of his dark blue waistcoat was now creased across the shoulders, whether from the ride itself or simply from accommodating his massive muscles Lucinda could not say. His leather riding breeches were in fairly good condition, though they did mold to his legs in such a way that Lucinda found it troubling.

He looks good enough to eat, Lucinda thought to herself, realizing that His Grace most likely would not give a fig whether her hair was finely coiffed or not.

He sat down next to her, running a hand through his thick hair, then turning his gaze to hers. "Good morning."

Lucinda slicked her tongue over her suddenly dry lips before answering. "And good morning to you. What brings you to Hyde Park at such an early hour, Your Grace?"

He looked tired to Lucinda, his eyes still soft from sleep and his jaw rough with hair. Something in her begged to reach out and run her gloved finger over the light beard. Would it be soft, as surely his deep black hair was, or coarse? She wouldn't—no, couldn't—find out.

"What wouldn't bring me, Lady Lucinda? The fine weather. A healthful ride. You," he answered, resting one booted foot on the opposing knee.

His leg now touched hers, the fitted breeches and her bright green merino riding costume all that separated their skin. Her fingers tingled and she instinctively moved to touch him. With effort, she restrained herself, clenched her fingers, and tucked her hands beneath her skirts. She offered a small smile to the duke. "I find my hands in need of warmth just now. I am chilled—that is to say, my hands are, and I fear these York gloves are doing little to help."

He looked slightly puzzled at Lucinda's stammering, then understanding dawned. "Let me be of service," he said, pulling one hand into his and then the other, cupping both and gently rubbing back and forth with his own.

This is what I get for playing with fire, Lucinda mused silently, the rhythm of his ministrations lulling her into a pleasant fog.

"Are we quite alone?" he asked, his tone gruff but not angry.

Lucinda sensed that she should rouse herself, but the feel of his hands on hers was overwhelming. "Yes."

His hands stopped and tightened around hers. "The women I choose to court are not allowed to cavort through the woods like fairies, unattended and in a state of some dishabille."

Now he sounded angry, the flecks of green in his eyes

clouding to a deep moss. Lucinda bit her lower lip in response, her own eyes unable to hold his absorbing glance.

Lucinda very nearly felt embarrassed and apologetic.

Very nearly.

Her initial response shifted into something altogether different, something akin to outrage and sheer, hot fury. She pried her hands from his and took a deep breath. "You have absolutely no right to speak to me in such a superior tone," she ground out, her hands balling into fists.

The duke was looking just past Lucinda's head at the copse of trees behind them. His eyes were practically black, the pupils dilated with rage. Lucinda began to reconsider her words, though her anger at his ridiculous remark was warranted, on that she would not budge.

And all at once, he grabbed her by the shoulders and heaved their combined weight against the back of the bench, upending the seat until they were delivered to the soft ground below. "You impertinent, impossible woman," he bit out, just before he pulled Lucinda to him and kissed her.

Oh, God, this is madness, Lucinda thought, wondering whether she'd hit her head and was now imagining the duke's surprisingly soft yet firm lips on hers, his tongue as it nimbly attacked her own, his hands as they freed her buttons, revealing her thin white habit shirt beneath.

Lucinda's leg hitched over his hip, confirming what she'd feared: This was not the product of a particularly nasty spill, and she'd no hope of saying no, as her body clearly had other plans.

The duke growled low into Lucinda's mouth, obviously pleased with her counterattack. He heatedly untied the bow at her neck, then pulled his mouth from hers, his lips traveling the length of her neck before he set to work on her shirt buttons.

Lucinda's body pulsed with diminutive fireworks bursting into vivid colors with each button he released.

She ran her hand through his hair, stopping at the nape to entwine a lock between her fingers. She'd intended on pushing him away, but somehow the need growing inside of her wouldn't let her. She squeezed her eyes shut, a pleasurable sense of dizziness pushing her toward something that both thrilled and terrified her.

"Are you quite sure that it is Sol who holds your heart entirely, my lady?"

Garenne moved swiftly, silently down the wooded trail. Pain stabbed his skull in a series of knife-sharp jabs. He swung his head to the right, then left to assure he was alone, and brilliant comets of light flared on the edges of his peripheral vision. He narrowed his eyes against the resulting disorientation and snarled silently as his throat constricted, making it difficult to swallow.

He should have followed Clairemont home from the ball and killed him when he'd had the chance.

How the man had sensed his presence among the park's trees was beyond comprehension. But the duke had, looking directly at Garenne before throwing the woman to the ground. There'd barely been enough time to control his rage, to stop himself from throwing his knife directly into the bastard's neck.

It would be maddening to the average man, but Garenne knew himself to be exceptional. It was not his fault that Clairemont's presence at the ball had forced the attempt. Nor was it a lack of skill that had led to the failure. Clairemont was to blame and, in time, Garenne would make him pay. But for now, he knew that all of his focus must be on the woman.

Pressure built inside his skull, rage exacerbating the inevitable reactions brought on by frustration.

He came across a hare, frozen with fright in the middle of the path. Garenne threw the knife with expertise, landing its tip in the animal's left ear and pinning it to the ground.

He walked to where the rabbit lay, wounded and terrified. He bent down to retrieve his knife with one hand, the other coming to encircle the rabbit's neck. He squeezed hard, then flung the limp animal into the foliage.

The pain eased and the lights impacting his vision ceased flashing. Once again, he could consider the situation dispassionately.

"Clearly, I will require assistance. A few choice operatives should accomplish the desired goal.

"Soon. Very soon," he whispered to himself before making his way from the park.

7

"Perhaps the blue?" Lucinda held up a length of deep-hued sapphire ribbon, the satiny end trailing from her gloved fingers. The bright blue gleamed against the rose pink bodice of her walking dress.

Pomeroy Milliners sold the finest ribbons in the whole of London, their countless offerings varied enough to satisfy even Lady Hertford, the Prince Regent's notoriously discriminating mistress. And while Lucinda knew full well that this particular shade of blue suited her perfectly, she welcomed the opportunity to distract Amelia from her current line of questioning.

"Your skill at evading inquiries is impressive, but hardly a match for me. I know you too well." Amelia slipped the ribbon from Lucinda's fingers and returned it to the glass-topped case counter. "Now, please explain how allowing the Duke of Clairemont to court you is in any way advantageous."

"Shhh." Lucinda lowered her lashes and her gaze flicked over the shop. Across the room, ladies and their maids crowded around a table where a new shipment of ribbons was decoratively displayed with a rainbow of matching gloves and lace-trimmed handkerchiefs. Their chattering filled the air, conveniently covering her murmured conversation with Amelia.

Nearer at hand, however, the narrow-faced clerk behind the counter had sidled closer. Lucinda was sure the woman's apparent absorption in rearranging spools of purple and blue ribbons was wholly feigned.

Convinced the clerk had heard Amelia's question, Lucinda smiled sweetly when the woman glanced sideways, her cheeks flushing as she met Lucinda's gaze.

"I believe I would like to see something in red," Lucinda said, politely but firmly.

She waited until the clerk had disappeared behind the heavy curtain that separated the storage area from the remainder of the shop before she answered Amelia. "How could it *not* be to my advantage?" she asked, turning to stroll between the tables heavily laden with ribbon. The move took them farther away from the counter and, in an excess of caution, also put more space between them and the other shoppers. Gossip spread through the ton with amazing speed; Lucinda refused to aid it by being carelessly overheard.

Amelia hurried after her, took a firm hold on the skirt of her pelisse, and tugged.

Pulled off stride, Lucinda halted abruptly and turned to look at her friend. "Was that truly necessary?" she asked mildly.

Amelia let out an exasperated sigh and slipped her arm through Lucinda's, steering them toward a settee, comfortably upholstered in gold and white striped silk and situated conveniently along the opposite wall.

"Sit," she commanded, and waited for Lucinda to do so before settling beside her. She tugged off her right glove and touched her palm to Lucinda's forehead. "Are you feeling well?"

Lucinda's swift gurgle of laughter had her glancing quickly at the crowd of ladies filling the shop's aisles before answering, "Yes, quite well, thank—"

"Have you been imbibing? Running wild through the heath by the light of a full moon?" Amelia's eyes grew rounder as she whispered, "Did the Devil himself visit you in a dream?"

Lucinda couldn't help herself; she tilted her head back and let out a most unladylike laugh. The trio of sour ladies examining the selection of velvet ribbon two aisles away turned as one to gape at her. The eldest frowned, her gray brows lowering over dark eyes that snapped with disapproval.

"I beg your pardon, but my friend possesses quite an imagination and took me by surprise," Lucinda said in apology. The older woman sniffed, but she and her companions nodded and returned to perusing the selection.

"Amelia, what on earth would lead you to believe that any of those outrageous claims would be true?"

The look of concern disappeared from Amelia's face, replaced by a glint of mischief. "How else would one explain your sudden lapse in judgment? 'How could it *not* be?'" she repeated in a gently mocking tone. "How *could* the duke's courtship be advantageous to you, a woman who has always declared that marriage holds no interest for you whatso—"

"Of all people, Amelia, you're the one I would expect to be happy for me," Lucinda interrupted. "Wasn't it you who told me: 'Your one true love is out there, just waiting for the day you'll find him.'?"

Amelia rolled her eyes in response. "Of course, but I wasn't speaking of His Grace, Lucinda."

"But why? He's wealthy, handsome—"

"And a hedonist," Amelia continued in an urgent whisper. "Rumored to have coaxed a woman out of her clothes with merely one word. Is this your one true love?"

"Impossible," Lucinda balked, and then couldn't resist adding, "Who was the woman?"

"Lady Swindon," Amelia answered dramatically. "And she's only one of many."

Lucinda's mind raced back to the park bench, when the duke's lips had been on hers. He'd completely undone her in less than five minutes. Lady Swindon was clearly either weaker or wiser than she.

"I am no Lady Swindon, as you are well aware," Lucinda said, desperately trying to harness her thoughts before they betrayed her.

The lanky clerk appeared through the curtained doorway and came toward them, her arms laden with ribbons in every shade of red.

"Are you absolutely certain this is all you have?" Lucinda asked, desperate to secure their privacy once more.

"I'll look again, my lady," the clerk answered before disappearing back into the storeroom.

"Exactly my point," Amelia shot back in a hushed tone. "You are a woman of discriminating sensibility with no inclination to take a husband. So why are you engaged in this ill-conceived association with Clairemont?"

To disappoint Amelia was unthinkable; to lie to her, impossible. Lucinda took her friend's hand in hers and squeezed. "If I confide in you, you must promise to tell no one, not even your husband," she said earnestly, all amusement gone.

"Is that quite necessary? I share my deepest, most private thoughts with John—"

"Not even John," Lucinda insisted.

Amelia narrowed her eyes consideringly. "Very well. I promise. But only because I am sure you wouldn't ask this of me were it not absolutely necessary."

Lucinda leaned closer until there wasn't a hairsbreadth between their skirts on the settee. "I've come to an agreement with the duke regarding King Solomon's Mine," she whispered.

A look of confusion clouded Amelia's face. "What on

earth does a horse have to do with you finding your one true love?"

"Nothing, actually. I've not changed my opinion in regards to marriage, Amelia. I am and will always be deliriously happy for you and your John, but it simply isn't something I want." Lucinda paused, glancing about to ensure no one was listening. "Clairemont has acquiesced to his mother's wishes for an heir—which requires him to find a bride."

Amelia sat back and absorbed this piece of the puzzle, clearly still befuddled. "Well, I'm delighted he has agreed to marry, but I fail to see how this has anything to do with the horse."

"We've come to an understanding. I allow him to court me. If, at the end of the allotted time, I've fallen for his innumerable charms, we marry. If not, I win King Solomon's Mine and secure the stallion for our breeding program."

Amelia's mouth curved into an O of comprehension as the last piece fell into place. "Lady Lucinda Grey, you know that I hold every confidence in your ability to do anything you set your mind to, but this is no ordinary man you're dealing with."

"Oh, Amelia, I'm fully aware of that. But I've declined proposals from nearly every eligible bachelor in London. Surely I have one more refusal left in me." The heat that had flared when the duke traced her bare skin with his fingertips lingered on Lucinda's body and flared anew with the mere mention of him. Her awareness of just how unordinary the man was could not be denied but she wouldn't, couldn't, confess her weakness to Amelia.

Amelia squeezed Lucinda's hand. "And the Furies, what do they have to say about your ambitious scheme?"

"They had their reservations," Lucinda began, a wry

smile curving her lips. "That is, until I told them that the duke is a particular friend of your husband's."

Amelia's eyes flew wide with alarm. "You didn't!"

Lucinda chuckled. "Really, they're not that terrifying, are they?"

"You have to ask?"

Lucinda patted Amelia's hand and stood, pulling her friend after her. "I'm only having a bit of fun, though Lord Northrop's friendship with the duke may be of some help to me."

Amelia flashed a wicked grin. "Leave it to me," she said knowingly, then stopped. "But Lucinda, you will take care, won't you? I've never considered fighting a duel, but to save you from the clutches of Iron Will, I would do so without question."

Lucinda knew that despite Amelia's light tone, her friend's concerns were real. They matched the very ones taking shape in her own heart, and for the first time in her life Lucinda wondered whether she'd taken an irrevocable misstep.

"I know, and I would do the same for you without hesitation," she answered. "But first . . ." She looked toward the counter, where the exhausted clerk had arranged what was surely every last red ribbon in the shop's inventory for their review. "I believe we have need of many red ribbons."

How women could spend such a vast amount of time doing what amounted to child's play was beyond Will. Lady Lucinda and Lady Northrop had been occupied in Pomeroy's for nearly an hour, leaving Will to loiter on New Bond Street like some young buck desperate for attention. "Purveyors of the finest ladies' millinery, ribbons, and bows," Will quoted, reading from the gilded scrollwork on the wooden sign above the shop's entry.

He bit out a curse, muttering under his breath.

If someone had told him a fortnight ago that he would find himself within ten miles of such a ridiculous shop, Will would have laughed. And then, most likely, hit the man for having the temerity to suggest he'd dangle after a woman while she trolled the shops for fripperies.

But the incident in the park had been too near a thing for Will's liking. Garenne wouldn't take the failure lightly. Will's unorthodox method of thwarting the Frenchman would likely fuel his determination to complete the mission.

Will planned to keep Lucinda under Young Corinthian guard day and night until the Frenchman was in custody and her safety assured. Which was why he found himself outside Pomeroy's, wishing to God that Lady Lucinda had opted to spend her time at home in her parlor.

Still, the crowded avenue offered many shops in which a man of Will's social and financial position could claim an interest. "Haberdasher, tailor, fanciful snuff-boxes," he recited as he surveyed the shops surrounding Pomeroy's.

"Unfortunately," Will muttered under his breath, "I couldn't give a bloody damn about any of it."

Still, anyone seeing him would have to agree it was plausible that he would be found at one time or another on New Bond Street, a fact that would not be lost on Lady Lucinda.

Lady Lucinda. The taste of her lingered on his tongue. Her sweet surrender in the park had been as surprising as it was unforgettable. He ached at the memory of her—the lush curves of her body lifting against him, her skin flushed with desire.

But the park had been the wrong place, the wrong time. Just plain wrong. Will had come to know Garenne's habits too well to have lingered in the grass with Lucinda. Though the Frenchman wouldn't allow himself to be drawn out, he was no less dangerous. He would waste no time before attacking again.

Will had alerted Carmichael and his fellow Corinthians about the foiled attempt, arranging for more men to be assigned to the case. He knew that he did not *need* to be here, watching her, but he felt a certain sense of duty to the case. She required looking after. And he was the right man for the job.

A gaggle of fresh-faced young misses approached, giggling and eyeing him with interest as they walked by. Will ignored them and looked past the group to the tall, impeccably dressed gentleman strolling toward him, a few yards behind the chattering girls.

"I never would have pegged you for a dandy," Lord Marcus MacInnes, the Earl of Weston, drawled as he neared Will, coming to stand next to him. "Yet here you are, Clairemont, shopping. On New Bond Street. Will wonders never cease?"

Will eyed Weston, relieved to have the seasoned Corinthian on the case. The Scotsman's fashionable appearance and devil-may-care attitude had proven to be the perfect cover for Corinthian business in the past, and Will had high hopes it would serve their efforts well now.

"You've caught me, then," Will responded sarcastically. "Though one has to wonder just what you're doing here."

Weston grinned. "Well played, Clairemont."

The door to Pomeroy's opened suddenly and Lady Lucinda and Lady Northrop stepped over the threshold, followed by their maids, who carried several wrapped parcels. The sight put an abrupt halt to their conversation.

"Drop back and follow us," Will said in a low tone, keeping his facial expression relaxed and uninterested.

Weston clapped Will on the back and laughed. "Of

course," he replied, his jovial action belying the true nature of their interaction.

Will moved quickly, easing behind a passing tall, elderly gentleman escorting a very rotund lady gowned in black. He used the couple as concealment until they were close to Lady Lucinda's party. Then he slowed, letting the space lengthen between himself and the elderly couple.

"Lady Lucinda, Lady Northrop." He approached the two women and their maids.

He held back a smile at the surprise and, if he wasn't mistaken, pleasure that appeared on Lucinda's face.

"Your Grace," Lady Northrop began, her expression markedly less cheerful than Lady Lucinda's. "I must admit to some surprise at finding you here," she said.

Will bowed, smiling at Lady Lucinda before turning to Lady Northrop, a look of bewilderment clouding his face. "Indeed? I cannot imagine why."

Lady Northrop's ears turned scarlet at the tips as they almost always did whenever they met. "Surely I am not the only one to marvel at the sight of Iron Will strolling down New Bond Street. Or would you have us believe you've suddenly become obsessed with the cut of your waistcoat?"

Will spread his hands, palms out, in a plea for mercy from Lady Northrop. "Ah, you've caught me out. In truth, I could not have cared less for any of this." He paused, gesturing at the surrounding shops. The fashionable set thronged the walkways and street, to see and be seen. "But of late I've found myself quite taken with the notion of self-improvement."

He looked at Lady Lucinda, lifting an eyebrow in a silent request for confirmation. "Lady Lucinda, have I not demonstrated a marked desire to prove myself a gentleman in every way?"

He dared her to answer truthfully. The narrowing of

her eyes told him she knew he was referring to their interlude in the park.

"I wouldn't dream of judging you, Your Grace, though your 'marked desire' is most convincing." She finished off the sentence with a serene smile, and he half expected her to drop into a polite curtsy.

"Be that as it may," Lady Northrop cut in, "I pray you will remember that a well-cut coat alone does not make the man. A true gentleman is one in both manners and heart."

"Time spent with you is always edifying, Lady Northrop," Will assured her solemnly. He offered an arm to each lady. "Would you care to instruct me further while enjoying ices? We're nearly to Gunter's."

Lady Northrop looked confused for a moment, clearly searching for the words to refuse him without violating the code of manners drilled into all genteel young girls long before they entered society.

"That would be most gentlemanly of you," Lady Lucinda responded, taking Will's arm.

Lady Northrop's mouth opened and closed in a vaguely fishlike fashion as the two waited patiently for her response. Finally, she settled her gloved fingers on Will's coat sleeve. "It would be rude of me to deny your request at this juncture, would it not?"

"Yes," Will and Lady Lucinda said in unison.

"Very well." Lady Northrop glanced over her shoulder before catching Lady Lucinda's eye. "Perhaps we should have your Mary tell the coachman we'll be a bit longer and then send our maids home?"

Lady Lucinda agreed, and moments later Will escorted the two women down the street toward Gunter's.

The three walked in silence the short distance to Berkeley Square, curious looks from fellow pedestrians meeting their every step.

Will leaned toward Lady Northrop, dropping his

voice to a murmur as he asked, "Lady Northrop, have you engaged in some sort of scandalous behavior that I should be aware of?"

Lady Northrop's eyebrows shot up, and she gaped at him.

"Everyone is looking at us," he explained, all innocence.

Her eyes narrowed, and her mouth opened, but she lost her opportunity to reply when Will drew them to a stop.

"Ladies," Will said, holding open the door and stepping back to gesture them inside.

The fashionable crowd inside turned to see who was entering, their heads swiveling almost as one and then nodding in the expected polite greeting to both Lady Lucinda and Lady Northrop.

Their expressions of surprise, shock, and utter dismay when they recognized Will were laughable. He fought back the urge to bare his teeth at them, simply for the amusement of hearing them all gasp, and instead intercepted a waiter. "A table for three," he said gruffly.

The waiter jumped to attention, motioning to a fellow server to make room in the already crowded parlor for the trio. A table and three chairs were brought out and set near the window; the waiter bowed to Will's party and gestured for them to follow.

Will could have sworn he heard a unified intake of breath as they made their way to the table, utensils full of fanciful sweets stopping just short of gaping mouths.

"Lady Northrop, I beg your pardon," he said, settling his frame into his chair after ensuring the ladies were comfortably seated.

"What for?" Lady Northrop asked suspiciously.

"Clearly it is Lady Lucinda who has inspired such interest," Will said sardonically.

Lady Lucinda responded by arching a brow at him in amusement. Lady Northrop sniffed her disbelief and the two turned to question the hovering server about the cakes available.

No sooner had the trio ordered than the tinkling of bells signaled a newcomer. The door swung wide and a footman appeared, dressed head to toe in scarlet livery, his gold buttons and embroidery bright enough to reflect and perhaps substitute for the midday sun. The man swept the room with a supercilious gaze, stepping back with a low bow to usher in a woman.

Her spectacular mane of auburn curls was fashionably bound beneath a charming deep forest green hat. Her matching pelisse clung to the curve of her shoulders, draping expertly over the gown beneath. The woman surveyed the shop's occupants, her emerald green eyes reflecting the pleasure she felt at such attention.

She walked across the room to join a group of women clustered at a table, the hum of whispers beginning anew.

"Lady Swindon certainly does know how to make an entrance," Lady Lucinda commented.

Lady Northrop rolled her eyes in response and unfolded a linen napkin. "That is one way of looking at it," she confirmed, arranging the snowy white square over her lap.

Will kept his eyes on the window, hopeful that the two were finished.

"Are you acquainted with Lady Swindon, Your Grace?" Lucinda asked.

Will's instinct was to growl a particularly fervent oath, but even he knew that such a response was beyond the outer bounds of propriety. Fortunately, the waiter arrived with the requested ices and plate of cakes before he could speak. The brief interruption allowed him time to manage a more polite reply. "Yes, we are acquainted."

"Would you be so kind as to introduce me?"

Will turned to Lady Lucinda, not quite sure he'd heard her correctly. "I'm sorry?"

Lucinda dabbed at her mouth, looking up at him through her lashes. "I'm not acquainted with Lady Swindon, though I have heard a great deal about her. I find her interesting, and would like to meet her."

Will slowly continued to spoon the cold ice into his mouth. When he'd reached the bottom of the bowl, he looked at Lady Northrop, whose bland stare told him she wasn't about to offer help in any way. He turned his attention to Lady Lucinda, who eyed him expectantly.

He wondered how long he would have to pretend he hadn't heard her before she repeated the request.

Lady Lucinda smiled sweetly. "I do wonder, Your Grace, if you would introduce us?"

A great deal longer than this, apparently.

"Bloody hell," he muttered under his breath before dropping his spoon on the table with a clatter. "She is not like you, Lady Lucinda, not in any way."

Lady Lucinda looked into his eyes, her brows furrowing. "Whatever do you mean, Your Grace?" she asked softly.

"She may have a title, but she does not possess any of the qualities that someone in her position should."

"Not unlike you, Your Grace," Lady Lucinda responded. "And yet, look at how well we are managing."

"Oh, my," Lady Northrop whispered, her gaze focused just beyond Will's shoulder.

Will and Lady Lucinda turned to see what had upset Lady Northrop, only to find Lady Swindon herself approaching.

Will's last encounter with the woman had not gone well. She'd convinced a footman to allow her entry to his town house and Will had found her disrobed and wild-eyed in his bed, begging him to take her back.

She'd been reasonable enough in the beginning, joining in long nights of lusty sex with unabashed enthusiasm and no expectations beyond the carnal. Which was exactly what Will had hoped for from the young, beautiful widow.

But then she'd married the aging Lord Swindon, turning her from a widow to the wife of a respected acquaintance. He'd ended the affair as gently as he could, but the woman clearly still held a grudge, if the expression on her face was any indication.

"Lady Swindon." Will said politely, standing. "You're looking well."

She acknowledged the compliment with a gracious nod, her emerald eyes taking in the trio. "Your Grace, how kind of you to say so," she responded coolly before turning to Lucinda. Her frosty gaze examined Lady Lucinda's face as if committing it to memory. "Lady Lucinda, your reputation precedes you."

Will shifted, resting one hand on the back of Lady Lucinda's chair. The implied intimacy of the act was duly noted by the redhead and her eyes narrowed.

"Lady Swindon." Lady Lucinda nodded, a sincere smile on her lips.

Lady Swindon's creamy complexion pinkened as she glared at Will. "Really, Your Grace. She is charming. So very charming," she murmured in a tone that could cut glass, before turning her attention back to Lady Lucinda. "You'll have quite a time of it taming this one, Lady Lucinda."

"We shall see," Lady Lucinda replied resolutely, then glanced at Will and Lady Northrop. "Your Grace, I do believe it is time for us to be off." She turned back to Lady Swindon, inclining her head in a gracious nod. "Good day."

Lady Swindon forced a smile before returning to her seat.

"Lady Lucinda," Will murmured as they rose and she took his arm, "I believe I underestimated you."

Lucinda looked up into Will's face. "Do not let it happen again, Your Grace."

8

The Young Corinthians Gentlemen's Club was not the most exclusive club in the city. Its membership boasted titles from baron to duke, but these barons and dukes (and quite everything in between) were not always of spotless reputation and respectability, which was why so many of them held the club in such affection. They darkened its doors at all hours of the day and night, comfortable in the knowledge that their fellow patrons could not afford to be judgmental, and, therefore, would not be.

The men enjoyed the comfortable armchairs and daily newspapers, complimentary bottles of sherry, and a limited selection of well-cooked English dishes. The brandy was a touch above good and the gambling opportunities were plentiful. The Corinthians Club was what every gentlemen's club should be: an escape from the daily duties that men in such a position endured.

It neither stood above the other clubs nor fell beneath, but rather maintained a constant level of comfort that its members had come to expect.

In all ways but one very important, and very clandestine, exception. For within the walls of the club the Young Corinthians conducted their business, perfectly hidden within the normal daily rhythms of catering to London aristocrats.

Staffed entirely by Corinthians and with a sufficient number of secret passageways, concealed entryways, and meeting rooms to satisfy even Carmichael himself, the club, it could be said, was an indispensable member of the Corinthian team.

To Will, it was simply home. He'd never really felt comfortable in the ducal mansion. The specter of his father cast a shadow so dark and wide it was well nigh impossible to escape the late duke's influence without walking out the door.

And so Will had—walked out the door, that was, hastening to the Corinthians Club at every available opportunity, business or not. He'd spent more birthdays there than he cared to admit and celebrated the successful conclusion of countless missions. In many ways, the club afforded Will a life he'd never known outside of its walls. The enduring relationships and satisfying work he'd found in Carmichael's organization were far more meaningful for him than anything his family offered.

Little else outside the Young Corinthians held a place in Will's heart.

Until now.

He appeared to be obsessed with Lady Lucinda.

Clearly this had come about because her life was in grave danger. Any man, or at least any man trained by the Young Corinthians, would find it difficult to ignore a woman in such straits.

It had nothing to do with her beauty.

Or her sense of adventure.

Or her intelligence.

Or her—

He stopped. He literally stopped moving. He had, in theory at least, been reaching for his glass of brandy. But he had stopped, because it seemed to be the only way to force his bloody brain to stop as well.

Of all the things he needed in his life, a mental catalog of the many attributes of Lady Lucinda Grey was not among them.

"Are you planning on drinking that brandy or have you decided to perform a magic rite for its continued safety and good health?"

Will looked at Carmichael, then looked at his arm, still frozen in space, hovering over the table.

He looked like a damn fool.

"Sit," Will said, motioning to the chair near him.

"What were you doing?" Carmichael inquired, settling in.

Will lifted the heavy crystal glass to his lips and swallowed, the liquor burning pleasantly down his throat. "Thinking, Carmichael. I can't recommend it highly enough."

Carmichael lifted a brow. "Work or pleasure?"

"Both, actually," Will replied, then halfheartedly retrieved the day's paper from the mahogany side table next to his chair.

"I trust you're not mixing the two."

Will took the paper in both hands and opened it wide.

Carmichael called to a footman to bring him a brandy. "You don't read the paper, Will."

"I do," Will replied gruffly.

The liveried servant set Carmichael's drink on the table and disappeared.

"Give me a moment," Carmichael said, then took a hearty sip of his brandy, swallowed, paused to consider, and shook his head decisively. "No, you still do not."

"Bloody hell."

"You know where we stand on such things. Personal interest has no place in Corinthian business."

Will dropped the *Times* in his lap and reached for Carmichael's brandy. "Just a moment, won't you," he said before throwing his head back and draining the glass. "Yes, I still do. Now, shall we talk about something else?"

"As you wish."

Will appreciated Carmichael's concern, but he could not bring himself to discuss the problem that was Lady Lucinda. Not only would Carmichael likely tell him in great detail why Will's interest in her was forbidden to an agent, but Will feared he would be disappointed in him. To engage in anything other than what the mission demanded with any asset—which clearly defined Lady Lucinda—was forbidden. But to contemplate relinquishing one's position in the Corinthians for a woman? The mere thought of surrendering his significant role within the brotherhood for something as inconsequential as love was simply too ridiculous for words. Such things had always mystified Will.

Northrop's choice of Amelia over his field position was beginning to make some sort of odd sense to Will— and this scared the hell out of him.

Regardless, he knew his duty and all that he owed to the Corinthians, and to Carmichael. To fall short in the eyes of his mentor was too much to risk.

Will roughly folded the paper and leaned forward, resting his elbows on his knees. "The incident in the park, then."

"Anything of particular interest?" Carmichael asked.

"No, though he's doing what I'd expected of him, I'll give him that," Will answered. "One attempt and nothing more. Garenne can't abide failure of any kind."

Carmichael nodded in acknowledgment. "His next move?"

"He prefers to work alone. He won't want to hire associates, but considering the mark, he may have to." Will paused to rub his temples. "Kidnapping a well-protected, prominent member of society is a far different proposition than assassinating an agent in the field. If he chooses to hire assistants, depending upon their number and skill, he could strike at any time. And my guess would be that he'll choose somewhere less public."

Carmichael toyed with his gold watch fob. "You're comfortable with the number of our men assigned to the situation?"

"He's not human, old man, so no, not even a thousand agents would put my mind at ease," Will answered. "But we'll catch him, that I know for sure."

"Alive, Will," Carmichael's low murmur cautioned. "He's no good to us dead."

Will resisted the urge to argue the point, methodically rubbing his temples once more in an attempt to dispel vivid thoughts of just what he would do to Garenne if given half the chance. "Yes, alive. If possible." He dropped his hand, fixing Carmichael with a hard stare. "If I have to kill him to save Lady Lucinda, I will."

Carmichael shrugged. "Of course."

A sudden burst of laughter erupted from the gaming room, the volume and intensity signaling the late hour.

"Now come with me," Carmichael said in a lighter tone. "I believe there's a five-pound note I've need to win back."

Will stood up from his chair and stretched. "Ever the optimist, Carmichael."

"Hardly. But I know a thing or two about odds, and you're bound to hit upon a losing streak one day," Carmichael answered, making his way to the gaming room just beyond.

"As I said, ever the optimist."

Lucinda had never dreamed that he would accept her invitation. Iron Will agreeing to attend an assembly at Almack's? Inconceivable.

But he had. Lucinda now stood with the duke just inside the assembly's upper rooms within the King Street building that housed Almack's. They faced Lady Jersey, as she eyed him skeptically from head to toe. No visitors to Almack's would be admitted tonight without Lady Jersey's approval.

Lucinda offered the woman a sweet smile when the patroness flicked her a sharp glance before returning her narrowed gaze to the duke. Clearly her perusal was an attempt to find fault with His Grace's appearance. In truth, his reputation alone should have barred him from the assembly.

But he was obviously escorting Lucinda, a fact that Lady Jersey could not overlook. Lucinda also knew Aunt Victoria had tortured the woman's mother for years with a particularly juicy bit of gossip involving the countess and an Italian opera singer from their youth. So Lucinda was not terribly surprised that the woman was having a difficult time of it.

Still, Lucinda had demanded that he play by the rules. Which meant he had to comply with the sartorial regulations, which had led to him donning the knee breeches that he currently wore. Trousers would never do at Almack's and she was beginning to understand why. The cream breeches molded to his legs in a most appealing way, *to say nothing of his—*

"Lady Lucinda?"

Lucinda pulled her thoughts from such an inappropriate path and focused on Lady Jersey. "I do beg your pardon, Lady Jersey. Would you be so kind as to repeat your question?"

"I said," the birdlike woman began, flicking her fingers dismissively in a distinct air of irritation, "that the duke is granted a Stranger's Ticket for the evening."

The duke offered Lady Jersey a dazzling smile and bowed. "Lady Jersey, always a pleasure."

"Hmph," the woman replied, gesturing for the two to remove themselves.

Lucinda curtsied with just the right mix of deference and serene confidence, then allowed the duke to escort her into the main assembly room, crowded with the cream of society.

"Was it the breeches?" he whispered in her ear. "I'm told I look especially fetching in breeches." His warm breath brushed her neck as he spoke and her skin prickled, her pulse racing.

Lucinda reined in her shivering nerves, relieved to spot her aunts not far away. She seized the distraction, lifting her fan to gain their attention. "I warn you, Your Grace," she said as she drew him with her through the throng, "you'd do well to be on your best behavior within the hallowed halls of Almack's."

He flashed her a wicked grin. "Must I? Even as pertains to you, Lady Lucinda?"

Her mouth formed an O of surprise. The shocking and, to be perfectly honest, delicious nature of his comment was outrageously pleasing. "Your Grace . . ." she whispered repressively, trying to restrain the rush of excited curiosity as to his meaning.

"I do adore the way you say that," he replied huskily, pasting a bored look on his face as they came to stand with her aunts.

"Well, well, Lady Jersey is wiser than I believed her to be," Victoria said in greeting, eyeing the duke with amusement. "And you, Your Grace, polish up quite well, I must say."

Will bowed before the aunts then flashed a charming smile. "High praise, indeed, especially from you."

"Do not become too used to it," Victoria replied, slyly winking at Lucinda before turning to her sisters. "Ladies, tepid lemonade and abysmal cake first, or straight to the tables?"

Charlotte gave Victoria a chiding look before answering. "The tables, I believe. Bessie, do you have a preference?"

Bessie was far too engrossed in admiring the duke's

breeches to hear Charlotte's query. The slight smile of appreciation on her face made Lucinda swallow her laughter. She knew just how her aunt felt.

"Aunt Bessie," Lucinda said a bit more loudly, waving her fan as unobtrusively as possible to gain her aunt's attention. "Shall we?" she asked, holding out her arm for her aunt.

Bessie pulled her gaze from the duke and took Lucinda's arm, the entire group moving toward the card room with its gaming tables. "Yes, quite," she said, then added, "I'm sorry, where are we going?"

"To the tables," Lucinda replied, then whispered, "Do try to keep up, Aunt."

"It's hardly my fault, dear. You are the one who insisted he wear those breeches," Bessie answered in a hushed tone, the smile returning to her lips.

"Fair enough."

They were, in a word, dangerous. Will now knew what the Furies did to pass the time. No sewing or needlepoint, painting or reading for this trio. No, clearly the three habitually played cards well into the wee hours, if their current individual winning streaks were any indication. Will looked out at his fellow five-card loo players and sighed. "Poor bastards," he said under his breath, watching the Marquess of Billingham accept his loss and Charlotte's latest win with as much grace as he could muster.

"Did you say something?" Lady Lucinda asked softly, her eyebrow arched in a most attractive way.

"You knew, and yet you did not warn me," he murmured, bending his head toward her, the intoxicating scent of her skin mingling with the heated air.

She merely smiled in response. Will existed in a simmering state of arousal in her presence and the wicked curve of her lips badly threatened his control.

"You brought me here for this very reason, didn't you?" he asked, leaning in closer. He was much taller than she was, and seated this close, the sight of her breasts as they rose and fell more rapidly in time with her quickened breathing did little to ease his current state. The faster flutter of her pulse beating at the base of her throat only heightened his desire. "It wasn't enough to watch poor Billingham fall to the Furies. You wanted to embarrass Iron Will."

Across the table, Billingham's wife tapped him on the shoulder and the marquess reluctantly stood, vacating his chair to stroll off with his spouse.

Lady Lucinda gently blew out a breath, then folded her hands in her lap. "Come now, it's all in good fun," she responded, her teasing tone laced with desire.

"Is it fun you're after, then?" Will asked softly, resting his hand on the curve of her knee beneath the cover of the table. "Be careful what you wish for."

She turned toward him and licked her lips before speaking, the sight of her tongue urging Will on. "Are you warning me?"

"Good evening, all."

Will turned abruptly to see Lady Northrop slipping into the marquess's abandoned chair, Northrop standing just behind.

Lady Lucinda smiled in welcome and greeted her friend. "Amelia, Lord Northrop, how lovely to see you this evening."

Will nodded to Northrop, rolling his eyes when his fellow Corinthian asked whether this was the duke's first trip to Almack's. "Surprisingly, yes," he answered sarcastically.

"Better late than never, I always say," came a sultry voice behind Will, the look of distaste on Lady Northrop's face telling him what he already knew.

"Lady Swindon," he replied before pushing back his

chair and standing. "I hardly expected to see you here this evening."

She adjusted a glove slowly, eyeing Will with a predatory stare. "You're not the only one with friends in high places, Your Grace," she answered, peering down at Lucinda with a disingenuous smile. "Lady Lucinda, you look lovely this evening. I do adore the country influence we're seeing this year."

Lady Lucinda acknowledged the thinly veiled insult with a cool glance and brief smile. "You are too kind, Lady Swindon."

"Oh, I don't know about that." She turned her attention to Will, her catlike eyes gleaming with malicious enjoyment. "Perhaps we should query the duke on such matters. We are, after all, particular friends, are we not, Your Grace?"

"Lady Swindon," Will's voice was lethal. "I believe it's time for you to go." He took hold of her arm and turned her around. "I'll just deliver Lady Swindon to her carriage and return directly."

Lady Lucinda nodded in agreement, her face devoid of emotion. "Of course. Good evening, Lady Swindon."

Will did not allow Lady Swindon time to respond. Arm in arm, he moved her inexorably toward the edge of the room and the exit beyond. "Just what do you think you're up to, Sarah?" he growled.

She pressed her shoulder against him and leaned in. "Perhaps I should be asking you the same question. Lady Lucinda Grey, really? She's hardly a match for your particular tastes."

He marched her down the hall toward the exit, the gilt-edged mirrors lining the walls reflecting their forms. "I hardly think it's any of your concern."

She stopped abruptly, taking him by surprise as she yanked him into an alcove, nearly toppling a potted palm in her haste. "You are wrong on that point, Clairemont. And I shall prove it." Her lips pressed hard against his, her hands reaching beneath his coat to clutch at his waistcoat.

He heard a gasp of dismay just as he savagely wrenched his mouth from hers and pushed Lady Swindon away from him. He turned and nearly cursed aloud.

Lady Lucinda stood in the empty hall, only feet away, her mouth covered with her hand, her eyes filled with emotion.

"Lady Lucinda, this is not what it seems."

Lady Swindon's low, satisfied chuckle sent Lady Lucinda running down the hall, toward the other end of the building.

"I'll deal with you later," Will growled to Lady Swindon. "Leave. You won't like what happens if you disobey."

He saw her eyes widen in sudden fear. Assured she'd not linger, he hastened to catch up with Lady Lucinda. He saw her approach the staircase leading to the upper floor and hesitated, hoping she would slow if she thought he was not in pursuit.

Unfortunately, she only quickened her pace, lifting her narrow skirts and taking the stairs as quickly as she could. He followed, reaching the top floor in time to see her disappear through a large oak doorway. He surveyed the empty, silent hall, making sure there was no one about, then let himself into the room, closing the door and locking it quietly.

It was a storage room of sorts, tables and chairs filling nearly the entire space. Lady Lucinda stood across the room, looking out the window at the dark night.

"Lady Lucinda," he began, walking slowly toward her, his movements muffled by a worn carpet.

She turned to look at him, anger practically rising in visible waves off her body. "I do not wish to speak with you," she said succinctly.

Will pulled a flask from the inner pocket of his coat and took a drink. "Bloody hell," he growled, coming to stand next to her.

"How dare you use such words in my presence," she began, eyeing the flask. "And you know very well that spirits are not allowed here."

"And you must know that Lady Swindon means nothing to me. If I wanted her back I would have taken her weeks ago."

Lady Lucinda pressed a hand against the cold windowpane. "She is brash. And bold. She would think nothing of doing this," she ground out, reaching for Will's flask and taking a long drink.

"Lady Swindon is everything I am not," she finished, her voice cracking, the words husky from the brandy.

"Precisely," Will answered, reaching unsuccessfully for the flask. "My time with Lady Swindon came to an end the moment she married. An end, Lady Lucinda, and of my own doing."

She took another long drink, the burn of the alcohol reflected in her pained expression. "But you were lovers—"

"Lady Lucinda," he interrupted, reaching out again. "This is not who you are."

"Perhaps not now, but I could learn."

Will closed the gap between them. "Do not make such ridiculous statements—"

"If you'll only be patient, I am confident—"

He reached out and cradled her face in his hands. "Lady Lucinda, do not say such things. Hell, don't even think . . ." He paused, collecting his temper. "You are everything a man could ever want and more."

She covered his hands with her own and looked up into his eyes. "Show me."

*   *   *

Lucinda did not know if it was the effects of the brandy or simply her heart winning out over her head, but she needed the duke in a way that she'd never felt before.

Happening upon him with Lady Swindon in the alcove had been torture, rage and jealousy filling her entire being until she'd had to run away or risk making a fool of herself.

"Lady Lucinda," he said, his voice low and husky.

She gently urged him closer. It did not matter that she knew little of what she was doing. Nor did she weigh the consequences that would surely come with such a bold move. Lucinda abandoned all that she knew of what she *should* do, and instead let her heart lead her astray.

She went up on tiptoe to reach him and pressed her lips against his, pouring all of the torrent of emotion she was feeling into the kiss.

His body tensed, muscles going hard with seemingly iron control as he hesitated, pulling his mouth from hers and looking deep into her eyes. "You do not want this," he ground out, his breathing labored.

"You're wrong." She rested her cheek on his, her lips nearly touching his ear. "I want this. But more important, I want you."

"You do not know what you ask of me," he growled, his hold on her arms tightening.

"Please."

He took her mouth with such seductive force Lucinda nearly wept. His tongue sought out hers, leaving her breathless with anticipation. She was barely aware he had released her arms, but then his hands moved to her waist, rough caresses causing fresh sparks of need to ignite in her veins.

She ran her hand through his hair, stopping at the nape to entwine a lock between her fingers. She squeezed her eyes shut, a pleasurable sense of dizziness pushing her toward something that both thrilled and terrified her.

His mouth left hers and his lips trailed a slow assault down her neck, kisses so sweet yet so seductive Lucinda thought they would surely drive her mad. She was vaguely aware that he walked her backward before urging her gently to the floor and onto the soft, thick pile of a Persian carpet.

She opened her eyes and watched as his head bent toward her, sighing as his mouth moved over her throat, then lower, to the slope of her breasts above the gown. He tugged the bodice lower. He sucked at first, then licked the shape of her entire breast before moving on to the other one.

"Yes," she urgently whispered, every inch of exposed skin screaming for his attention. "More."

His hands stroked down the length of her, over the inward curve of waist and the outer curve of hip and thigh. She shivered beneath the pleasure of clever hands before he reached the hem of her pale blue evening gown and slowly pushed it up, first to her knees, and then her thighs, stopping just below her waist. He lifted away from her, just far enough to take in the sight of her, and his eyes hazed with desire. His gaze seared her skin and her heart beat faster.

Desperate for release, she caught his hand in hers and kissed the palm. She took one finger in her mouth, sucking lightly at first, then harder, the salty taste of his skin surely the most intoxicating flavor she'd ever encountered.

"Bloody hell," he growled.

Lucinda watched the duke pull at his neckcloth and rip it from around his neck. He pulled his finger from her mouth, caressing first her top lip, then the bottom before tracing a path between her breasts and down to her belly and beyond, coming to rest just below her corset.

He towered over her, supporting himself on his knees while one hand reached for her breasts, gently tugging at a nipple then releasing, drawing a circular pattern in and out, heightening the desire.

She felt the sudden brush of cooler air between her thighs. The duke placed his finger where only moments before her chemise had been, rubbing gently, the exquisite friction coaxing Lucinda to new heights.

Somewhere in her mind reason screamed for her to stop, but she could not. She wanted this—wanted him—more than she'd ever wanted anything before in her life.

"Please," she sobbed, looking into the duke's eyes.

His fingers quickened their pace, driving Lucinda's tension higher, then he bent to kiss her mouth, the flick of his tongue stirring the sudden explosion of Lucinda's entire being.

Pleasure radiated from the juncture of her thighs outward, pulsing through her body. The sensation seemed to build on itself, wave after wave of intense emotion assaulting her anew.

She threw her arms around him, pulling him down on top of her. Stars burst before her heavy lids as she kissed him with every last ounce of energy she had within her, moaning under the pulsating pleasure.

Long moments later, he dragged his mouth from hers, dropping his head to rest below her breasts. "What have I done?" he asked, the low timbre of his voice vibrating against Lucinda's sated body.

"Nothing that I did not ask for," Lucinda responded, slowly sitting up and urging him to do the same. "I needed something in a way I'd never experienced . . ." she began, hesitating in an attempt to find the right words. "I needed you, and I will not, cannot, apologize for it. Neither should you, unless you—"

Lucinda stopped, doubt suddenly filling her. Had he only taken pity on her? Obliged her out of lust and some twisted sense of duty rather than any real feeling for her?

"Do not, for a moment, think I do not want you, Lady Lucinda."

Lucinda couldn't think beyond this moment, the ramifications of what had just transpired too numerous and earthshaking to entertain. When at last his lips left hers, she rested her head on his shoulder and sighed contentedly. "In that case, I do believe it's time you called me Lucinda."

9

Nearly eighteen hours had passed, but Will could still smell her on his skin, taste the salt of her sweat in his mouth, hear her panting in his ear.

She'd caught him off guard, the need so achingly apparent in her eyes that even Iron Will could not say no. He could take some relief in the fact that he'd left her maidenhead intact. "Cold comfort," he growled, rolling the cue ball with such force that it crashed into the remaining balls, sending them careening across the baize surface to bounce off the sides of the billiard table.

Will stalked to the sideboard near the fireplace in Clairemont Hall. He hastily poured two fingers of brandy into a cut-crystal glass and tossed half of it down, returning the decanter to the silver tray before dropping into the leather chair angled next to the hearth.

"Christ," he whispered, nearly unable to believe his reaction to her. He'd wanted to bury himself so deeply inside of her that their mingled cries could be heard in heaven itself.

But more than that, his own need for connection matched hers, his heart and soul echoing what he saw in her eyes.

He stood abruptly and savagely threw the crystal glass into the fireplace. A thousand tiny shards rained down over the flickering flames, pinging against brick and stone.

"This cannot be." He turned toward the door, halting abruptly to drop to his knees. *This cannot be!*

Desperate for something, anything, to release his anger upon, he roughly took up a nearby billiard cue and snapped it in half, flinging both pieces to crash against the wall. He sat back on his haunches and covered his face with his hands, the dawning recognition of such unfamiliar emotions washing over him anew.

What was happening to him?

Love, you giant damned fool. Love, he thought, unable to even speak the words out loud.

He raked his hands through his hair before standing. "And danger." Dangerous for him for so many reasons. But worse, dangerous for Lucinda.

Will could not be the man she wanted, that was certain. His faults could fill a thousand books. His father had been right about one thing: Will could never be what a duke should be.

But more than that, he could not be the agent he must be with such feelings hammering away at his heart.

Or could he? Will propped himself against the billiard table and looked deep into the fire. Perhaps it was those very feelings that made him the perfect man for the job. After all, what other man would have a more vital reason for keeping her safe than he?

He gripped the edge of the table with both hands, his knuckles turning white from the effort. This was madness. Lunacy. He'd steeled himself from such involvement countless times before, flirtations and physical encounters serving to fill the void that years of emptiness had created.

And when it hadn't been enough? Will had found comfort in the Young Corinthians, the endless hours of intelligence work numbing him beyond the ability to feel.

And yet, somehow, some way, he could not let

Lucinda go. With every single detail he discovered, he only yearned to know more of her.

To give in to the madness could be his salvation, a new life, where love filled his soul rather than loathing and rage. But what of his old life? His debt to the Young Corinthians could not be repaid from behind a desk.

He unclenched his grip, leaving the table to walk across the deep red and taupe patterned carpet, stopping in front of the window that looked out on St. James's Square. He caught his reflection in the glass. Hair mussed, his neckcloth missing, his jaw in desperate need of a shave. And those eyes. "Nearly as dark as the hell from which you came," his father would say.

"She couldn't love you, you fool," he gruffly whispered, looking past his image to the square below. Streetlights were just being lit, the dusk silently settling into the deepening expanse of night.

He'd tortured himself for naught, he realized. A woman such as Lucinda would not, could not, love a man such as he.

A carriage rolled to a slow stop in front of the house, the Clairemont crest barely visible in the waning light. "Bloody hell," he growled, watching the footman jump down from his perch to open the door. "As if I am in need of further distraction." His brother, Michael, emerged first, fingering his neckcloth and smoothing back his meticulously groomed hair before offering his hand to the remaining occupant.

A dainty gloved hand appeared, then one slim arm draped in a scarlet wool shawl. Finally the remainder of Will's mother came into view as she stepped down onto the pavement bricks. Her hair was just as it had always been, though silver locks now glimmered among the ebony tresses visible beneath her bonnet. She'd aged somewhat since he'd last seen her, and yet one could not deny that the duchess was still a striking woman, even at the advanced age of five-and-fifty.

She paused to smooth her skirts, looking up at the house with a mixture of emotions playing across her face.

Will turned away from the window and moved across the room slowly, reluctant to meet his unexpected guests. He knew how difficult it was for his mother to be here; the memories of life with his father were extremely painful ones. But the strain of entertaining his family was more than he cared to take on at the moment.

He met Smithers in the hallway, the man's dismay punctuated by the grim set of his mouth.

"Your Grace," Smithers began, stepping in time with Will, "your family—"

Will chuckled, despite Smithers's obvious discomfort. At least he could always count on him to behave exactly the same, every day. It was oddly comforting to Will and he clapped the man on the back. "My family, yes, I know. Thank you, Smithers—though this can all be left to Peterson, you know."

"If I may be so bold, the duchess and Lord Michael require special consideration, which is not Peterson's forte, Your Grace," he replied, a slight hint of irritation apparent in his tone.

Will laughed out loud this time. "No, Smithers, I suppose it is not."

The natural order of things put right, Smithers cleared his throat and picked up the pace. "Might I suggest the rose room for your mother and the—"

"Do as you see fit, Smithers," Will interrupted.

"Excellent, sir," the valet responded, then nearly ran down the hall to the stairs.

If only Smithers could manage the whole of my life, Will thought to himself, hesitating in the hall for a moment before making his way to the foyer.

*   *   *

When Will's father was alive, dinner demanded military precision. The candles were lit to cast a warm glow over the entire room. The food was prepared to entice and delight, every course agonized over by the staff until no fault could be found in their offerings. The crystal and china shone like jewels, the silver sparkled, and the table linens were pressed to hard-edged perfection.

Or else.

Will had detested every meal in the ornate room, the painted pastoral scene circling the four corners only serving to irritate him further.

One of the first dictates he had given upon assuming the title had been to never eat another meal in the formal dining room. He'd seen to the packing up of the room himself, taking great delight in swathing his father's chair in Holland cloth and distributing the ornate silver to a collection of street urchins he found down near the docks. They'd given him looks of disbelief when he'd approached with the rough sack of treasure, but quickly changed their minds when he began to dole out what would surely be a year's worth of meals for each of them.

It would have killed his father to see such a thing, which was exactly why he did it.

Though he had to admit, observing his brother and mother's attempt at normal behavior as they sat around the table in the morning room, he'd not considered the effect on the rest of his family.

"If I had known you were coming, Smithers would have seen to the airing of the dining room," he said, cutting a large bite of mutton in half before forking it into his mouth.

The duchess took a demure sip of her wine and gave him a small smile. "What is good enough for you is good enough for us, William," she answered quietly.

"And that is precisely the problem," Will countered, dropping his knife and fork to the table with an audible thwack.

"It truly is tiresome to have the exact argument over and over again, wouldn't you agree?" Lord Michael Randall pointed out, his face—the spitting image of Will's—a tight mask of frustration.

Will glared at his younger brother, the urge to throttle him tempered only by his love for the young man. They'd been inseparable as children, their boyish pranks proving too much for nearly every nursemaid south of Hadrian's Wall. And then their father's hatred for everything familial intensified, causing Will to distance himself from Michael in an attempt to spare the boy from the ugliness.

It had worked, though Michael had not understood his older brother's behavior, taking his cold treatment for dislike and betrayal rather than what it truly was.

Will had saved his brother's life, and sacrificed his love in the process.

The loss of his brother's respect had hit hard, but the realization that his mother would do nothing on his behalf hurt the most. No matter how cold his father's treatment, the magnitude of his insults, or the viciousness of his behavior, she sat idly by, absorbing the damage in quiet pain.

He'd often wondered as a child about his parents' relationship. His mother, so capable and assured with him and his brother, would be reduced to tears by his overbearing father. It was a transformation he could not understand—and one he came to detest.

"How long will you be in town?" Will asked abruptly, ignoring his brother's statement.

The crease between the duchess's eyebrows softened, the change in topic settling her. "Well, I suppose that depends entirely on you."

Will drained his glass of wine and motioned for a servant to take his plate. "You know me, Mother, ever the amiable host. Stay as long as you like. The old pile of bricks is as much yours as it is—"

"No," Her Grace smoothly interrupted. "You've misunderstood me. We received news of your courtship of Lady Lucinda Grey and had hoped our presence would be required in the not-so-distant future."

"Bloody hell."

"William—manners, please," his mother chided, falling into the parental role much too easily for Will's taste.

"My sentiments exactly," Michael muttered, spearing a piece of artichoke from his nearly empty plate.

Will propped his elbows on the table and leaned forward. "You mean to tell me that the gossipmongers took the time to spread such drivel all the way to Derbyshire?"

"I don't know why you're upset, William. It is wonderful news, is it not?" his mother answered. "Besides, Derbyshire is not as far from London as you make it out to be. And those gossipmongers you refer to are some of my closest friends, so I would thank you to be a bit more respectful when speaking of them. If it were not for them, we may not have heard for some time, which would have been more embarrassment than I could have withstood."

The look on his mother's face spoke clearly of the pain he'd caused in allowing her to find out such personal family news from anyone but him. The knowledge needled at Will's heart.

He ran a hand through his hair and looked at Michael, who simply stared back at him, his face now expressionless. "A fat lot of good you are, then?" he said dryly.

"Oh, I've talked myself blue in the face, but the

woman will hear nothing of it," his brother said. "For some reason Mother is inclined to believe persons whose comments suggest you may be less than concerned over familial ties, though I can't imagine why. And Lord knows I'm more than happy to continue performing the ducal duties—without the title, of course—so you're able to . . . I'm sorry, Will, what is it that you do?"

"Michael, please," the duchess said, the muscles in her jaw tightening. "We are here, together, as a family. That is what is important."

Will could not take any more, especially in light of the day he'd endured. "I apologize. Can we be done with it?"

"Of course," his mother answered quietly.

Michael nodded, the movement abrupt.

The duchess paused to let a servant clear her plate, then leaned slightly forward, a twinkle visible in her hazel eyes. "Now, when might we meet Lady Lucinda?"

"Bloody hell."

"Lucinda, even King Solomon's Mine could win against you today," Victoria chided.

Lucinda pulled herself from her thoughts in time to see Charlotte stifling a small laugh.

She winked at Charlotte before turning her attention to the cards in her hands. "I'm sorry. I'm afraid I've been woolgathering, Aunt Victoria." She played the four of hearts, wincing slightly at the headache pounding behind her eyes.

Victoria let out a "harrumph" of displeasure before adding her card to the table. "Woolgathering indeed. And over that Iron Will, I suppose. Tell me, is it absolutely necessary for you to meet his family?"

"Surely there is no need to be quite so cold, Victoria," Charlotte protested, an audible "tsk, tsk" punctuating her words. "The dowager and I came out the same year, you know. She was something, quite out of the ordinary, until . . ."

Charlotte looked down at the book in her hand, fingering the pages slowly.

"Until . . . ?" Lucinda asked, suddenly desperate to learn all that she could of Will, though equally anxious to keep such feelings from her aunts.

Charlotte reached for a length of moss green ribbon and placed it in her book before closing it. "Until she married the duke."

"And then?"

"And then that man drained her of everything that made her who she was," Victoria said bluntly, eyeing the cards on the table before looking up at her sisters and niece, all three frozen with looks of horror on their faces. "Well, he did, did he not? I didn't know her personally but according to the endless supply of gossip, the woman was the most vibrant of beings before marrying Clairemont and a miserable captive after."

Lucinda turned to Charlotte. "Is this true?"

"I'm afraid so. Despite having the attention of every eligible bachelor that year, she fell in love with Clairemont." Charlotte set the book on the small side table and adjusted her soft woolen throw. "No one could blame her. He was a duke, after all, and terribly handsome."

"And charming," Bessie added, her head tilted and eyes hazed over ever so slightly as she thought back to her younger days. "Oh, so charming."

"Yes, well, he was all of these things and more. Unfortunately, beneath the smiles and handsome façade, there beat a heart as black as the moors on a December night. No one believed his dalliances with other women would stop once he was married."

"No one except the duchess," Victoria interrupted, her voice softening. "She fell for the roué despite all the rumors of debauchery, and lived to pay the price. Poor woman."

Lucinda set a card on the table without looking at it. "He did not stop, then?"

"Oh, the exact opposite, I'm afraid. If the gossipmongers were to be believed, the duke tortured his wife not only with his affairs but with verbal thrashings, and, on occasion, physical violence, too."

"She could do nothing," Charlotte said. "His Grace threatened to take everything from her, even the children, if she dared to disobey him."

Lucinda fanned her cards out on the table, her brows knitting together. "She was trapped. And he knew it."

"Exactly so. I think it's fair to say that the day the duke dropped dead in his mistress's bed was, perhaps, the happiest day of Her Grace's life."

"And the boys?" Lucinda wondered aloud.

The three aunts looked at one another for a time, Charlotte finally speaking. "Dear, we would not want you . . . that is to say—"

"Regardless of their father's treatment, they are grown men, fully capable of making their own decisions, good or bad," Victoria interrupted, leaning across the card table to take Lucinda's hand. "We would not want to sway your regard for the duke based on the sins of his father."

"The boys?" Lucinda pressed, knowing the answer but needing to hear it regardless.

"There were rumors; servants and staff who shared stories with other servants and staff, who passed the information on to their employers. Your Iron Will took the brunt of it—out of choice, if memory serves. He adored his younger brother, by all accounts, and purposefully set himself between the father and the boy."

Could this be why he's strayed so far outside society?

Lucinda wondered to herself, pieces beginning to fall into place before her eyes.

Victoria squeezed Lucinda's hand with her own, then leaned back against the mahogany parlor chair. "This revelation should not be calculated into your dealings with the duke," she said, her firm tone in place once more. "No matter his history, he is who he is, and that, my dear, does not change."

Despite the lack of candlelight, Lucinda's eyes had adjusted to the darkness of her room. Moonlight filtered in around the curtains, throwing shadows here and there. She'd long since abandoned her games, naming this shadow a minotaur, and that one a lamb, all in an attempt to hasten sleep.

Slumber had not come, yet Lucinda could not bring herself to leave the bed, the warmth of her cashmere coverlet creating a cozy nest that provided some comfort in the absence of rest.

The invitation to attend the opera with Will and his family lay next to her pillow, the fine linen paper creased from her repeated readings. The day had been long and hard, in no small part due to the brandy she'd so foolishly imbibed the night before. But she knew she could not pin the entirety of her current state on the liquor.

No matter how many times she examined her feelings, replayed the events of the last days, or imagined any number of possible outcomes, Lucinda could not deny one truth: William Randall, the Duke of Clairemont, had conquered her heart.

"I love him," she said into her pillow, the sound of her voice ringing unfamiliar to her own ears.

The revelations earlier in the evening concerning Will's childhood had not, as her aunts had feared, swayed her. Not completely, that is. Their interlude at Almack's had started her mind racing, the intimacy of the encounter still overwhelming her, even now. They were not suited; all of the ton—including her three aunts—were in agreement that such a match would be unthinkable. Impossible.

Insanity.

Lucinda fidgeted with the cream ribbon at her bedgown's neckline. "Do you truly love Will?"

She looped the ribbon around her forefinger, tightening it as she went. "I do."

He might be just as his father was, utterly charming yet a monster underneath. He could ruin her reputation with hardly any effort, leaving her without the comfort of family and friends. He could simply not love her—the thought surprisingly painful, yet altogether possible.

He could change everything she'd expected for her life, something Lucinda found most frightening of all.

She released the ribbon and gently massaged her finger, slightly numb from the pressure of the binding.

Her feelings for Will were simple. They were pure. This was everything Lucinda had been missing without even being aware that something was lacking.

"I love him."

But could he love her in return?

10

It was decided that Charlotte would act as Lucinda's chaperone for the evening, though it had taken some time for the four women to reach an understanding. Lucinda had done her best to remain impartial, but she'd secretly hoped that it would be Charlotte who accompanied her. Bessie would have tried to seduce Will's brother, and Victoria may have used the opportunity to suggest the duke abandon the courtship altogether and simply hand over the horse.

Charlotte's previous acquaintance with the duchess had been the deciding factor, and the other two had reluctantly complied, leaving Lucinda free to fret over her dress and hair, her jewels and slippers.

She looked from the blush silk to the capucine silk in Mary's arms, feigning interest for the sake of holding off what would surely be a litany of questions from Mary regarding the duke.

Lucinda couldn't have cared less what she wore. Her feelings for Will made clothing seem a trivial matter that held little importance to her at the moment.

She'd not seen Will since attending Almack's. She blushed at the memory of her appearance, her cries of delight at the storm of emotions and pleasure he'd coaxed from her. Her body heated at the thought, small patches of perspiration forming in the most delicate of places.

"The capucine, my dear," Charlotte said from the doorway.

Lucinda turned, smiling at her aunt. "Do you think so?" she asked, posing a question in order to earn a few moments to compose herself.

Charlotte stepped into the room, her matronly rose-hued gown making the slightest of swishing sounds as she did so. "Does the capucine not suit your tastes?"

"No, not at all. It's just, well, that is to say," Lucinda began, and suddenly realized she'd run out of time. "No, not at all. It's lovely."

Mary dropped the rejected blush silk on the bed and carefully held up the burnished orange with both hands. "This one it is, then."

Charlotte motioned for the servant to hand her the dress. "Thank you, Mary, I'll assist Lucinda in dressing this evening."

Mary released the dress and swiftly curtsied before leaving the room. "Careful of her hair," she said over her shoulder, then smoothly closed the door.

Charlotte turned to look at Lucinda. "My dear, what ever is the matter?"

"I'm sorry?" Lucinda said, distracted, as she rose from the edge of her bed and crossed to the window. "With the dress, you mean?"

The swish of Charlotte's gown once more signaled her progress across the floor. "Not with the dress, my dear. With you. You seem quite distracted. Is it the prospect of meeting Lord Clairemont's family?"

Lucinda wanted nothing more than to tell her aunt the truth. She needed the counsel of a trusted confidant, but her dear, kind aunt could not be responsible for carrying such a secret.

Lucinda turned from the window and loosened her dressing gown, letting it fall to the floor. "No, it is not that, Aunt Charlotte. I'm simply tired, that's all. The last few weeks have found me in situations I am not accustomed to, and I fear I am much more a creature of habit than I ever would have cared to admit."

She finished with a practiced, bright smile, then raised her arms in preparation to receive the dress. "Do not forget the hair. Mary will scold both of us, you know," she finished teasingly.

"Oh, I know all too well, my dear. All too well."

It had been some time since Will's last appearance at the theater, even longer since he'd arrived with his family. The Grecian-inspired Royal Opera House stood proudly in front of them, four large, fluted columns supporting a portico under which a vast number of society's elite congregated.

Michael held out his arm for their mother as she exited the carriage. "Prinny himself laid the foundation stone apparently," he remarked, assisting his mother to the bricked pavement.

"Hardly a ringing endorsement, brother," Will said, stepping out to join them. "Come, it's beginning to rain."

Large, fat drops of water chased their progress as they made their way through the crowd. The glances and sly stares began almost immediately, the hum of low voices acting as the trio's own personal accompaniment.

Michael assessed the crowd around them as they mounted the stairs, then looked at Will. "Are you always so popular?"

Will nodded to a Young Corinthian as they crossed paths. "Well, I am, after all, Iron Will. Though I would think your presence here this evening, as well as Mother's, is a particularly juicy tidbit for these imbeciles. How long has it been since you were last in town? Four months? Perhaps six?"

"We were here for the Yuletide, as you well know,

which was barely four months ago. And our presence here was entirely thanks to you, if I remember correctly." Michael paused, meticulously wiping the rain from his coat. "You could not be torn away from town, requiring Mother to travel in the century's most severe snowstorm—"

Will shook his head, holding lightly to his mother's elbow as they ascended the stairs. "Is there something you wish to discuss, Michael? Or are you merely making conversation?"

"This Grimaldi, is he as good as they say?" the duchess asked, cutting through the impending argument with quiet, practiced skill.

Will's sharp gaze located a Corinthian agent stationed near the landing and he nodded discreetly, receiving a brief nod of recognition in reply. "Better. I had the pleasure of attending a private performance by Grimaldi. He is a comic genius, to be sure." He paused, slowing his pace. "Although I fear you may disapprove of his antics, Mother."

The duchess allowed Will to steer her toward the entrance to the Clairemont box. "Do you truly, or are you merely being polite?"

"You wound me, Mother," Will replied, clutching at his chest as though a death blow had been delivered to his heart.

His mother's light laughter made bystanders turn their heads as the three walked through the parted red velvet curtains and reached their seats.

"And you would do quite well out there," she said, gesturing with her hand toward the stage. "I enjoy a good laugh just as well as the next person."

Will looked at her with mock disbelief. "Really?"

"Yes, William, I do," she answered in an altered tone, the teasing quality of her voice having vanished.

"As do I," a feminine voice came from the back of the box.

The three turned to see Lady Charlotte Grey enter the box with Lucinda following behind.

"Mother," Will began, "Michael, may I present Lady Charlotte Grey and her niece, Lady Lucinda Grey."

The duchess smiled endearingly. "Charlotte, it has been far too long since we last met." She moved toward Lady Charlotte, both hands outstretched.

"I could not agree more," Lady Charlotte replied with feeling, moving to take Will's mother's hands in hers. "You look as lovely as the first time we met."

The duchess quietly clucked her tongue. "You are too kind, Lady Charlotte," she said, then turned her gaze to Lucinda, "And you, my dear, are just as I'd hoped."

Lucinda graciously smiled and came to stand next to her aunt. "Your Grace, now I fear you are the one who is too kind."

The three ladies softly laughed, looking from one to the other with instant affection. The low lighting from the candles reflected off their dresses—Lucinda's dress perfectly complemented by the soft rose of Lady Charlotte's and the deep brown of his mother's. It was as if Thomas Lawrence himself were readying to paint the trio, their ease with one another as pleasing to the eye as it was to the soul.

Will didn't know whether to be elated or terrified, the conflicting emotions discomforting. "Do not forget my little brother, ladies," he said, oddly compelled to dispel the heartwarming scene.

"Lady Charlotte." Michael bowed. "And Lady Lucinda."

"Lord Michael," Lady Charlotte replied, dipping her head in unconsciously regal acknowledgment.

Lucinda stepped forward and curtsied with easy grace. "Lord Michael, I am most happy to make your acquaintance." She rose, offered her hand to Michael, and smiled brightly.

He bent to kiss her hand, with a smile to match Lucinda's. "My mother was correct, you are lovely indeed." He waited just a moment too long for Will's comfort before he released her hand.

"And you, Lord Michael, are very much His Grace's brother," she answered in kind, the slightly teasing nature of her words vexing Will further.

The sound of the gong from the stage signaled the call for the audience to find their seats, putting an end to the party's friendly conversation.

"About bloody time," Will muttered under his breath, escorting Lady Charlotte the few steps to her seat then returning to Lucinda. "Lady Lucinda," he said, offering her his arm.

She smiled in warm response and linked her arm through his, allowing him to guide her to the front of the box. He waited for her to sit, then dropped into the miniature seat next to her.

"Oh, my . . ." she murmured. Will immediately wondered whether in the process of attempting to settle his frame comfortably in the ridiculously small seat he'd managed to tread on her gown.

About to apologize, he belatedly noticed Lucinda wasn't looking in his direction, but rather out at the theater. He followed her gaze and realized what had caused her unease.

It appeared the entire audience was not buzzing with anticipation over the impending performance, as they should be.

No, their attention was concentrated on the Clairemont box, every set of opera glasses in the whole of the Royal Opera House trained on them. The sight brought to mind countless curious owls avidly eyeing a particularly delectable mouse.

"Lean ever so slightly to your right," Will whispered to Lucinda, who, despite clearly being confused, did as he asked.

He leaned in the same direction and the two watched every last owl do the same, following them with marked determination.

Lucinda muffled a laugh and centered herself in her seat before turning to Will. "This could prove to be quite amusing," she said, a wicked grin curving her lips.

"Oh, yes. The stupidity of the ton is an endless source of entertainment, particularly when you are as popular as I am." Will winked at her.

She laughed out loud, causing all three of their box mates to turn.

"I . . . that is to say . . ." Lucinda began, desperately trying to piece together a proper explanation. "I simply cannot bear the anticipation! Everyone of my acquaintance talks endlessly of the great Grimaldi. Are you not all as excited as I to be here tonight?"

It was clear from their faces that the three were skeptical of her comment, but they smiled politely and returned to their conversation.

"You really do need to practice your prevarications, Lucinda," Will whispered, keeping his eyes on the audience. "It is a skill that can be quite useful, especially for those in my social circle."

"You called me by my first name."

His gut told him to look at her but his brain demanded he keep his eyes on the stage.

"I like a man who can follow directions," she continued smoothly.

The massive red and gold curtain that divided the stage from the audience slowly began to open, and the crowd hushed, preventing Will's response.

What was the enchanting woman playing at? Will's body was literally humming from the effort of sitting still next to her. He'd spent almost the entire day attempting to decide upon a course of action. His past relationships with women were of no help, intimate displays of affection being merely an expected part of the equation there.

But Lucinda was different for so many reasons. Or was she? Perhaps he'd been wrong in assuming she would be affected by their interlude.

He glanced at her discreetly. She looked to be perfectly comfortable despite the fact that he'd pleasured her in the storage room above Almack's.

The entire audience erupted with laughter, as did Lucinda, Lady Charlotte, his mother, and Michael, giving Will the opportunity to look at her directly.

She turned and gave him a dazzling smile, her eyes dancing with merriment. "He is wonderfully wild, is he not?"

"Indeed," Will answered, his light tone failing to betray his thoughts.

He gripped the spindly arms of the chair, loosening his hold when they audibly creaked in protest.

If Lucinda had deeper feelings for him, there would have been telltale signs, Will was sure. The woman wasn't practiced in the ways of deception. He'd witnessed her face flush with color over lesser things; her eyes shielded by her lashes when she wished to conceal the truth; her searching for words that would hide what she was thinking.

No, that small sliver of hope for something he couldn't quite explain had been in vain. *Be thankful, you fool,* he thought to himself, releasing the chair and folding his arms across his chest. *She's doing you a favor.*

The audience erupted with laughter again, and this time Will joined in. He, unlike Lucinda, was well versed in the art of deception, and he'd be damned if he would let something as trivial as his emotions compromise the quality of his work.

"Are you enjoying yourself?" he asked Lucinda.

She leaned in conspiratorially, her shoulder connecting with his. "Immensely."

"In that case," he replied, turning to look at her. "Perhaps you'll do me a favor. After all, Grimaldi is quite the most difficult ticket to obtain in town."

She turned to face him, her eyebrows furrowing. "What might that be, Your Grace?"

"Assure me that we've come to an agreement concerning your morning rides."

She pulled back, the absence of her shoulder leaving Will cold. "I thought I made myself clear."

Will smiled charmingly. "Really, because I'm quite sure that I made myself clear as well. It is neither safe nor appropriate. And, as your suitor, I do have some say in the matter."

The color began to rise from her chest, slowly creeping its way up to settle in her cheeks. "I do so appreciate your concern. But let us remember, you are not my husband, Your Grace."

"Not yet," he growled. Why was she being so disagreeable? He was doing his bloody best to play by the ton's rules—and if that meant he would not have to rise at an ungodly hour in order to keep her alive, well, all the better.

"Are you expressly forbidding me from my morning ride?" she furiously whispered, her face turned toward the stage.

Will took a deep breath, his cravat suddenly tight. "I am."

Her jaw clenched. "And if I do not obey?"

"Lucinda," he began, itching to rip the bloody cloth from his neck. "Is it even necessary for me to answer?"

"We shall see."

*   *   *

THE WILY WOLF TAVERN
CHARING CROSS, LONDON

Will lifted his tankard and drank deeply, realizing belatedly that claiming a need for ale as an excuse for taking his leave from his mother and brother had not entirely been a ruse.

After receiving word of Garenne from a Young Corinthian at Covent Garden, he'd escorted a chilly Lucinda and her aunt to their carriage, then accompanied his mother and brother home, only to excuse himself and immediately head out into the dark night.

He set the pewter tankard on the rough-hewn, scarred tabletop and took in his surroundings. He'd heard of the Wily Wolf, a popular gathering place for London's criminally inclined, and he had to admit, it lived up to its reputation.

Scant light threw ominous shadows around the interior. Smoke from the tallow candles hovered in a thick cloud against the ceiling and hazed the room, preventing clients from getting more than a minimal view of their fellow drinkers.

It was a sizeable room, though Will had counted a total of only twelve tables and a large bar that ran along the back wall; hardly surprising in such an establishment, where privacy was a necessity.

Will gestured for the serving girl to bring him another ale and eased back onto the hard wooden bench. He allowed his eyelids to droop, the half-hooded appearance affording him the opportunity to observe while appearing uninterested.

He knew most of the cutthroats present; his Young Corinthian duties had brought him into contact with many of them. One-Eyed Jack, named for the eyeball he'd lost to the knife of a business associate, slumped over a plate of alehouse food in the back. His stringy gray hair fell across his face, nearly covering the large black patch concealing his empty socket.

The man sitting opposite One-Eyed Jack had his back to Will, but from his size and build it could only be Monty Milburn, or "The Mountain" as he was called by friend and foe alike. Monty often worked with Jack, hitting the respectable neighborhoods of London with a ragtag army of street urchins. From bank notes to valuable jewelry, the two made a living off the ton, a fact that made Will smile quietly.

Jack and Monty were harmless enough. The two sitting across the room from them were not.

Owner of the brothel Giselle's, Clive Baskers was a ruthless, moneygrubbing bastard who, by all accounts, enjoyed killing far too much. Rumor had it that more than one man had gone missing from the rooms above his gambling hell. Since the dead men were always from the lower class, Baskers had no need to worry that the authorities would bother with the matter.

Will watched the brothel owner for a moment. His gaunt frame rattled each time he coughed and spat into a worn handkerchief in his hand. But tonight, Will was more interested in the man who accompanied Baskers— Philip Gaston, a Frenchman of questionable lineage who owned a stake in the brothel. Gaston had sworn allegiance to no one, offering up information to the highest bidder regardless of their loyalties.

He'd frequently provided intelligence to the Young Corinthians through a network of communication that ensured he was kept at arm's length and never given the opportunity to guess the true identities of the agents.

Despite his belief that the Corinthians' net of secrecy held fast, Will was thankful for the rough workman's clothing Smithers had provided him in the carriage. A secret compartment beneath the cushioned seat contained everything Will might need in the line of duty.

Clothing, assorted weapons, money, and a number of other items occupied the compartment, all magically replenished by Smithers when necessary.

Will fingered the lapel of the nondescript coat he was currently wearing, absentmindedly noting the difference between the coarse wool and the smooth quality of the evening attire he'd donned for the theater earlier in the evening.

He would not be so stupid as to entertain thoughts of Lucinda outside of the confines of Corinthian business again, he brooded, tracking a pair of drunken seamen as they staggered toward the long bar. Her mercurial mood had left Will confused and frustrated—a far cry from what he'd been hoping for.

But he would not allow a woman, not even Lucinda, to distract him in such a way ever again.

The serving wench came toward his table, her tray heavy with full tankards. She set one in front of him on the table. "Can I offer you anything else?" she asked, leaning over to show her impressive breasts.

"No, thank you, love," Will replied, reaching for the tankard.

"'Ave it your way," she answered in her thick Cockney accent, then lowered her voice. "You're needed out back, I'm to tell you. By a man with the breath of a dragon. He dinnat give a name, just said you'd know 'im."

Will reached inside his coat and pulled out several coins. He tossed enough for the two ales on the table, then added another. "Thank you."

The wench eyed the money greedily. "Anytime. Anytime," she replied, scooping up the coins and dropping them into her ample cleavage.

Will took one last swig of ale before sliding out of the booth. He tugged the brim of his hat lower over his brow and made his way toward the door, careful to not move too quickly. The last thing he needed was for one of these men to become curious.

Garenne pushed his stew about, forking a chunk of mutton into his mouth and chewing. His beard itched, as did the snarled wig atop his head, but he hardly noticed as he swallowed the gristly meat. Watching Clairemont from across the tavern had proven enjoyable for any number of reasons, not the least of which was the fact that the giant knew nothing of his presence. *"Idiot,"* he muttered to himself, nearly choking on the inferior cut of meat.

It galled Garenne to admit that such a man had kept him from success, but he would not have to suffer at the hands of the duke for long. The man had made a disastrous mistake interfering with plans for Lady Lucinda Grey, but he would pay. Slowly, methodically, and, with any luck, painfully. The duke would pay.

It was a pity that Garenne himself would not be the one to deliver the death blow, but there were details to decide upon and he would not leave one out of place.

Garenne tossed a coin onto the planked table and moved toward the door. No, everything would be in order and the woman would be caught. Or else.

Once the tavern's heavy door slammed shut, the dark night shrouded Will. The moonlight was faint, thick clouds nearly concealing the pale curve. Will picked his way around the decrepit building, dodging refuse and a trio of scavenging, half-starved dogs along the way. The rear of the tavern was cast in shadow, the meager light glimmering from two dirty windows above the establishment not enough for Will's liking.

The hair on his neck stood up, a sign he had learned to trust years before. He spun, backing up against the wall, and pulled a knife from a sheath sewn inside his coat.

"Gaston, I trust you know better than to screw with me," he said sternly, quickly assessing his surroundings and calculating his escape routes.

A flash of silver caught the light. Will braced himself as a dark figure flew out of the blackness at the back of the alley, followed closely by a second and third. Will pressed against the wall and waited, dropping to his knees at the last second.

The first man missed Will and hit the wall hard, the sound of his face connecting with brick filling the air. He crumpled on the ground to Will's right, moaning.

Will drove forward, slamming his fist into the second man's groin and sending him flying backward into a massive pile of rubbish. But before Will could spin to face the third, he attacked from behind, slashing a knife across Will's back and slicing deep before grabbing his shoulder and dragging him around to face him.

He kicked Will's knife from his hand, a second vicious kick catching Will's chin. Will dropped to the ground, stars whirling as his sight dimmed, and before he could recover, the man straddled him.

The attacker's lips curled in an evil grin, his bared teeth gritting with exertion as he struggled to hold Will down.

"He said you'd put up a fight," he spat out, gloating as his fingers closed on Will's throat and he raised the knife. "You gentry coves are all the same."

A potent mixture of anger and bitterness raced through Will's veins.

He roared, startling the man sitting on his chest just enough to make him slacken his grip. Will grabbed a thick piece of firewood from the ground beside him and swung.

The savage blow clubbed the man on the side of his head, sending him flying backward. Will shoved upright and hit him in the rib cage, then the leg. The attacker screamed.

"We are not all the same, you useless bastard," Will panted, leaning over the man.

He readied himself to deliver the death blow, his arm arching over his head with the wood in hand.

At the last moment Will lowered the weapon and stood back. "You're not worth the effort."

He moved toward the alley, cutting across two streets to where a hackney waited. "The Young Corinthians," he told the driver, slamming the door himself.

The cab came to life, the pull of the horse throwing Will back against the seat. He cried out in pain, his injuries just starting to make themselves known.

Sheer force of will was keeping him conscious despite the blackness that threatened, beckoning just at the edge of his vision. He began to count, this time starting at one hundred.

"You're bleeding," Weston observed as he helped Will into the back parlor of the Corinthian Club. "Profusely, actually."

Will winced with pain when Weston's arm pressed against the wound on his back. "I'm well aware of that," he ground out, allowing the man to aid him as they mounted the stairs.

By the time they reached the lower floor and the two made their way to a bookcase, the third from center of the shelves lining both sides of the hallway, Will was leaning heavily on Weston's strength. Without comment, Weston reached for the slim volume of Shakespeare's sonnets. He pulled hard on the false book, triggering a hidden mechanism, and the section of the wall swung out, revealing a second hallway, lit by Argand lamps.

"Shall I carry you from here?" Weston asked, winking at Will.

Will fought off the urge to punch the man, knowing he'd only injure himself further if he did so. "Do and you'll live to regret it."

They entered the last room on the right in silence. Carmichael and the Corinthians' physician met them at the door.

"On the table, Your Grace."

Will followed the physician's orders and awkwardly eased facedown onto the table, unable to silence a small grunt of pain.

Wordlessly, the physician took out a knife and cut his shirt off. "Hmm," the man muttered deep in his throat, then reached for a cloth, dipping it into a basin of water.

Will flinched when he began to clean the wound, a sharp wave of pain nearly knocking him unconscious.

Carmichael handed Will a silver flask. "Drink this."

"All of it," the physician added, finishing with the cloth.

Will turned his head to the side and swallowed the contents of the flask, the brandy slowly warming him from the inside out.

"How did this happen?" Carmichael asked, the anger in his voice barely contained.

Will lowered the empty flask to the tabletop, next to his face. "The usual way. A knife. A stiletto, if I'm not mistaken."

His flip response met with clear disapproval, Carmichael's mouth tightening to a grim, thin line. "More important, perhaps, *why* did this happen?"

"I've been told that meetings with Gaston are usually quite predictable," Will began, flinching as the physician began to stitch his flesh back together. "I had no reason to believe this one would be any different."

"Need I remind you that Garenne is here, in London?"

"Of course not," Will growled in response.

Weston pulled a slim flask from his coat and offered it to Will. "Gaston is a right bastard, but he's never betrayed us before."

"Well, now he has," Carmichael hissed, turning his back to the trio.

Will emptied the second flask and handed it to Weston. "We'll take further precautions, old man. You have my word."

Carmichael turned back, his eyes shuttered once more. "Let us hope you live long enough to make good on that."

11

"I want him to come," Lucinda spoke out loud, ripping the petal off an errant wildflower that she'd pilfered from Tristan's shaggy mane. "I do not want him to come," she continued, another poor petal meeting its untimely demise.

It was a dreary, gray morning, the lovely spring flowers in the fields that bordered Lover's Walk in Hyde Park doing little to lift Lucinda's spirits.

She looked up at the sky, noting the full clouds that threatened rain at any moment. She slowed Tristan to a plodding walk and allowed him to wander off the path and drop his head to the green grass.

She'd barely slept the night before, the evening spent with Will and his family occupying her thoughts entirely. Lucinda could not say what she'd expected from the duke, but it was certainly not what had transpired.

He'd been the perfect gentleman—charming, polite, and utterly devoid of any sign of a connection beyond what was expected. Then his demeanor had changed drastically, his assumption that he held any real power over her as a suitor irritating at best.

She'd struggled to keep from whispering her feelings in his ear the moment Grimaldi had taken the stage, Will's use of her given name pure music to her ears. And then he'd transformed into what, she couldn't quite tell. It was all quite upsetting.

Tristan abruptly stopped grazing and raised his head,

his ears pricking forward at the sound of someone approaching.

Lucinda tossed the flower to the ground and reached for the reins. Tamping down her nervousness, she blew out a breath and sat straight in her saddle. A raindrop landed on her nose. "Perfect," she muttered, tucking a lock of stray hair behind her ear.

To her surprise, the horse cantering toward her was not the majestic King Solomon's Mine. The mount was a stout chestnut, his rider's build not as bulky as Will's, and the man was fairer in coloring. Lucinda narrowed her eyes in an effort to make out the man's identity but could not, and resigned herself to turning Tristan about in order to face the oncoming rider.

The stranger pulled the chestnut to a walk and slowly approached. "Lady Lucinda Grey?"

"Yes," Lucinda answered hesitantly.

The man smiled, his handsome face lighting with apparent pleasure. "You've nothing to fear, Lady Lucinda, though I suppose I have the look of a beastie this early in the morning. I am Marcus MacInnes, the Earl of Weston." He tipped his hat, managing an elegant bow while seated, his sun-streaked golden hair falling into his face. "Clairemont sent me to see to your safety."

Lucinda relaxed back into her saddle, not sure if her relief was due to Lord Weston's legitimacy or the absence of Will. "Safety, Lord Weston? From what exactly? The beasties you made reference to?"

His green eyes flashed with amusement. "Oh, yes, there's the beasties and any other number of woodland sprites, Lady Lucinda. Don't tell me you've yet to see one in this fair park?"

"I don't recall such a sighting, Lord Weston, though I suppose it is entirely possible I did come across one of your sprites and simply did not recognize it for what it was," Lucinda replied, allowing the whimsical tone of their conversation to ease her mind.

"Impossible," he said with a laugh. "When you meet a sprite, you'll know it. Now, shall we get you home before the weather turns?"

It was Lucinda's turn to laugh as she glanced at the darkening skies. "Lord Weston, has the weather not turned enough for your liking, or would you prefer snow before returning to the comfort of your town house?"

Lord Weston walked the chestnut behind Tristan and reined him alongside Lucinda's mount. "I spent a fair amount of my youth in Scotland, Lady Lucinda. This," he waved negligently at the menacing sky, "is nothing compared to the ferocity of a Highland storm. But I've no doubt Clairemont would have my head on a pike were I to let you catch a cold, so shall we?" He smiled, gesturing for Lucinda to take the lead.

She clucked at Tristan, lifting the reins and turning him back onto the path. "How is it you know the duke?"

"Doesn't everyone know Iron Will?" he countered, joining her.

"That, Lord Weston, is not what I asked."

Lord Weston laughed again, the melodious deep baritone falling easily on Lucinda's ears. "He said you were a woman with a quick wit and sharp tongue. Will and I met at Eton, or to be more precise, we met in the headmaster's office at Eton, on a regular basis, as it were."

"Partners in crime, then," Lucinda confirmed.

He grinned and winked at her. "Not exactly, no. It took some time, and much blood, before we recognized our shared goals."

"Which were?"

"To beat the life out of anyone we could," he said matter-of-factly. "We were good at it too," he added, giving her a knowing look. "The moniker Iron Will isn't handed down lightly."

A giggle flew from Lucinda's mouth.

"Are you laughing at me, Lady Lucinda?" Lord Weston asked, wiggling his thick blond eyebrows up and down.

Lucinda forced a frown. "Of course not, my lord. That would be . . ." She hesitated, searching for just the right word.

"Heartless? Cruel? Unspeakably unkind?" he offered helpfully.

"You are very kind, Lord Weston," she said simply.

"And you are too generous," he answered, underscoring his sincerity with a smile. "Though I am not surprised. Will said as much."

Lucinda fidgeted with her reins. "The duke is quite chatty, is he not?"

"Not usually. But when it comes to you, he's a veritable font of knowledge."

"It does makes one wonder, then, why he could not summon the interest required to rise and meet me this morning."

"Oh, well, Will *is* a busy man," Lord Weston began, "what with being a duke and all."

The chestnut nosed at Tristan, blowing out a huff of air when he failed to receive a response. "That's a handsome horse you have there. Thoroughbred?" Lord Weston asked.

"Yes," she replied, almost certain that he'd changed the subject on purpose. He did not want to divulge anything more about Will, although Lucinda did not know why. And there seemed little point in trying to question him further.

"Yes, he is. And yours? He's a beauty. Reminds me quite a bit of Sebastian's Fury."

Lord Weston's expressive face registered surprise. "Fury was Pokey's sire. You know horses?"

"Pokey?"

He leaned forward, covering the chestnut's ear with his palm. "Shhhh," he cautioned in a loud whisper. "Poor Pokey did not inherit his sire's gift for speed. He's sensitive, though, so I try to spare his feelings when I can."

"Ah, I see," Lucinda murmured before raising her voice. "Well, my lord, Sir Pokey is, without a doubt, the most gorgeous chestnut I've seen of late. Such strength, such character—he truly is one of a kind."

Lucinda could have sworn the horse's ears pricked up at the lengthy compliment and his stride took on a prouder attitude. She smiled with delight.

Lord Weston mouthed "Thank you" as he stroked Pokey's neck. "He is indeed, and we thank you kindly for your generous words."

The rain began to pour in earnest, and the wind picked up, ruffling the skirt of Lucinda's blue velvet riding habit. "Shall we, Lord Weston?"

"We shall," he returned, settling his hat more firmly as he pulled the brim lower on his brow.

They urged their mounts into a faster trot and made haste for home.

"My dear, we visit Clairemont House today," Charlotte called from the drawing room.

Lucinda slowed her steps, her bedraggled riding habit dripping water on the marble foyer floor, and stopped just beyond the threshold to the room. Somehow, Lucinda had convinced herself that if she forced all thoughts of Her Grace's kind invitation from her mind, perhaps Charlotte would forget as well.

Clearly, that had been wishful thinking.

"Do we have an engagement?" She stood in the doorway, feigning confusion. Attempting to tuck up her rain-soaked hair was a useless effort, as was smoothing her sodden, wrinkled skirt. Her efforts did little to right the ruined garment.

Charlotte looked up from her needlepoint, her shock at Lucinda's appearance quickly giving way to concern. "Good heavens, Lucinda, you're soaked through to the skin." She hastily rose from the settee and crossed the room, yanking at the bellpull.

Mary appeared instantly, taking one look at Lucinda's soggy state before urging her upstairs.

"We must get you out of those clothes, my lady," she instructed, pausing mid-flight to stop a footman and demand that hot water be brought up.

Lucinda lifted her sodden skirt as she trudged up the stairs, Mary urging her from three treads above as Charlotte huffed from behind.

The moment they entered the bedchamber, Mary undressed Lucinda, then went to supervise the filling of the tub. Once it was full, she summoned Lucinda and waited to leave until her lady was safely immersed in the steaming hot water.

Charlotte came to stand next to the tub. "You soak every last ounce of rainwater off of you, young lady. I need to see how the gardener is managing my rosebushes this morning, but I will come and check on you shortly. I want you warm and dry by the time I return."

"You enjoyed your time with Lady Clairemont," Lucinda said, not making it clear whether her words were a statement or a question.

Or had it been an accusation?

Charlotte paused, dropping her gaze to look at Lucinda. "I did, very much so." She turned her gaze back to the doorway and began walking, stopping just short of the hallway. "It is as if she is experiencing life for the first time, now that her husband is gone."

"She has her freedom," Lucinda answered quietly.

"Exactly."

Charlotte disappeared around the corner, leaving Lucinda to stare at her toes.

Her aunts had extolled the value of a woman's independence since she was a child, until it had become her credo. Freedom was more than most women could hope to attain.

The pursuit of absolute freedom had been the impetus for her involvement with Will, King Solomon's Mine being the key. With the stallion they would not only establish a credible reputation within the male-dominated equine world, but they would improve upon that world, breeding quality horses and providing for the studs into their retirement years. Will could not give her what the prized stallion surely would.

"That is it, then," she said out loud, letting the water trickle through her fingers. "You choose a horse over a man."

In some measure, the choice had been made for her, since Will's feelings clearly did not match her own. But she took some small comfort in uttering the words nonetheless.

She reached for the perfumed soap, a new feeling of resolve blooming in her breast. She would have tea. She would, before this charade had run its course, have danced, flirted, made polite conversation, and demurely deflected countless empty compliments.

"It is a small price for freedom," she said, quietly but firmly, then began to scrub in earnest.

Clairemont House overlooked St. James's Square and was surrounded by sumptuous homes that only the cream of the ton could call their own. Hidden from the street by a sizeable iron gate, the short drive curved in a graceful arc, affording guests the opportunity to view the house and extensive grounds as they approached. Despite the dazzling quality of its fellow structures, Clairemont House stood out. The façade was entirely of Portland stone, the architecture fashioned in the neo-classical style, complete with eight massive columns and as many windows framed in ornamental carvings.

"Don't gape, dear," Charlotte said to Lucinda, straightening her own bonnet ribbons as the carriage came to a stop.

Lucinda pursed her lips, taking in the house before her. "Aunt Charlotte, I am not one given to gaping, but this . . ." She blinked, gesturing to the view beyond the carriage door. "It is—"

"Impressive? Yes, I know. I still remember my first ball here. Such grandeur, such opulence." Charlotte's features turned wistful for a moment before she returned to her practical self. "It's as breathtaking inside as it is on the outside, so I suggest you take a moment before we disembark to collect and prepare yourself."

Lucinda sat back against the wheat-colored squabs and took a deep breath, then expelled it with all the force she could muster.

"Better?" Charlotte inquired.

"Yes, thank you," Lucinda answered, though a question niggled at her. "You spoke of attending a ball here, yet I have never heard of any events being held at Clairemont House. Why is that?"

Charlotte looked to the house again. "It's my understanding that the duchess refused to host parties of any kind once the boys were sent off to school."

"Good for her," Lucinda said, following Charlotte's gaze.

"Yes, I would have to agree," her aunt said with a firm nod. "Are we ready, then?"

As ready as I will ever be, Lucinda thought to herself. "Yes, of course. A cup of tea would be most welcome."

Charlotte's fist thumped the ceiling of the carriage twice. The liveried footman jumped down immediately, lowered the step, and opened the door. Charlotte descended first, taking the driver's arm and allowing him to assist her safely to the ground.

Lucinda took one last, deep breath and stepped out onto the graveled forecourt to join Charlotte. Together, they strolled to the impressive front door, where the beautifully carved knocker announced to the world that the duke was in residence.

A house footman held open the massive oak door, bowing to usher them over the threshold. An anxious-faced butler waited just inside, his build and demeanor reminding Lucinda of a nervous bird she'd once seen at the Kew Botanical Gardens.

"Madam," he said, bowing to each of them in turn with quick, efficient bobs of deference. "This way, if you please."

He led them through the sumptuous foyer, their slipper heels tapping lightly on the black and white marble floor. Lucinda tilted her head back to better admire the Doric frieze that adorned the ceiling high above. They reached the impressive staircase, a wonder of engineering in stone that possessed a gorgeous balustrade done in trompe l'oeil.

The butler slowed, stepping aside when they reached the stairs. He gestured for them to ascend, then followed. Charlotte gripped the ornate iron baluster, while Lucinda counted the steps.

"Sixty-two," she said under her breath as they reached the first floor.

"Pardon? Did you say something?" Charlotte asked somewhat breathlessly, though to her credit she did not faint on the spot.

"No, nothing. Nothing at all," Lucinda replied, bending her head to conceal her gaze from Charlotte. She tightened her grip on her rose print skirt, lifting it to clear the toes of her slippers as she climbed, and attempted to hide her fatigue.

She rather suspected that she hadn't managed a single good night's rest since meeting Will. She tossed and turned, trying to remember every word they'd spoken, and then worse, thinking on each one until she was dizzy. And if she managed to finish that, she spent the next hour berating herself for being unable to sleep.

It was madness, and it had to stop, but for once in her life, she could not make her feelings bend to her will.

They reached the top of the stairs and followed the butler down a long hall lined with Grecian busts, stopping midway. Lucinda paused to allow her aunt to enter the room first.

"Lady Charlotte Grey and her niece, Lady Lucinda Grey, Your Grace," the butler announced.

Lucinda looked to the end of the room, where a massive fireplace took up nearly the entirety of one wall. Graceful wood furniture was arranged before it, the duchess seated in a chair nearest the window. Lord Michael rose.

Lucinda's gaze swept the length of the room from one end to the other, frowning when she didn't find Will.

"I'm afraid you'll have to excuse my brother," Lord Michael said, strolling toward them. "He's been detained by business and will not be able to join us."

He met them halfway down the long room and escorted them to join his mother. Both Charlotte and Lucinda dipped a curtsy to the duchess before taking seats, side by side, on the embroidered, blue silk cushions of the settee.

"I hope the duke's business matters aren't of serious concern for him," Lucinda said, unable to contain her disappointment—and, if she was being completely honest, a healthy dose of irritation. How was she to stop loving him if she was never given the opportunity to observe what she assumed were his many shortcomings?

Her Grace smiled politely. "No, no, nothing is amiss. Simply a matter that required his strict attention, that is all."

Two footmen and the butler entered the room. One held a large tray with a gleaming silver tea service while the other two brought forth a variety of sandwiches, tea cakes, and other delicacies.

The duchess waited until they had deposited the trays and departed the room, then sat forward in her seat and saw to the tea, pouring with consummate ease as she made polite conversation.

Lucinda participated in the discussion of the latest on-dits, though her mind couldn't help but wander. What business could be keeping Will? To the best of her knowledge he was not in the least committed to the duties a duke would normally shoulder.

She accepted from Her Grace a delicate china plate holding a cucumber sandwich and nibbled. Was it possible he had simply grown tired of their game? A sense of indignation washed over her. If that was the case, she would refuse to release him from their agreement, and King Solomon's Mine would be hers.

"Lady Lucinda?"

Was he avoiding her?

"Lady Lucinda?"

Lucinda looked up to discover Will's brother addressing her. She swallowed her bite of sandwich quickly and smiled. "I'm sorry, Lord Michael. You were saying?"

Amusement tugged at the corners of his mouth. "Would you join me in a stroll about the room?"

Lucinda arched an eyebrow and tilted her chin. She might have pleaded a reluctance to leave the conversation, but was curious to know what Lord Michael wanted. So she gave him a small nod of acceptance and rose.

He tucked her gloved hand through the crook of his arm and led her toward the far end of the room, beginning a clockwise circuit.

"A shilling for your thoughts," he said in a low tone.

Lucinda glanced out the window, desperate to keep the discouragement of Will's absence to herself. "And just what would lead you to believe I am thinking on anything in particular?"

Lord Michael let out a low chuckle. "Come now, Lady Lucinda, you and I have no need to play games."

She turned back to face him. "You've your brother's laugh."

"And you lack the talent for subterfuge."

"Fair enough."

The two remained silent as they passed Charlotte and Her Grace, though they needn't have bothered. The ladies had their heads together and were giggling like two young girls.

"Now then," Lord Michael continued. "Where were we?"

"You were prying, I believe," Lucinda answered succinctly.

"Yes. Do continue. You were going to tell me what thoughts absorbed your attention so completely."

Lucinda drew a deep breath, holding it for a moment before expelling it in a heavy sigh. "I suppose there would be no harm in sharing my dilemma with you. It's just that . . . well . . . ." she began, hesitating as she leaned in to murmur privately, "the Foster masquerade ball is nearly upon us and I have yet to decide on a costume."

Lord Michael's serious expression turned to confusion and then amusement. "That is a dilemma. A much larger one than I'd first assumed."

"Yes, well, not being a woman, how could you have

known the paramount importance of choosing just the right attire?"

"A gown is a much larger dilemma, indeed, than my brother could ever be."

Lucinda, to her credit, did not break her stride, though the mention of Will made her heartbeat stutter. "I do not believe we were speaking of the duke."

"Indeed we were not." He paused. "But now we are."

Lucinda narrowed her eyes at Lord Michael. "In addition to his laugh, you clearly share the duke's ability to manipulate a conversation to your advantage."

"I will take that as the compliment I'm sure it was meant to be," he replied. "But I believe we were speaking of His Grace."

Lucinda came to a complete stop, forcing Lord Michael to follow suit. "I am at a loss for words."

"Then allow me to help you," he murmured, looking out over the extensive gardens at the back of the house. "Do you intend to marry my brother?"

Lucinda let out a squeak of surprise, though thankfully they were far enough away from Charlotte and the duchess not to draw their attention. "Lord Michael, I do not believe we have known each other long enough to speak with such frankness."

"Come now, Lady Lucinda." He eyed her consideringly. "Avoidance is hardly attractive in an intelligent woman such as yourself."

She raised her chin and met his stare. "I believe, Lord Michael, that you must address your questions to your brother."

"Forgive me, Lady Lucinda. Perhaps I should have asked, if the offer is made, will you accept?"

Lucinda's heart raced, the tattoo it beat out faster than she would have preferred. In a desperate attempt to end the questioning, she purposely turned to the garden view framed by the window. "Your gardens are beauti-

ful. And the beds of tulips and daffodils are exceptionally fine—they are truly lovely this time of year."

"Yes, quite," Lord Michael answered impatiently.
"Lady Lucinda, allow me to apologize. I do not usually
act in such a forward manner, but when it comes to my
brother, time is of the essence. Despite his assumptions
to the contrary, the duchess cares very deeply for him
and would like nothing more than to see him happily
settled."

Lucinda nearly nodded her head in agreement. It was
exactly how her aunts had described it, and after meeting Will's mother, she now shared their opinion.

Lord Michael continued. "You are the first woman
His Grace has shown any real interest in. Some indication that the courtship is progressing toward the desired
outcome would be most welcome."

"The natural outcome of most serious courtships in
our social strata is marriage," she began, looking back
at the duchess and Charlotte. The two women were
now unabashedly watching her and Lord Michael converse. She managed a brief smile before turning back
to her escort. "But, as you know, nothing can be assumed when dealing with the duke. What I can confirm
is that, for my part, the courtship is progressing as expected."

Lucinda congratulated herself for providing such a
vague, yet perfectly polite answer. Lord Michael's questions clearly indicated he wasn't privy to the details of
her and Will's agreement. And if Will had not shared the
truth, she certainly was not prepared to do so.

Lucinda released Lord Michael's arm, turning to look
up at him when they were still several yards from Her
Grace and Charlotte, but far enough removed to allow
private conversation. "Is that the information you
hoped to gain, my lord?"

"Hardly," he answered. "It appears I must question my brother on the topic."

"And you're brave too," Lucinda exclaimed lightly. "I marvel you've not married."

He chuckled, the low, gruff quality sounding so much like Will that Lucinda's heart caught.

"I suspect it's not bravery on my part," he replied. "You mentioned that I am like my brother in many ways. Pigheadedness, I'm afraid, is one of those qualities we seem to share."

He turned toward her, and she smiled, thinking that he was ready to allow the conversation to drift toward less personal waters. But then his eyes met hers, and there was something so stark and raw in his expression.

She wanted to cry. She had no idea where it came from, this sudden burst of emotion, but it was all she could do to hold it back, to cling to some semblance of her dignity.

"I suppose," he said, his voice catching slightly on his words, "that despite my brother's oft-demonstrated dislike for all things familial, I cannot help but want the best for him."

"He loves you, you know. Deeply," she blurted out in a soft murmur, her hand flying to her mouth as soon as the revealing words were uttered. As much as she wanted to tell him of all that her aunts had shared concerning the duke's painstaking efforts to keep his brother safe, she dared not speak another word.

"Michael, Lady Lucinda—do rejoin us before we eat the remainder of the pastries," the duchess called. Charlotte's good-natured harrumph of confirmation regarding the disappearing confections made Lucinda laugh despite the tears that hovered on her lashes.

"I should not have said that," she murmured, brushing her fingertips across her lashes. "Please accept my most sincere apologies. It's not my place to speak of such intimate matters."

"Do you lie?" he asked simply, his face devoid of any emotion other than polite interest, though a rough urgency ran beneath his words.

"No. Why would I, my lord?" Lucinda answered, then turned to rejoin the two women.

"I don't know," Lucinda heard him mutter.

She did not turn back, despite her deepest desire to do so.

It hadn't been the best of days, Will reflected grimly, wincing as he shifted beneath the sheets on the massive ducal bed.

After being stitched and dosed with brandy, Weston had accompanied him home and dragged him to his bedchamber, aided by Smithers. The brandy had made the wound more bearable, but it had done its work on his wits as well. His dissection of the evening's events with Carmichael would have to wait.

He'd woken with a pounding headache and enough bandages wrapped about his chest and back to rival those of an Egyptian mummy. Those at least he could hide, even if the wound hurt like the very devil.

The problem was his face. His jaw was riddled with angry bruises. The black-and-purple mottled pattern made his appearance even more menacing, Will thought with disgust.

He wouldn't have been averse to using the box of stage paints packed away in the armoire across the room. He'd made use of the charcoal and pots of paint a time or two in Corinthian dealings. But on those occasions, he'd had the cover of night to help conceal what would surely be detected in the brightness of day.

And the wounds were far too fresh to offer any believable explanation for their appearance. If he could avoid Lucinda for a day or two more, he could pass it off as a boxing injury. But any sooner and she'd never believe him.

Much as he disliked it, there seemed no other option than to remain in his room until he looked a little less battered.

"I'm assuming from the looks of things that the lion won?"

Will sat up, wincing when the movement pulled the stitches and stretched the wound on his back. Gingerly turning his head, he saw his brother standing in the open doorway, one shoulder propped against the doorjamb.

"Hardly." Will fingered his jaw and winced. "Though he did land a few good blows."

Michael strolled into the room and walked to the glowing fireplace, taking stock of the pewter candlesticks poised at each end of the stone slab mantel before dropping into a leather armchair facing the bed. "Is this the business that so desperately needed your attention?"

"And if it is?" Will countered. He threw back the sheet and swung his legs over the edge of the bed, grunting at the protest of torn skin and muscle. His head swam, and he sat without moving, fighting the sensation.

Michael stretched out his legs, crossed his booted feet, and propped his elbows on the arms of the chair. He templed his fingers just below his chin and contemplated Will. "Far be it from me to advise you in the ways of women, but . . ."

"But?" Will pushed, the slightest hint of irritation present in his voice.

"I don't think Lady Lucinda would take it well if she knew you'd returned to your old ways."

"Bloody hell," Will bit out, standing too quickly. His body clenched with pain and his vision danced with tiny black motes. He steadied himself with one hand on the bedpost and waited for the burning sensation on his back to subside. "Don't involve yourself in my dealings with Lady Lucinda," he snarled.

Michael rubbed at his lower lip with his forefinger, clearly restraining himself from responding in kind. "Mother wants to see you happily settled," he said, then, in a quieter voice, added, "As do I."

Will gripped the bedpost tighter. Michael's words carried a weight and sincerity he'd rather ignore.

"You care for Lady Lucinda, do you not?" Michael asked, breaking the heavy silence.

Will was unsure how to answer him. His brother's words revealed genuine interest; his demeanor held a depth of emotion Will had not witnessed in him for too many years.

He released the bedpost and slowly walked across the floor, the fine wool carpet providing little warmth against his bare feet. He came to stand in front of the fire, his back to Michael. "I do."

"Then for once in your life, do what is right for you— for your heart. Do not endanger what will make you happy."

Will was glad he'd turned toward the fire; his face surely revealed far more than he wanted to express at the moment. Why had his brother's feelings for him changed, turning from contempt to care overnight?

Will searched for a rational explanation, but his exhausted brain failed to find one. He simply could not comprehend the emotion brought on by Michael's words, so he beat it down as best he could and forged on.

"Very poetically put, little brother." He turned away from the fireplace and winced when the flames heated his wound. "Clearly tea with the ladies was most beneficial."

Disappointment flickered on Michael's face briefly before the boredom and mild irritation that Will knew so well returned. "Yes, well, I'd venture to say even the most hardened of hearts would melt in Lady Lucinda's presence."

Will nodded in response.

"Oh, wait, that's already been proven, hasn't it?" Michael continued, crossing his legs, the leather chair absorbing the movement.

"Michael," Will began, his tone one of warning.

"I do wonder, though, what she sees in the likes of you. Because, let us be completely honest: The woman could have any man she wanted. And yet, she has chosen you," his brother added.

Will knew when he was being baited. Michael was, without a doubt, doing his damnedest to upset him. The question was, *why*.

"Yes, well, it is the mysteries in life that make it all so interesting, wouldn't you agree?" he replied, his tone deceptively light.

"Quite," Michael replied. "Though, I do think that I should make one thing perfectly clear: I find Lady Lucinda delightful—a fact I shared with her today during our walk about the room—"

"Michael," Will interrupted, coming closer to his brother.

"She was quite thankful for my proposal."

Will raked a hand through his hair, then folded both arms over his chest as he counted to ten. "And what offer might that be?"

Michael uncrossed his legs and stood, their eyes meeting. "Well, I think we all know what will come of this *courtship*," he said, disdain dripping from his tone. "I wanted her to know that I would not abandon her, though the entirety of the ton surely will once you're finished."

Will stretched to his full height, barely a hairsbreadth

above his brother's. "Enough!" he yelled, grabbing at Michael's arms and holding him in a vicelike grip. "I would rather die than do Lucinda harm."

"Your very presence in her life harms her more than—"

"Do not speak of things you know nothing about!" Will hissed, his hands tightening about Michael's arms.

The grim set of Michael's mouth slid into a satisfied smirk. "I lied. No such proposal was made to Lady Lucinda," he said smoothly, "though it is encouraging to see that you are in possession of a heart after all."

Will wanted to hit him—lay him out flat on the floor of the ducal chamber and be done with it. But it was not so simple. It never was when it came to his family.

"I am in possession of a temper, little brother," Will replied, belatedly releasing Michael's arms. "And I am tired. I do believe I'll go to bed. You'll have to wait a bit to get the best of me."

"I wouldn't be so sure of that," Michael said, his voice barely above a whisper.

Will watched Michael's back as he walked from the room, the uneasy feeling that he should stop him weighing heavily on his heart.

"Are you quite done with the preserves or would you rather eat them straight from the serving dish, my dear?"

Lucinda looked to her plate, where her toast was now swimming in strawberry preserves, and set her knife down. "It is wonderful jam, Aunt Victoria."

"But hardly a meal in itself," Victoria countered, beckoning for the serving dish.

Lucinda took a bite of toast and began to chew, hesitating for just a moment before passing the jam to Victoria.

"Impertinent little chit," Victoria said, taking up her own knife and spreading a minute portion of the sweet preserves on her toast.

Lucinda offered a small smile in response, the disappointment of Will's absence yesterday lingering.

"Ha!" Bessie yelled, then clapped the table with her hand, holding *Bell's Weekly Messenger* in the other. "It appears our Lucinda has gained the attention of the society pages."

"Gossip rags, you mean?" Victoria replied, rolling her eyes in Bessie's general direction before taking a bite.

Bessie ignored Victoria's remark and continued on. "Your outing to the opera with the duke caused quite a stir."

She turned the paper so that the rest of the table might see the story and accompanying illustration.

Charlotte lowered a forkful of eggs back to her plate untouched and squinted at the drawing. "Is that meant to be Lucinda and the duke?"

"He resembles an ape of some sort," Victoria commented dryly, "though perhaps the most attractive ape I have ever seen."

Lucinda gestured for Bessie to pass her the paper, the excitement exhibited by her aunts hard to ignore. "Aunt Victoria is correct. The sketch of the duke bears a striking likeness to a very large ape," she confirmed, taking another bite of toast while she studied the picture. "I must say, the artist made me look rather fetching, though the discrepancy in our height is rather severe, wouldn't you agree?"

Stanford came through the door, a silver tray in his hands piled high with the day's mail. He set the tray down near Charlotte, removed a letter from the top, and rounded the table to Lucinda. "My lady, a rider delivered this just a moment ago and asked that it be given to you directly."

Lucinda set down the paper and took the missive from the servant. "Thank you, Stanford."

The man bowed and took himself off, leaving the four women alone.

"More regrets from the duke, I suppose," she said quietly.

She broke the wax seal and unfolded the note. The black handwriting was not Will's—the small, blocklike quality very unlike Will's large, firm strokes.

"Oh, no." She barely breathed the words, unaware she'd spoken them aloud as she read. Her heart slammed, and her lungs seized with fear as Lucinda gripped the missive tightly.

In unison, her aunts jumped from their chairs and hurried to cluster around her.

"Whatever is the matter?" Charlotte asked as all three bent nearer to read over Lucinda's shoulder.

"It's from Perkins. Something is terribly wrong with Winnie," she answered, holding back tears.

Lady Winifred, or Winnie to those who adored her, was perhaps the single most valuable mare in the family stable. She was bred to the county's top stallion and due to foal any day.

Samuel Perkins was in charge of the horses' care at Bampton Manor, overseeing everything from their food to their exercise schedule. His diagnosis of a complication involving the unborn foal was extremely worrisome.

The stable manager was a capable, calm man and not given to flights of fancy or worry without cause. That he'd felt compelled to inform Lucinda of Winnie's illness spoke volumes about the depth of his concern.

"I must go at once," Lucinda said in a panic, dropping the letter to the table and pushing back her chair to stand. "Should I write to the duke? We were to attend the Whitney musicale this evening."

Victoria retrieved the note from the table and tucked it into her sleeve. "No, my dear. We will see to everything. Now go."

"No, you're right. Of course," Lucinda replied tearily.

The three aunts stood back and made room for Lucinda, who ran from the room in haste.

"I will accompany her," Charlotte said to the other two. "Please, alert the servants. We will leave the moment we're packed."

"What, in God's name, is in Bampton?"

Will's man in the Grey household gave him a weary look from across the ducal bedchamber. "A horse. A sick horse, to be more precise."

Will leapt from bed, wincing at the fresh flash of pain

from his wound. "And Lady Lucinda is the only person in all of England who can cure this equine?" He stalked across the room to where the man stood.

The agent took two steps back. "It is a mare of some importance to her apparently."

"Smithers!" Will yelled viciously, his eyes remaining on the man. "Apparently," he repeated, his tone lethal.

"Your Grace," Smithers said breathlessly as he entered the room. "A note from Lady Charlotte has arrived."

Will grabbed the offered note and ripped it open, reading the contents quickly.

He crumpled the correspondence in his fist then tossed it to the floor. "You," he said gruffly to the waiting agent, "Lady Lucinda is traveling to her home in Oxfordshire. Take two men and follow her."

The man nodded firmly and turned to go.

"Smithers, my clothing."

The vague feeling of light-headedness he'd experienced last night returned; only this time it was punctuated by a loud gasp from Smithers.

"Your Grace, you seem to be bleeding."

Will cocked his head in an attempt to view his back; the little he could see was covered in white bandages, a crimson stain spreading rapidly.

"I'll summon the doctor at once—"

"There is no time for such trivialities!" Will said angrily. "You'll find fresh dressings on the end table."

A frantic Smithers ran for the bandages, returning to stand in front of Will. "My lord?"

"Blast, Smithers," Will growled, reaching around for the soaked fabric and pulling. He grazed the edge of the wound, spitting out an expletive in reply.

"All right, then," Smithers said quietly, his composure returning though his face remained deathly pale. "Do turn around, Your Grace."

Will was finding it hard to stand upright, Smithers's hesitation doing little to help. "Now, man!"

All at once, Smithers ripped the bandages from Will's back, the pain causing him to see stars. He steadied himself with one hand on the wall and took a deep breath. "Good man. Now fetch me that brandy," he said, gesturing toward the decanter on the far table.

Smithers did as he was told, walking as fast as he could to retrieve the brandy then returning.

In one swift move Will uncorked the crystal decanter and poured the liquid over his shoulder, the burning sensation dropping him to his knees and ripping a deep, guttural grunt from his throat.

"Your Grace," Smithers gasped, leaning over to offer his aide. "The stitches have been upset."

"The bandages. Now," he demanded through clenched teeth, ignoring the valet's concern.

Smithers set about reapplying the bandages quickly and efficiently. "I've done all that I can, Your Grace," he said, offering Will his arm. "I do think that a doctor—"

Will waved off the help and awkwardly rose. "We've wasted enough time as it is. Bring me my clothing."

To his credit, Smithers did not argue, choosing to retrieve a shirt, breeches, boots, and neckcloth in silence.

Will took the proffered clothing and dressed as quickly as he could, affording minimum care with his wounds. "Give my mother and brother my apologies," he ordered the valet, then walked to the door.

"Your Grace, I have not packed your things. You cannot leave without—"

Will continued to walk, savagely pulling open the door and sending it crashing into the wall. "Send them along after me," he shouted, his fatigued body barely able to keep up with his agitated state. "Or do not. I don't bloody well care either way."

*   *   *

Antoine Garenne was many things. Patient was not one of them. He took a drink of the abysmal red wine and pursed his lips in distaste. He must wrap up his business in this godforsaken country and return to France—if for no other reason than to get his hands on a decent bottle of wine.

He'd killed the fools who had failed to take care of Clairemont—a charitable act, really, considering the damage the giant had done to them.

But the lady's unexpected trip to the country was, quite simply, more than a man could take.

He paused to look out the dingy window of his rented room. On the narrow street below, a trio of prostitutes called out to passing men, their lewd and explicit invitations to potential customers rising on the damp spring air.

The band of pain around his head, reduced by a bout of vigorous coupling, gained strength, cinching tighter. His grip on the wineglass tightened and anger roiled in his gut.

He'd use the days that Lady Lucinda was absent from London to refine details for two potential kidnap schemes. And if the Duke of Clairemont died during either of them, so much the better.

He tipped the glass up and swallowed with difficulty, his throat constricted by rage.

"Lovie."

Garenne pushed himself away from the scarred table and stood, crossing to the rumpled bed, where a nude prostitute lay. "It's a bit cold without you," she said coyly, her garishly painted face only serving to make her more disgusting to Garenne.

"We would not want you to be cold," he replied, leaning one knee on the sagging bed and reaching for a pillow.

The filthy whore had eased some of the pain, but not all. He required more of her.

The woman smiled lewdly at him as he brought the pillow nearer. And when he brought it down hard over her face she complied, the many twisted demands she'd endured in the past hour telling her that he meant no harm.

But when he failed to release her, she began to struggle, her arms flailing in an attempt to free herself, her legs kicking out at the air. Her response pleased Garenne. After all, without a struggle there was no thrill, no satisfaction. No pleasure.

Her legs stilled, then her arms, signaling the arrival of death. Garenne waited a moment, then lifted the pillow away from the woman's face and threw it across the room. He took in the frozen look of terror on her face and smiled, the irritation of the mission easing slightly.

He stood and walked to the window. Squinting through the dirt and grime, he eyed the women across the street. Standing within the pool of light cast by the newly lit lantern, the small group included a round, buxom redhead, a tall blonde, and a petite black-haired one, all more than willing and expertly able.

"I'll bury myself in the black-haired whore. Or perhaps the blonde tonight?" A slow smile curved his thick lips. "All three it is."

"Bloody British rain," Will cursed, tugging his hat brim lower on his forehead. Sol pinned his ears back and snorted, clearly in agreement with his master.

"You've no one but your beloved Lucinda to blame for this," Will said to the stallion, brushing water from his mane. Given that the horse was soaked, the action did little good and was more a rough gesture of affection. "Well, Lucinda and a mare named Winnie."

He'd ridden at breakneck speed, not stopping until he reached the Rosemont Inn despite the dizziness that threatened to unseat him. He was terribly tired, and the pain from his wound was unbearable, the countless hours spent astride only having added to his misery.

The rain quickened, accompanied by a tepid wind from the north. Will turned up the collar of his greatcoat just as the dim light from the Rosemont's muddy yard came into view.

He turned Sol into the yard and slid from the saddle, nearly falling to his knees in the dank mud. A young man approached and Will handed him the reins.

He reached in his pocket and pulled out several coins. "Has a Lady Lucinda Grey taken a room for the evening?" he asked pointedly, dropping half a crown into the flat of the man's palm.

The man stared at the coins in Will's hand, scratching his head in earnest. "There's only one lady of quality that's taken a room for the night. Blonde, blue eyes, traveling with a companion—an older woman."

Will dropped the remaining coins into the man's hand. "Thank you. Take care of my horse and there will be more where that came from."

"Yes, sir!"

Will thumped Sol on the rump and walked toward the inn. *Strange candles, those, that they would dim as one drew near.* He squinted at the lights that flanked the front door, blinked once, then again, but they continued to dim.

Before Will knew what was happening, the night sky had engulfed him and he was falling, though there didn't seem to be a damn thing he could do about it.

* * *

Lucinda stared up at the darkened eaves of her room in the Rosemont Inn, restless and weary.

The trip to Bampton Manor always felt endlessly long, and today's journey was no exception. Lucinda had wanted to travel straight through, stopping only to secure fresh horses. But Charlotte had objected, insisting Lucinda would be of no use to Winnie if she arrived exhausted and addle-brained from lack of sleep.

"Shouldn't the patrons be abed by now?" Charlotte asked, stifling a yawn.

Lucinda rolled to face her aunt, tucking one hand under her feather pillow. "I highly doubt that anyone is thinking on what they *should* do, Aunt."

The Rosemont's tavern was exceedingly popular, though it had nothing to do with the quality of the establishment. On one of her many trips between London and Oxfordshire, Lucinda had discovered that the Rosemont was the only watering hole for some twenty miles.

The carousing had started innocently enough with a snort of laughter floating up here and there through the floorboards. But in the last hour the intensity of the evening had taken a turn for the worse.

"Too true, dear girl," Charlotte answered. "Too true."

The bed dipped slightly as Charlotte rolled from her back to her side. "I suppose absolute silence would fail you as well with all that must be on your mind."

"Winnie, you mean?" Lucinda asked apprehensively, fingering the rough bed linens.

"Yes, my dear. Who else would I be referring to?"

Lucinda chewed her bottom lip. "Precisely."

"Although," Charlotte began, "there is the duke."

Lucinda froze, thankful for the darkness that filled the room. "The courtship is proceeding as planned," she lied, squeezing her eyes shut. "Sol will be ours by summer."

"Perhaps you did not hear me, my dear. I mentioned the duke, not the horse."

Lucinda turned her face into the pillow, frightened that she might cry. "The duke? Well, he is . . ." She swallowed, urging the lump in her throat to move lower. "That is to say—"

"My lady!"

The sound of their coachman's voice was punctuated by three loud raps upon the wooden door.

"Rogers?" Lucinda and Charlotte said in unison, the bed nearly breaking in two from the force of their combined exodus. They fumbled about in the dark for their dressing gowns, Lucinda finding hers first, then dashing toward the door.

She unlocked the door and swung it open. "Rogers, what is it?"

"I am sorry to disturb you both, but the innkeeper has need of you," he said, averting his eyes. "Seems there's a gentleman that's fainted and they don't know who he is."

Charlotte knotted the robe's sash about her waist and came to stand next to Lucinda. "Rogers, I don't mean to be obtuse, but how on earth might we be of assistance? In all likelihood there are several individuals passed out below-stairs."

"Beg your pardon, my lady. This gentleman didn't drink himself to sleep. He's injured. But he asked after Lady Lucinda before planting himself facedown in the yard."

Both women gasped in horror.

Charlotte reached for Lucinda's arm. "Who on earth could it be?"

Lucinda patted her aunt's hand reassuringly despite the macabre curiosity she felt. "I can't imagine. But surely there is a reasonable explanation."

Rogers continued to stare at the door. "Er, will you go and see him?"

"Oh, of course," Lucinda replied, taking Rogers's offered candlestick. "We'll be but a moment."

Charlotte closed the door firmly and turned to where her things were. "Have you any idea—"

"None at all," Lucinda interrupted, struggling to pull her nightgown over her head.

"Come, let me help you," Charlotte said, walking to where Lucinda stood by the rumpled bed and reaching to pull at the gown. As soon as they were both dressed, Lucinda hurried toward the door, readying to open it.

"My dear, a moment," Charlotte said, prompting her to turn back.

"Yes," Lucinda replied, her brows knitting together.

"I know that it has been a trying time for you, what with Winnie and . . ." she paused, taking Lucinda's hands in hers. "Well, I do worry that the sight of a grievously injured man may be that proverbial straw."

Lucinda tried to smile. "Are you calling me a camel?"

"Lucinda!" Charlotte attempted *not* to smile. "What I am trying to say is, there's a limit to the number of misfortunes one person can endure."

Lucinda gripped her aunt's hands tightly as if to keep herself from falling. "Aunt Charlotte," she began, looking down at their joined hands. "Sometimes in life, the only option one has is to continue on. Would you not agree?"

"Wholeheartedly," Charlotte confirmed, freeing her hands and reaching to caress Lucinda's cheek. "When did you become so wise, my dear?"

"Precisely fifteen seconds ago," Lucinda answered, offering her aunt a lopsided smile. "Shall we?"

"We shall."

The two walked to the door, opening it slowly.

Rogers stood in the hallway. "Come with me, then, ladies."

They followed him down the dimly lit corridor, the sounds from below having quieted somewhat.

"Here we are," Rogers said, gesturing to the last door on the right. He opened it and stepped aside, allowing Lucinda and Charlotte to enter. "I'll be in the hallway if you need me."

The women nodded at the coachman, then stepped across the threshold. A man in dark traveling clothes stood with his back to the door, obscuring the bed just beyond.

He turned at the sound of their entry. "Splendid. One of you is Lady Lucinda Grey, I presume?"

"I am she," Lucinda answered hesitantly.

"Well, come along, then," he urged impatiently. When Lucinda failed to obey him immediately, he let out a rather loud harrumph of displeasure. "Ladies, I am a man of science and, as such, social graces are not my forte. Please, forgive me," he said, quickly bowing. "Dr. Elijah Forrester at your service."

Lucinda and Charlotte bowed and made to properly complete the introduction. "Lad—"

"All right, then. Who might this man be?" Dr. Forrester interrupted. "I've a patient in Dunsford who requires my attention."

Lucinda stepped past the doctor and turned to look upon the man, the flickering candlelight casting him in shadows, though the hideous bruising on his face was readily apparent even in the dim light.

She gasped and stepped forward, her hand flying to her mouth. "Will?!"

Charlotte rushed to the bed. "Good Lord," she uttered with horror, steadying herself against the doctor.

Forrester propped Charlotte upright and cleared his throat. "You know this man, then?"

"He is the Duke of Clairemont," Lucinda said haltingly.

The doctor gaped at her. "The . . . who?"

Lucinda brushed past him, blinking rapidly in the hopes that Will's injuries were nothing more than a trick of light. "Who did this to him?"

The doctor reached for his kit on the side table and began to rummage through it. "We might never know."

"Surely you're not implying that he . . ." Lucinda paused, her voice shaking with the effort. "That he will not wake?"

"Well, one never can tell in these sorts of situations," he replied simply. "Only time will tell."

Lucinda reached to stroke Will's hand, noting the smudges of dirt and blood on his hands and face. "Is there nothing that we can do?"

Dr. Forrester produced a small leather pouch from his kit and gestured toward Will. "Actually, yes, there is."

He handed Lucinda the pouch then reached for Will's shoulders, pulling him to a seated position. "Now, if you'll hold him thusly I will stitch up his back."

Charlotte reached for Lucinda's arm. "My dear, the duke is undressed—"

"Aunt Charlotte," Lucinda pleaded in a low tone. "The doctor needs my assistance."

Charlotte's brows knit together as she considered her options. "All right."

Both Lucinda and Charlotte leaned forward in order to see the wound, the amount of coagulated blood encircling the gash making them gasp.

"Why was this not seen to immediately?" Charlotte demanded, fanning herself vigorously with her hanky.

The doctor gestured for Lucinda's help. "No one could identify the man. How was I to know if he could afford my services?"

Lucinda bent down and exchanged places with the

doctor, the substantial weight of Will's debilitated body coming to rest against her as she faced him.

"He is the Duke of Clairemont," Charlotte said angrily. "He could very well die and you would be held—"

"Please," Lucinda cried, halting her aunt's indictment. "It is of no consequence now." She looked up at the doctor and swallowed. "Just do what needs to be done."

The room fell silent as the doctor prepared the needle and set to work.

She held Will about the waist with the greatest of care, the feel of his bare, sweaty skin on hers oddly comforting.

Resting her chin on his shoulder, she breathed in his familiar scent and tried to will him awake. She watched the doctor draw the thread through the wound over and over again, panic rising in her stomach with every stitch.

You cannot die, she screamed in her head, tightening her grip about his waist. *Please, hold on. There's so much I need to say.*

"That should do it," the doctor said, dropping his instrument on the side table and picking up a length of linen. He bandaged the wound and pulled Will from Lucinda, the absence of his body leaving her bereft.

Charlotte put her hand on Lucinda's shoulder and squeezed. "What signs are we to look for, Doctor?" she asked worriedly.

"Well, if the duke does not wake up, then we've a real problem," he answered, swiping at his needle with a cloth then returning it to his kit.

"He will," Lucinda whispered. "He has to."

Dr. Forrester held his palm to Will's forehead. "I do hope you're right," he said.

But he was shaking his head as he said it.

A heavy hand on his aching forehead forced Will to awaken, and then the pain began in earnest.

"Christ," he blew out, struggling to sit up, then wishing he hadn't, the pain from the torturous wound on his back multiplying in intensity.

He opened his eyes to find three hazy forms leaning over him. He squinted, bringing his view into focus—one stranger, Charlotte, and *Lucinda*.

And that was when he found his voice. "What in the name of all that is most holy is going on?"

"Dr. Elijah Forrester, Your Grace," the man said, reaching to press on Will's jaw. "You were found in the yard. Luckily, Lady Lucinda was able to identify you."

"Lucinda, I am eternally indebted to you," Will replied through gritted teeth, the man's probing fingers doing little to ease his discomfort.

"I am assuming those bruises on your face and the mighty gash on your back were not the result of your fall in the yard."

Will ran his hands through his hair. *Well, now. Collapsing has never proven to be quite so convenient.* "A band of highwaymen, Doctor. Some two miles back. I trust you'll find a few strewn about in the bushes."

The women gasped, Lucinda's hand moving to cover her heart. "Your Grace, how you can you be so cavalier when you—" She broke off, gathering her composure. "You could have been mortally wounded."

Will was enjoying this far more than he should. "But I am not mortally wounded, correct?" he asked, looking to the doctor.

"No, not mortally," the doctor replied, turning to his kit and pulling two bottles from the bag.

"The blood loss from the wound on your back is what caused you to faint. Odd thing that gash," he began, giving Will a questioning look before setting the bottles down on the side table.

Will eyed the doctor with a superior glare. "I've incurred my share of injuries in the boxing arena and beyond. This latest round of scrapes hardly signify, I assure you."

"Very well, then," the doctor answered succinctly, any questions he may have had concerning the wound having conveniently disappeared. "Ladies, if you'll follow me below we'll see to the instructions for the duke's care."

Lucinda whispered something in Charlotte's ear, to which her aunt answered firmly, "No." A second bout of whispering began, the request being granted, though with conditions.

"Rogers will be right outside. The door will be open at all times. Do I make myself clear, dear?"

"Yes," Lucinda answered quietly. "Of course. You have my word."

Charlotte looked to be rethinking her decision, but the doctor's prodding won out, the aunt shuffling from the room while Lucinda stayed behind.

"Lucinda, to say that I'm shocked would be an understatement," Will teased, wincing with pain as he attempted to sit up.

She moved to adjust his pillows, the smell of her filling Will's nose.

"Why are you here?"

"In this bed—"

"You know what I am asking of you," she interrupted, pushing her long, golden hair from her face.

Will settled into the fluffed pillows. "I would hardly be a proper suitor if I allowed you to gallivant across the countryside alone."

"You knew that Aunt Charlotte accompanied me—"

"And how would she have fared against the highwaymen, hmm?" he asked accusingly.

She massaged her temples, the fatigue plain on her face. "Will."

"Yes?"

She situated herself on the edge of the bed, careful to not touch him. "I cannot do this."

A sudden sense of dread filled the pit of Will's stomach. "Lucinda?"

"You told me once that you admired my honesty, did you not?"

Will thought back to their first walk in the park when he'd paid her the compliment. "I did."

She folded her hands in her lap and took a deep breath, her gaze suddenly fixed on his. "I have not been honest with you of late. I have tried to be someone that I am not. Played at games that I knew nothing about. Inspired feelings in you for false reasons. And none of it has turned out as I planned."

Will reached out, placing his palm on the small of her back. "I am sorry."

"You've nothing to apologize for. Reacting to my many moods and attempts to manipulate your feelings must have been exhausting," she pressed on, her eyes filling with tears. "I am the one who is sorry."

He would do anything to make her pain go away. *Anything but tell her the truth, you loathsome cad.* God, to sit there was torture, the knowledge that he was the one who'd manipulated her from the start burning a hole through his heart. "Lucinda, please, there's no need to apologize. You are tired and overwrought with concern for your horse—"

"Will, let me finish before I lose my courage," she urged quietly.

Will tensed, anxious to hear the words he'd been sure he never would, but terrified as well.

She laid a hand on his cheek gently, the soulfulness in her eyes nearly making Will weep. "I ask nothing of you—only, know that I care for you deeply. And, I think I always will."

Will could not find enough air to fill his lungs, the

weight of her declaration nearly knocking him back into unconsciousness. "Lucinda, I . . ." he began, choosing his words carefully.

"Lucinda dear," Charlotte called out from the hall. "The duke needs his rest now. Do come to bed."

Lucinda stood up and Will reached for her gown, but he missed it.

"Please, don't—"

"Do I need to fetch you myself?" Charlotte said, peeking around the door.

"Rest well, Your Grace," Lucinda said, offering him a wistful smile then turning to go, the door shutting quietly behind her.

Will groaned with frustration. "Not bloody likely."

The next morning came too early for Lucinda, the deep sleep she'd fallen into after speaking with Will not something she was eager to leave behind.

But she had, with much poking and prodding from Charlotte, and the two had readied themselves for the day, taking a light meal in their room, then meeting Will in the yard.

Will had used every argument he could to keep from riding in the carriage with Lucinda and her aunt to Bampton Manor, but Charlotte had insisted. And when a Fury insisted, well, not even the Duke of Clairemont could say no.

Sol's reins were tied to the carriage and the three set off for Oxfordshire, Lucinda on one seat, with Will and Charlotte opposite.

Lucinda had tried in earnest to keep up with the steady stream of conversation, but she'd failed miserably, nodding off just after Charlotte made mention of the returning rain and not waking until they'd pulled into the circular drive of Bampton Manor.

She'd seen to their guest, instructing the servants to escort Will to a suitable room, then insisted that her aunt rest, before taking her leave and running as fast as she could to the stables.

In the past, the familiar smell of hay and horses had always been a comfort to Lucinda. But not today. The rain beat down outside, drumming a military tattoo on the roof.

She stood in Winnie's stall, watching the mare as she attempted to shift her cumbersome weight. She'd arrived to find Perkins watching closely as the veterinary-surgeon examined her. Though she was due to foal, she was not acting in a manner that led anyone to believe this would be an uneventful birth.

The mare ignored her oats and ambled awkwardly nearer to stand with her head next to Lucinda's. She stroked the chestnut's silky flaxen mane and kissed her irresistibly soft nose. "Whatever is the matter, Winnie?"

The mare nuzzled Lucinda's chin, cheek, and temple, huffing warm breath that stirred Lucinda's hair above her ear, then dropped her head low, her right eyelid drooping.

Will appeared, propping his elbows on Winnie's gate and gently clucking to the mare. "How is she?"

Lucinda gave Will a look of disappointment. "I instructed the servants to lock you in your room."

"I escaped."

"Why does that not surprise me?" she said wryly.

"Because you know me too well," he answered. "Now, how fares Lady Winifred?"

Lucinda took a long worrisome look at the mare before answering Will. "We can't be sure, but we believe it may be related to the foal. It's something to do with her right side. She's not able to move as she should."

Will slowly reached for Winnie, the mare allowing him to rub her forelock. "And you? Are you all right?"

Now I am, Lucinda thought. "As well as can be expected."

She yawned unexpectedly, her hand coming to cover her mouth. "I'm so sorry," she offered, meeting his gaze.

Will stepped closer. "You need your rest. I'll stay with the mare."

"I was not attacked by highwaymen mere hours ago nor can I currently lay claim to several spectacular bruises and one hideous wound on—"

Will placed his index finger on Lucinda's mouth. "Have you eaten dinner?"

She shook her head. "No."

"Slept in a comfortable bed since leaving town?"

She begrudgingly blew out a breath.

Will lifted his finger and replaced it with a gentle kiss. "Four hours. That is all that I ask."

"But if she worsens—"

He moved toward the gate and let free the latch, swinging the door wide enough for Lucinda. "I will send someone for you at once."

Lucinda readied to argue, but Will came up behind her, kneading her shoulders with his powerful hands. "Go."

"Do I have your word?" she asked, leaning into the feel of his touch.

"Of course, Lucinda. If the mare worsens and there is something to be done, I will send for you immediately."

He dropped his hands and pushed her gently forward, closing the gate behind her.

Lucinda lingered, watching the mare wearily. "What do you mean 'something to be done'?"

"If Winnie's condition worsens and there is *nothing* that can be done for her," Will said gently, reaching out and caressing her shoulder, "would you want me to fetch you, though it would mean leaving her side?"

"Of course not," she answered immediately. "I would not have her without the comfort."

"Then we are in agreement. Now go. You will be of no use to Winnie unless you take care of yourself," he said simply.

She could not argue with his logic nor the exhaustion that inhabited every last bone in her body.

She reached for Winnie once more, lovingly patting her soft head then turning to go.

Will kicked his chamber's door shut and removed his sodden coat, revealing the white shirt beneath, now soaked in blood.

Winnie had remained stable for some time after Lucinda had gone, making Will hopeful that she would fully recover. And then she'd staggered toward the gate of her stall and collapsed against it. Will had yelled for Perkins, but the few moments it took the man to run the length of the barn aisle to Winnie's stall were too many. The mare was gone, the only thing left to do being to save the foal.

Perkins had disappeared into the tack room and returned with the necessary tools. When it came time, Will pulled the sleek chestnut-colored foal free without injury. Perkins had left Will with the foal momentarily, returning shortly with a mare whose own foal was nearly weaned. The little one had curiously sniffed the mare as she did him, the two falling into a companionable silence before the foal nosed his way to suckle at her teat.

It was so beautiful, and yet Will could not appreciate it fully, knowing the pain the foal's beginnings would bring to Lucinda.

A soft knock at the door interrupted Will's thoughts. He crossed the room and quietly cracked open the door.

"She's in the library, Your Grace." One of his men

stood just outside, the light from a slim candlestick he carried illuminating his face.

Will nodded his thanks and turned from the door. He crossed the chamber and picked up his discarded shirt from earlier in the day. He dressed quickly then stepped out into the hall.

The waiting agent handed the candlestick to Will. He opened the door carefully, and the two moved silently down the hall.

They didn't encounter anyone on their way to the library, the lateness of the hour shrouding the household in sleep and darkness.

But not Lucinda, Will thought to himself with dread as he silently padded his way down the gallery where her long-dead ancestors eyed him from their gilded-framed portraits lining the walls.

The two men descended the mahogany staircase and crossed the entry hall, avoiding a massive stone sculpture of a horse in the process. They stopped in front of the library's closed door and Will handed the candlestick to the agent. He opened the door and stepped in, searching the room for Lucinda. He could not see the glow of candlelight anywhere. The room was huge, with tall bookcases standing at right angles to the walls and creating aisles down the carpeted length to the cluster of chairs grouped in front of a fireplace at the far end.

A faint sound caught his attention. The soft crinkling noise came again and he followed it, silently crossing to the opposite corner. He reached the last of the bookshelves and saw a spill of soft candlelight gleaming on leather book spines. Inching silently closer, Will leaned to his right to see beyond the rows of books.

The source of the sound was immediately apparent. It came again as Lucinda turned a page of the large book lying open on her lap.

Will stepped out into the light, clearing his throat as he did so.

Lucinda looked up in surprise. "Will?"

"I'm sorry to disturb you," he said in response, the agony of the news he must share weighing heavily on his heart.

"Is it Winnie?" she asked anxiously, moving to sit on the very edge of the settee. "I'm sure you're disappointed that I did not sleep longer, but I do believe I've discovered what's troubling her," she continued, gesturing to the large leather-bound book in her hands. "It has to do with the foal's placement in relation to her stomach and the—"

"Lucinda," Will interrupted, stepping forward farther into the candlelight then leaning down on one knee, reaching to take Lucinda's small hand in his. "Lucinda," he began, his throat thick. "She was gone in an instant. I wanted you there—but I could not leave her alone."

Lucinda's eyes pooled with tears and she let out a wail of protest.

"No, please tell me it's not true." She stopped abruptly, her voice cracking with emotion. "Not Winnie," She stood, her embroidered wrapper parting to reveal a nearly translucent white cotton night rail.

He couldn't bear to see her like this, hurt and in pain. "My God, Lucinda, you don't know what I would do to make it a lie," he began, standing again to meet her gaze. "But it's the truth."

"No. Not Winnie," she whispered, then fell silent as emotion clearly overwhelmed her. She closed her eyes tightly and wrapped her arms about herself, looking as though she thought to block the world from her battered heart.

"Lucinda," Will uttered quietly, not sure of what else to do.

She began to cry, soft whimpers of distress escaping her mouth.

"Lucinda."

"Say my name again," she pleaded, her eyes opening to meet his.

"Lucinda."

She edged closer to him and reached out, her arms coming to encircle his waist.

Will enfolded her in his warmth and bent his head to gently kiss the top of her head, her silken hair smelling of spring. He uttered words of comfort into the soft shell of her ear, eager to end her suffering.

She raised her head to his and looked into his eyes, a wealth of pain and sorrow, questions and something Will could not quite guess at reflected in her own. Slowly, she rose on tiptoe, then placed her lips on his tentatively.

He cupped her face in his hands and kissed her.

Will knew he should be gentle, but such constraint felt impossible, the need building inside him too powerful to resist.

He hesitated, pulling his mouth from hers and looking deep into her eyes. "You do not want this," he said in earnest, his breathing labored.

"You're wrong," she began, resting her cheek on his, her lips nearly touching his ear. "I want this. But more important, I need you."

Lucinda wrapped her arms around him, pressing the length of her body against him. She returned his bruising kisses with unbridled enthusiasm, her tongue first retreating, then darting out to meet his, learning the sensuous rhythm with an eagerness that drove Will beyond rational thought.

Her fingers pulled at his shirt and Will's blood burned. He broke the kiss and yanked the garment up and over his head to toss it behind him to the floor, the pain from his wound lessening with each second.

Her hand reached for his, moving it to the ribbons at her neck. He tugged and the ribbons fell loose, releasing the front of her wrapper. The garment fell open, exposing an expanse of creamy skin. He caught the hem of her wrapper and night rail in both hands. With her gaze locked on his, she raised her arms and he pulled her nightclothes up and off. He closed his fists, bunching the fabric, and bent his head, breathing in her scent before he looked at Lucinda.

She had slender legs and sleek thighs, hips that cradled the flat curve of stomach where the small indentation of her belly button seemed flagrantly female. And her breasts were perfect, high and firm, the nipples a deep dusky pink.

She touched him, her fingers shyly caressing his upper chest. She encircled his nipple with her forefinger, tugging gently. Will's heart rate pounded in response to the exquisite sensation.

Slowly, she trailed her hand down his ribcage to his waist. She pulled the buttons on his breeches before freeing them, one by one.

She reached the final button and hesitated.

"Lucinda," he groaned, his voice hoarse.

She obliged, releasing the button.

Will stood and freed himself from the breeches, his cock fully erect from the erotic foreplay.

Lucinda's eyes rounded and she stared, her gaze stroking over his body with slow absorption, as if she were memorizing every inch of him. She completed the perusal and returned to his crotch, a mixture of emotions playing across her face.

"Are you afraid?" Will asked, aware this was undoubtedly the first time Lucinda had seen a nude male.

She slowly smoothed her hand down her belly, stopping at the juncture of her thighs. "Never." She beckoned and opened her arms wide to receive him.

He hesitated though he could hardly bear to do so. "There is no going back after this. Once we join, nothing will ever be the same for either of us."

Lucinda gave him a pleading look. "I've no desire to go back, Will. Now come to me."

The reasons for avoiding involvement with Lucinda disappeared, practical logic overthrown by what Will could not deny in his heart. He wanted Lucinda more than any other woman he had ever encountered. But beyond the lust, he loved her. He'd never given her the words, but he needed to show her now with his mind, body, and spirit—their lovemaking a testament to his true feelings.

He pushed Lucinda gently down onto the settee and straddled her. He bent over her, nipping at the soft, fragrant flesh on the inside of each thigh before seeking out her damp core with his tongue. Her sudden, sharp intake of breath was quickly followed by panting as each lick of his tongue sent her pleasure higher.

"Yes, yes, yes," she moaned, clutching at Will's shoulders. Her nails bit into his skin with each rhythmic stroke of his tongue, the pain only heightening his desire.

Will covered her breast with his right hand, toying lightly with the nipple, then kneading, tugging, and finally pinching it between his forefinger and thumb. He moved to the other breast, roughly fondling it until Lucinda uttered a breathy "Please!"

She moved restlessly beneath him, instinctively spreading her legs further before her body went rigid, her cry of surrender signaling her climax.

Will released her nipple and slowed his pace, savoring the flavor that was uniquely Lucinda before raising his head.

"Oh, God, Will," she said simply, then pulled him on top of her, pressing a kiss to his lips. "Come to me."

Lucinda could not have known what those words

meant to him; the thought of ever surrendering himself so completely to one person was simply not possible only weeks before.

He eased his cock inside her slick folds, his hips thrusting slowly, going deeper with each movement. "I give myself to you, Lucinda. Heart and soul."

She kissed him again, a gentle soul-searing kiss that Will knew he would never forget.

He quickened his pace, grinding against her. "Lucinda, are you all right?" he managed to ask.

She hooked her legs around his waist and tilted her hips, moving in time as if they'd done this dance before. "Yes." Her response was a throaty, nearly breathless whisper.

She took hold of his testicles, massaging them rhythmically. Her breathing sped up to match his own heavy pants. "Come to me, Will, now!" she urged.

He entered her in one smooth thrust, and then the world exploded. The stars and the moon fell from the sky, the ground beneath them shook from the intensity of the moment. Lucinda squeezed her legs around his waist, lifting against him, and cried out. Will's groan of release followed a moment later.

"I love you," she whispered.

He blanketed her with his body, his face buried in her silken hair. "Lucinda," he said simply, repeating her name again and again.

13

As Will and the handful of Corinthians waited for the remaining two agents to arrive, the words "no rest for the wicked" felt tailored just for him.

He'd helped Lucinda into her night rail and wrapper after their lovemaking, and walked her back to her bedchamber. He hadn't wanted to leave her, but he'd resisted the temptation to linger in the interest of duty. He'd made his way through the darkened house and across the grounds to the barn. He'd not been the first to arrive at the prearranged meeting, but he'd not been the last, either—a testament to his superior strength if ever there was one.

A young barn cat wound around Will's legs, purring loudly. He bent to pick it up and sat down on an upturned bucket, tucking the warm fuzzy calico on his lap.

Superior strength, my arse, he thought.

He should not, under any circumstances, have allowed himself to make love to Lucinda. Never, in all of his time spent with the Corinthians, had he made such a fatal mistake. He knew damn well that the sight of her alone in the library, wearing little more than a few scraps of fabric, had tested his will beyond measure.

But he could have resisted that. It would have been hard. Hell, he would have been hard. For days, most likely. But he could have done it. He could have stopped before he took her virginity. He could have done it. He knew he could have done it.

The cat jumped from Will's lap and trotted across the hay-strewn floor, pausing to tilt its head and sniff the wind before heading off toward the tack room.

Will let out a long breath, watching the cat as it disappeared around the corner, its tail giving one final flick of farewell. Around him, the Corinthians continued to gather, but Will couldn't seem to take his eyes off the last spot where the cat had been.

Staring. Still staring. But seeing nothing.

Thank God he'd had the sense not to tell Lucinda that he loved her too. At least not in so many words. His body had communicated what his brain could not, and he knew, even if she perhaps did not, that the intimate joining of their bodies had been a silent testament to his feelings for her.

Even now, the concept defied comprehension. Despite any long-buried, secret desires that hid deep within his heart, Will had long ago given up on the likelihood that anyone could ever love him. If a man's own father was unable to feel affection for his son, then what hope was there?

And then Lucinda had declared her feelings in no uncertain terms, completely destroying what Will had settled long ago. But more than that, the tender feelings she inspired in him were in direct contrast to the single-minded, cold focus he needed to do his job. Spying was not for those inclined to softness or fancy. It was a dangerous vocation that demanded unwavering concentration, the ability to make the right decision no matter how difficult, and a deep conviction to do what was right—even if lives were lost along the way.

Cold, calculating, demanding, dangerous. The words described exactly who Will was—or rather, they were the qualities that had made him the most valued of all Corinthian agents.

Until now.

The last of the summoned agents entered the barn and joined the group illuminated in the low circle of light.

"I know you're all tired, so we'll make this as brief as possible," Will began. "Weston, what news of Garenne?"

Weston stepped forward, his right eye ringed with ugly black, blue, and livid red bruises. "Our sources confirm what we suspected: The Frenchman made inquiries several months ago in the area concerning Lady Lucinda, including the details of her estate grounds."

"Any sightings recently?"

"None that we can discern," Weston replied, "though the local frogs have béen active of late. None of our sources are willing to give the bastard up—at least, not yet."

. Will paused to take the information in. Garenne had not lured Lucinda from London with false tales, that much was clear. But it didn't mean that he wasn't lurking in the shadows even now. "I assume that whoever blackened your eye has been taken care of?"

"You know me better than to ask such a thing, Clairemont," Weston replied, a smile spreading over his swarthy face.

"Good," Will said with satisfaction. "Now, Parsons, your report on the surveillance efforts."

The meeting, true to Will's promise, was quick and efficient, the necessary information shared, plans for the morning reviewed, and the men sent back to their various posts to resume their duties.

Will slipped quietly back into the manor and made an unsuccessful attempt at sleep, only to be awakened two hours later when sounds from below signaled the house staff was up and readying for a new day.

Dressing quickly, he escaped the manor undetected and made haste for the stables, saddling Sol and leaving the property at a hard gallop.

He was glad for the forethought he'd shown when he'd left Lucinda at her chamber door and told her he would be gone this day due to business in the district. It would allow him the opportunity to interrogate informants who had yet to yield to his fellow Corinthians' wishes—always an activity that proved useful in ridding oneself of excess anger and frustration. And, more important, it would remove Lucinda from his sight, giving him the distance needed to make a decision he knew to be absolutely necessary.

But he dreaded it, all the same.

Weston appeared not far up the road at the agreed-upon meeting site, his gelding's ears pricking with interest at Sol's approach.

Will didn't slacken the stallion's speed, and Weston kneed his mount into motion, joining Will on the road as the two horses raced neck and neck toward town.

There were certain obligations that came with country life, and chief among them was replying in the affirmative when one's closest neighbor issued an invitation for supper. In Lucinda's case, this meant that when the Earl of Rowton, upon learning of her unexpected arrival at Bampton Manor, arranged for a meal in her honor, she had to say yes.

She was not quite certain how Lord Rowton had heard that she was in residence, but it didn't really matter. Her aunts had brought her up to be a good neighbor, and a good neighbor she would be.

And so here she was, climbing the steps to Rowton Manor, Charlotte at her side, trying desperately not to wince as she moved.

She was sore. Really sore. How was it possible that her regular riding schedule had not better prepared her limbs for the physical exertion of lovemaking?

"Where is His Grace?" Charlotte asked once she'd

surveyed the room and taken note of those attending. "He agreed to come, did he not?"

"Yes, of course," Lucinda assured her. He hadn't been particularly pleased about it, but she'd eventually wrenched a yes from his lips. It was what a proper suitor would do, she had said sweetly. That had been met with a scowl.

They *were* courting, weren't they?

His scowl gave way to grumbling.

So she'd launched into her good neighbor speech, sounding to her ear remarkably like her aunts.

He had acquiesced immediately.

He had said that he'd some business in town, although what she could not imagine, but he'd promised that he'd be there.

"I'm sure he'll arrive shortly," Lucinda told her aunt. "He mentioned that he might be delayed by some sort of ducal business."

"Here?"

Lucinda shrugged. As far as she knew, Will had no property in Oxfordshire, but the dukedom's holdings were vast, and she was quite certain she did not know the extent of it.

"Do you see Rowton?" Charlotte murmured in her ear.

Lucinda shook her head. She had known Lord Rowton for years. He was ten years her senior and had made no secret of his desire to join their properties. His father had suggested the match at her birth, and Rowton had taken up the cause as soon as Lucinda had reached a marriageable age.

She had not mentioned this to Will. It did not seem relevant, at least not while she was trying to convince him to accompany her.

"Ouch!" Lucinda looked over at Charlotte with some irritation. "What was that for?"

Charlotte retracted her elbow, which was presently dug into Lucinda's ribs. "Rowton, my dear," she murmured without moving her lips.

Lucinda's gaze followed Charlotte's. "Oh," she said under her breath.

Each pasted a smile on her face and prepared to greet their host.

There was nothing precisely wrong about Lord Rowton. He was an avid horseman, which was certainly a point in his favor, and he did not bore Lucinda with recitations of parliamentary proceedings while implying they were beyond her understanding.

In truth, Lucinda had to suppose that Lord Rowton had been the best of her suitors, or if not that, certainly the most convenient.

But that had been before Will. And with the memory of his body on hers still burned into her memory . . .

"Lucinda!"

She turned to Charlotte. "What?"

"You moaned."

"I did not," Lucinda shot back, horrified.

"Oh, you did. I assure you my hearing is—Lord Rowton! How nice to see you again."

Their host stood before them, smiling down at both. "Lady Charlotte," he began, nodding, bowing, and grasping her hand to kiss the air just above her fingers.

Charlotte had barely murmured a brief response before he turned to Lucinda, the look of adoration plain for all to see. "And Lady Lucinda. It has been far too long since our last meeting."

"Lord Rowton," Lucinda began, reluctantly offering her hand, "you are too kind."

His lips barely brushed her fingers, though they lingered too long for Lucinda's comfort.

She gently pulled back, not wanting to create a scene

but desirous to retrieve her hand all the same. "This looks to be quite a happy gathering, I must say."

"Indeed," he replied, gesturing for the ladies to accompany him into the room. "I was surprised to find you in residence at this time of year."

Lucinda eyed Charlotte wearily, her heart not quite prepared to speak of Winnie with the indifference necessary for such settings. "An ill horse, I'm afraid."

Charlotte cleared her throat. "Thank you for asking, Lord Rowton."

"And will you be staying on?" he pressed. "It really seems a shame to come all this way only to stay for a few short days."

Lucinda smiled sincerely. It was difficult not to admire his determination. "Aunt Charlotte wishes to stay on for the remainder of the week, and so we will."

"I'm *very* glad to hear as much," Rowton replied enthusiastically.

The three walked toward the pianoforte, where a plump, brown-haired woman was busily playing Mozart. She ended the piece with a dramatic tinkle of two keys and smilingly received the polite round of applause.

"Miss Winstead, you play beautifully," Lucinda said to the woman, her compliment failing to draw the round young woman's chocolate brown gaze away from Lord Rowton.

"Thank you, Lady Lucinda," she replied, dragging her gaze from the earl.

This could work to my advantage, Lucinda thought to herself, winking at Charlotte before proceeding. "Would you not agree, Lord Rowton?" she asked.

"I'm sorry?" The earl replied, his glass of wine halfway to his lips.

"I was just commenting on Miss Winstead's skillful playing."

"Oh, that. Well—"

"I could not agree more." The deep, masculine comment came from somewhere behind Lucinda.

The fine hairs on her nape stood up, her body coming to life as if he'd commanded it to do so.

She showed restraint though, waiting to turn until her companions did. "Your Grace," she began, not wanting to appear overly eager. "Do join us. I very much would like to introduce you."

He walked purposefully toward them, failing to acknowledge the buzz of surprise and excited whispers that were taking place about the room.

He joined them, standing between Charlotte and the seated Miss Winstead, who seemed to have removed her attention from Lord Rowton and refixed it firmly on Will.

Lord Rowton cleared his throat, and everyone turned to look at him. Lucinda thought he resembled a yearling she'd once owned. The young horse's reaction to castration had been to stand at the fence that separated him and the other geldings from the resident stallion and watch with quiet and decidedly bitter resignation as the virile Thoroughbred pranced about, displaying his undeniably large and functional manhood for all the world to see.

"I do beg your forgiveness, Lord Rowton," Lucinda began, pausing to push the thought of the defeated gelding from her mind. "Do you know His Grace, the Duke of Clairemont? He arrived in Oxfordshire most unexpectedly."

"Of course," Rowton replied, with remarkably little inflection.

Lucinda acknowledged his comment with a smile and a nod. "I assured His Grace that Aunt Charlotte and I would do everything in our power to show him all that we have to offer. An introduction to what makes our little corner of the country so special would not be complete without attending one of your soirées, would you not agree?"

"Welcome to my home," Lord Rowton said, nodding at Will. He did not appear terribly excited to have a duke in his midst, but he was nothing if not polite, and he added, "Any friend of Lady Charlotte and Lady Lucinda's is, without a doubt, a friend of mine."

"It's a pleasure to meet a close family friend of the Greys," Will replied with a polite, ducal nod.

Lord Rowton returned the pleasantry with a perfunctory bow. "If you will excuse me, I must tell my staff we'll be one more for dinner." He gave the group a vague smile, ventured one last, lonely glance at Lucinda, and took his leave.

"Well, I suppose that leaves you, Miss Winstead," Will said.

The young woman's eyes grew wide as saucers. "I'm sorry, Your Grace?"

Will gave her a devastating smile. "Forgive me. It's most improper to speak before being introduced, but I simply could not wait any longer."

Lucinda took pity on the blushing girl. "Miss Winstead, may I introduce His Grace, the Duke of Clairemont."

Will bowed over her hand.

"Your Grace . . ." Miss Winstead began as she rose from her bench, her voice trailing off into confused silence when Will refused to release her hand.

"I am a most devoted student of all things musical. And you," he said, gesturing for her to be seated once again, "are a truly talented musician. Please, gift us with another piece. Do not deny the world your talent."

Miss Winstead giggled and succumbed with blushes and an agreeing nod. She retrieved her hand from Will and thumbed through the sheet music, uttering an "Aha" when she found just the one.

Will left her, returning to stand between Charlotte and Lucinda. The three clapped softly as Miss Winstead readied herself.

"Just what are you playing at?" Lucinda asked Will from behind her fan.

Miss Winstead boldly began a piece by Handel, her pleasure at being singled out by a duke evident in the particular enthusiasm with which she played.

"Your Miss Winstead is a more accomplished player than most young women of her acquaintance," Will murmured. "If Rowton is ever to take notice of the chit, she'll need to make use of any assets at her disposal. I'm simply helping her along."

"How sweet—and quite clever of you, to boot," Aunt Charlotte commented. "If I did not know better, I'd say you're a bit of a romantic, Your Grace."

"You overestimate my capacity for kindness, Lady Charlotte."

A servant entered the room, tapping a small metal gong with a padded mallet. "Dinner is served."

"I think not, Your Grace," Charlotte said, her lips curving into a knowing smile. "My estimation of my fellow man, or woman, is rarely wrong." With that, she tucked her arm into the crook of Will's and allowed him to lead her away.

Will escorted Lady Charlotte to her seat, then looked about for his own, the many-armed epergne placed strategically in the middle of the table making it a rather more difficult task than it should have been.

"I do apologize, Your Grace," Lord Rowton began from his place at the head of the table, "but the servants were hard-pressed to rearrange the placement on such short notice."

Will walked to where Rowton sat, nodding in understanding. "Of course, Lord Rowton, think nothing of
it." He continued on, pausing to stand over Lucinda.

He leaned in slightly so that Rowton would not over-
hear. "Now, where do you think I might find my seat?"

Lucinda's expression, only just a moment before one
of happiness, turned serious as she gestured for Will to
move closer. "About that," she began. "You're seated
next to Lady Shipley, at the end of the table."

Will schooled his features to match Lucinda's. "Is this
information meant to inspire fear in my heart?"

"Well . . . That is to say . . ."

"Lucinda," Will urged gently.

"Do be kind to her, please," she asked solemnly.

Will raised his eyebrows in mock outrage. "You
wound me, Lady Lucinda. Truly," he replied.

"Oh, and do remember to speak directly into the
trumpet. And the louder, the better," she whispered urgently.

Will looked at her quizzically, but thought it best to
end their conversation before any more mysterious odd-
ities were introduced.

"If you'll excuse me, I must join my fellow dining
companions in what I can only assume is the northern
wing, if I am to judge by distance."

Lucinda laughed, then mouthed "Thank you" as Will
left her side and walked to his seat.

Lady Shipley enthusiastically swung the brass trumpet
about and raised it to her ear in anticipation of a conversation.

"Lady Shipley, how delightful to find myself sitting
next to you," Will offered, smiling at the woman as if
she were the only person in the room.

Confusion crossed the older woman's face. "You must
speak into the trumpet," she yelled, pointing at the ap-

paratus as if Will might confuse it with another ear trumpet in the room.

"Bloody hell." *This is going to be far more difficult than I'd anticipated.*

"What was that?" Lady Shipley yelled again.

"I could not agree more," a raspy voice offered from the seat at the very end of the table.

Will turned to take in the man. Slight of build with wispy tufts of white hair and a nose that was far too large for his face, the elderly man stared back at Will with a look of boredom.

"Shipley," the man said, then gestured toward his wife. "And you've met Lady Shipley."

"Alistair, you know it vexes me so when you leave me out of the conversation."

"Precisely," the baron answered, though his wife could not hear.

Will arched an eyebrow in response. "I am Clairemont."

"Ah, the man who has stolen Lady Lucinda away, then."

"I don't know that I would put our courtship in such terms—"

"No need to be polite on my behalf. Rowton had every opportunity to land the woman. Tactically, his campaign was an unmitigated disaster."

"Gentlemen," Lady Shipley pleaded, her voice quivering with curiosity. "Do tell me what you're speaking about."

The baron rolled his eyes then leaned forward toward the trumpet. "This is Clairemont, the 'devil of a duke,' if I recall your words, who's attempting to steal Lucinda away," he yelled, the polite conversations at their end of the table coming to a sudden halt, all eyes turning toward the baron.

Will could feel Lady Shipley shiver next to him, her

ample bosom shaking the table as she threatened to expire on the spot.

"Your Grace," she said in a shrill whisper. Rowton's wolfhound let out a pained whine from the corner of the room.

Will turned to the woman, offering her a sympathetic smile. "Lady Shipley, I have been called far worse, and, I might add, by far less charming individuals. And in truth, I am courting Lady Lucinda, though," he paused, looking down the length of the table with a possessive gaze to where Lucinda sat, "it remains to be seen whether or not the lady's heart will be won."

Lucinda's eyebrows shot shockingly close to the crown of her head while every other woman in the room sighed with sentimental enthusiasm. The men simply took the opportunity to begin eating.

"Ah, the soup," the baron said, a servant having appeared silently at his elbow with a silver tureen. Another servant carefully ladled a portion of the white soup into his bowl, then moved to fill Lady Shipley's.

Will waited patiently while his own bowl was seen to, then brought a spoonful of the fragrant soup to his lips, the scent of chicken broth and a hint of peppercorn filling his nostrils. "Tell me, Lady Shipley," he began, shouting into her trumpet. "Have you always resided in Oxfordshire?"

"Glutton for punishment," the baron said under his breath, then quietly slurped up a spoonful of soup.

Will acknowledged the man's comment with a perfunctory glance then turned his attention back to Lady Shipley.

"*That* is a fascinating story, Your Grace," she replied, her eyes bright with excitement.

The courses flew by in a blur of savory and sweet until the end of the meal was at hand. Will popped a walnut into his mouth and smiled at Lady Shipley.

He would have been hard-pressed to repeat most of what she'd shared, the pace at which she narrated simply too swift to follow. But one thing he knew without a doubt: He'd enjoyed himself, because *she* had.

Good God, what is becoming of me?

The women began to stir, Rowton's great-aunt being the first to rise from her chair and the others following suit.

"I do hope Miss Winstead will honor us with a song," Lady Shipley announced, nodding to her husband and standing.

Will rose and gave Lady Shipley a charming smile. "It was truly a pleasure, Lady Shipley."

"Oh, Your Grace, I dominated the entire conversation," she replied, color heating her cheeks.

Will could not argue. But more troubling, he didn't want to.

"When I remember Oxfordshire, it will be with great fondness. Do you know why?" he asked, speaking into the trumpet.

"The white soup?" she replied, clearly pleased with her cleverness.

"No, not the soup. You, Lady Shipley."

He bowed politely to the baroness, noticing as he rose that Lucinda was watching him. The smile on her face indicated she'd been doing so for some time.

He returned her smile, though the emotions playing across her face jangled his nerves.

Was he unsettled because he'd so thoroughly enjoyed an evening spent in the company of a woman such as Lady Shipley? Or unsettled because Lucinda had so thoroughly enjoyed his enjoyment?

Or maybe—

Ah, hell. The night was too fine to pick apart one's feelings.

"Come, Your Grace, do sit down," Shipley instructed.

"The port will appear any moment. Rowton's port is the best in the county—and the reason I allow myself to be dragged to these dinners at all."

Port is just the thing, Will thought to himself, then obeyed Shipley's command and reclaimed his chair.

14

"Our country air appears to have failed you," Lady Charlotte said, approaching the bench where Will sat in the morning sun.

The gravel path ran throughout the large kitchen garden just off the north end of Bampton Manor. He'd chosen this particular place to sit because he was sure no one would find him.

He shaded his eyes with his hand in an attempt to block out the bright sunlight. "And how is that, Lady Charlotte?"

She joined him on the stone bench. "The country is known for its restorative qualities. And you, Your Grace, look anything but restored." She settled herself on the bench, neatly smoothing out the fabric of her bishop's blue morning dress before folding her hands in her lap. "Did you attempt to rest in a tree?"

"I must say, Lady Charlotte," Will propped his elbows on his knees and grinned at her with honest amusement, "you are the most surprising of all the Furies."

"How dare you say such a thing!" she exclaimed, pretending irritation. Unfortunately, the smile tugging at the corners of her mouth gave her away.

"How dare I what? Make reference to society's affectionate name for the three of you?"

"No, not that," Lady Charlotte answered. "I no longer take notice of such silliness after all of these many years. No, I speak of your inference that I am the least colorful of the group."

Will ran his hands over his face, beard stubble rough against his palms. "With all due respect, Lady Charlotte, is that not a good thing?"

Lady Charlotte paused to consider, frowning at the rows of green herbs that neatly unfolded before them. "Mmmm, you may have a point, Your Grace."

The two sat in companionable silence for a short while, entertained by a honeybee that buzzed busily around a tuft of daffodils.

Will would have preferred not to have to speak, but he liked Lady Charlotte too well to be rude.

"Will Lady Lucinda be joining us?" he asked, looking at the manor.

The bee completed his business and flew off, his route cutting between the two.

"No, not this morning," Lady Charlotte said, flinching slightly when the bee came close to her shoulder. "Lady Thornton, a dear friend of Lucinda's from childhood, invited her to call."

Will already knew Lucinda's whereabouts; the report of her invitation from Lady Thornton had been relayed by Weston during their morning ride. Still, Will kept up the charade, pretending not to know Lucinda's plans rather than risk the elderly woman's suspicions.

Lady Charlotte squinted at Will, her assessing gaze traveling over his face. "You look exactly like your father, you know."

The muscles in Will's jaw contracted, his teeth clenching of their own accord. "So I've been told," he responded, his voice flat, unengaged.

"I meant that as a compliment," Lady Charlotte said quietly, returning her gaze to the rows of green shoots before her. "He was the most handsome man I had ever seen," she continued, her countenance softening. "Every single woman that season wanted him as a husband."

"Even you?" Will asked, surprise punctuating his question.

"Even me," she said. "But it was not to be. He had designs on your mother from the very beginning. No other woman compared."

Will laughed, a short, hard sound. "No, I'm sure they didn't. It is difficult to imagine any other woman being quite so perfect a victim for the Duke of Clairemont."

Lady Charlotte's gaze turned abruptly to Will, her eyes flashing with anger. "You'll do well to remember we speak of your mother."

Will stood swiftly, forcing down the urge to reach out and break something. "Pardon me, Lady Charlotte," he said tightly, "but it's not something I'm likely to forget."

Much as he'd tried.

His father may have been a monster, but his mother had been something much worse.

She had been . . . She'd been . . .

Nothing.

She had been nothing. She had watched when his father had beaten him, and then— No, she hadn't even done that. She had turned away. She had allowed it all to happen, never once lifting her voice in his defense.

He was alone in this world. The message had been clear. If he sought comfort, if he sought protection, he was on his own.

"I was lucky enough to count her as a dear friend," Lady Charlotte said quietly. "A force to be reckoned with, Her Grace was. Did you know that?"

Will began to count backward in his mind from ten to one. "Is that so?" he asked in response, hardly aware that he'd done so.

Charlotte stood and joined him. "She really was extraordinary, which is why, I would imagine, the duke chose her."

"She could have said no."

"You know as well as I that to refuse him would have been unthinkable. He was a duke. Never mind the fact that she loved him."

Having reached the number one, Will began to count again. "More fool she."

Lady Charlotte's fingers closed over his coat sleeve. "No one knew what existed beneath your father's charming exterior. He drew people to him like moths to a flame. She loved him and assumed he felt the same. We all did. It was not until after the marriage that he showed himself for what he really was."

"I've no need to hear this, Lady Charlotte," Will interrupted, looking down at the elderly woman. "I do not mean to offend, but I know only too well what kind of man my father was."

Lady Charlotte rearranged her shawl, holding it tighter as a slight breeze picked up from the north. "That may be true, Your Grace, but your mother is a mystery to you, clearly."

He came so close to telling her, in scathing terms, just why he was the only one who truly knew what went on in the house with his father and mother.

But her eyes as she peered up earnestly stopped him. They were so like Lucinda's in color and shape, yet uniquely her own.

"Your father was a tyrant, that much you know," Lady Charlotte began. "The demands he placed on your mother were . . ."

She hesitated, the distress such memories caused clearly written across her face. "Well, the duchess did everything she could to preserve herself, but it was pointless. He drained her of life, of confidence, of love—

of everything that she was, until there was not a recognizable trace of the vibrant girl she'd once been."

Will looked hard at the woman as she spoke. He concentrated on the information as if it were part of an assignment, the thought of the impact such revelations could make on an unguarded heart pushing him to focus.

"He seemed to take pleasure in robbing her of joy, and when you were born—"

"Stop."

Lady Charlotte grasped his hand in hers. "I do not mean to distress you, Your Grace," she said in a gentle tone, "but I feel it is important that you know the truth, no matter how painful."

Clearly, she was going to force him to hear her confidences through to the end. He wanted to run. Hell, he wanted to hide. But there was no escape. Funny how an unassuming old woman could manage what the most hardened of criminals could not.

Reluctantly, he accepted his fate and nodded for her to continue.

Lady Charlotte acknowledged his acquiescence and went on. "When you were born, your father used your existence against her, threatening to take you away from your mother if she didn't do exactly as he asked." She patted his hand then gestured for him to walk along the path with her. "She knew all too well what he was capable of and she could not risk losing you. And so she agreed, and lost herself in the hellish bargain."

Will felt numb; the anger he'd suffered for so many years over his mother's indifference wasn't easily defeated. He wanted to argue with Lady Charlotte. Couldn't his mother have escaped? Taken him to live with her parents? Hidden on the Continent somewhere?

But with brutal honesty, he had to acknowledge that these scenarios would have been impossible. His father had the power, and the legal right, to track her down like a common criminal and do with her—and the boys—whatever he wished.

"The duchess worked very hard to protect you, and all on her own, I might add," Lady Charlotte said, interrupting Will's thoughts. "He forced her to cut ties with all those she held dear, including me. Despite this, she spent every waking hour doing what she could to ensure your safety and that of your brother. It broke her heart to refrain from showing her love for you boys, but she knew your father's temper would only be more vicious if she had."

Will closed his eyes momentarily, the spring sunshine warming his face. Lady Charlotte's determined championship of his mother and blunt condemnation of his father was almost more than he could absorb. He'd made assumptions about his mother's reasons for her actions. Could he have been so completely wrong?

"Why didn't she tell me?"

"Would you have believed her?"

Will knew the answer without even stopping to think: no.

"You do not strike me as a man who dwells on the past, Your Grace."

"Meaning?"

"Meaning," the elderly woman began, "that while there is nothing to be done about what has transpired, there is always ground to be gained in the future."

Will smiled wryly at Lady Charlotte. "Am I to understand you see a heartwarming reconciliation in my future?"

"What you do with this information is, of course, solely your decision, but I would think a man of your intelligence would hardly let such an opportunity pass without some deliberation."

She tugged gently on Will's arm and turned toward

the house. "There is so much to be learned from your parents' actions, would you not agree?"

Will nodded absentmindedly, still trying to make sense of all he'd heard during the last few moments.

"A woman such as your mother, so intelligent and capable, is still vulnerable when it comes to affairs of the heart. Most women are."

"Yes, quite," he replied, then stopped. "Lady Charlotte, have you something else to say?"

She urged him into motion once again, continuing their stroll along the graveled path. "I'm certain you must realize how deeply my sisters and I care for Lucinda."

"Of course."

"You are in a unique position, Your Grace," Lady Charlotte said, pausing to snap a sprig of mint from a raised herb bed. She twirled it between her forefinger and thumb. "Do not let what happened to your mother happen again."

Will stiffened. Of course she would be concerned for Lucinda. Her beloved niece was being courted by the Duke of Clairemont, whose own father had destroyed a woman. Despite the logic of her concern, however, he felt only outrage and violent rejection of the possibility that he would harm Lucinda. "You think highly of me, then?" he answered coolly.

She looked directly at him. "Do not misunderstand me, Your Grace. You are not your father. But . . ." She hesitated, weighing her words carefully. "I have watched the two of you together. Lucinda cares for you—something she has not allowed herself to do with any other man."

She held the sprig of mint to her nose, her hand visibly shaking. "I should not be speaking to you of this, and normally I would never presume to invade your or Lucinda's privacy. But though I know you to be an honorable man—and I do, without a doubt," she continued, tossing the bit of greenery back into the garden bed, "a woman in love is a fragile thing, Your Grace, a very fragile thing indeed."

Will's heart could stand no more. He wanted nothing more than to ride straight to Gentleman John Jackson's and lose himself in the battering and blows until the physical pain was all he felt.

"Promise me you'll take care with her," Lady Charlotte said in a low tone, nearly pleading.

Will had always operated with the assured confidence of one who knew the difference between right and wrong. And now? All was in tatters and Will did not know how to put his world back together.

He relied on the only weapon left in his exhausted arsenal and answered the woman with convincing assuredness.

"You have my word."

A bar of bright sunlight marked the open doors at the end of the aisle between the stalls, but the stable's hay-scented interior was shaded and cool. Lucinda stood in Cleopatra's stall, braiding the rough silk of the mare's black tail as Winnie's foal watched her curiously from where he hid.

Cleopatra stood patiently, reaching out to nuzzle the foal now and again.

"Winnie would be proud, Cleo," Lucinda commented, the weight of such a loss slightly lessened by the lanky foal at Cleo's side.

The mare swished her tail lightly, twitching it from Lucinda's grasp.

"Now look what you've done," Lucinda scolded.

She caught up the thick length of hair and started

over, secretly pleased that her time with Cleopatra was extended.

"How is the colt today?"

Lucinda looked up. Will leaned lazily against the stall gate, his amused half grin making her want to kiss him right where his lips curved upward.

She smiled in response. "He is exceedingly handsome, is he not?"

He slid the lock free and pushed the wooden gate open, strolling inside the stall with its deep layer of bedding straw. He slowly approached the colt, extending a hand toward him. The colt looked ready to bolt, then sniffed Will and decided against it, his pink tongue darting out to lick at Will's palm. All at once the colt relaxed, moving toward Will until he threatened to climb into his lap.

"You've an admirer," Lucinda laughed.

Cleo pinned her ears back and glared at Will, hardly happy about her new ward's enthusiasm.

Will backed up and allowed the mare to nose the colt closer to her side.

"Do not take offense," Lucinda offered, finishing the braid. "Cleopatra is only doing as any good mother should."

"Cleopatra?" Will lifted an eyebrow. "Surely not the same Cleopatra who bested an entire pack of stallions— in both the Ascot and the Doncaster Cup?"

Lucinda smiled, delighted he'd recognized Cleopatra, and gestured for him to hand her the length of red ribbon looped over the gate.

"The one and only," Lucinda replied, taking the ribbon from Will's hand and securing the end of the mare's braid. "Though, with any luck, that distinction will be short-lived," she added. "In due time, she'll be foaling champions."

"And the sire?"

Lucinda smiled. "King Solomon's Mine, of course."

"Bloody hell."

Lucinda's smile widened. "Really, Your Grace."

"Call me Will, you silly chit." He covered her hand with his much larger one, capturing it against the mare's warm hide. "The surprising bit here is not my interest in horse breeding, but yours."

"Does it make me less appealing? That I have a brain and choose to employ it for such a masculine pursuit?"

"You know damn well it only makes you more irresistible to me," he answered in a gruff tone, his eyes heating. "Or have you not learned all there is to know about the infamous Iron Will?"

Cleopatra shifted her weight and a loud gurgling sound echoed through her belly.

Distracted, Lucinda didn't answer Will; instead, she slipped her hand from under his and circled the horse, stopping on the far side of the mare. She frowned, worry creasing her brow as she examined her beloved mare's midsection.

"Lucinda, it's nothing more than her digestive tract," Will said in an assuring tone. "Cleopatra is not Winnie."

She bent low to scan the mare's stomach. "But what if it is the grass? Or perhaps the oats. All of the horses receive the exact same oats."

As she rose, from the corner of her eye she glimpsed Cleopatra's braided tail, slowly rising.

"Oh—!"

Too late. The cloud of noxious gas that exited noisily from Cleopatra's posterior slowly filled the stall with a decidedly horsey smell.

"I suppose this means we've identified the stomach ailment?" Will said, his face solemn, though his eyes laughed at Lucinda over Cleopatra's wide back.

Lucinda felt her cheeks grow hot as she struggled to find an appropriate response. "Well . . ." she began, then burst out laughing, the worry she'd felt only moments before dissipating with each giggle.

Will cocked an eyebrow, feigning disappointment, and attempted to maintain an unmoving expression. He failed miserably, his deep, throaty laughter joining hers.

"You," he told her when their mirth subsided, "are a bad influence for a man struggling to act like a gentleman."

"You would be hard-pressed to find anyone who would disagree with you on that point, were they made aware of the last few moments."

Somehow, Cleopatra's impolite emission had put Lucinda at ease. Throughout the day, she'd been unable to focus on anything other than thoughts of Will. Could she expect intimacy would now play a regular role in their relationship? Because, God help her, she certainly did hope so. And most important, what happened next?

In all honesty, Lucinda had failed to entertain the possibility that she might fall in love with Will, so there had never been the need to think beyond a brief courtship and the eventual claiming of King Solomon's Mine before they parted ways.

But she had fallen in love. Fallen so completely, in fact, that she barely recognized herself now, the need for him akin to her requirement for air or food.

"Will," she began, finding the courage to look into his dark eyes, "what are we meant to do now?"

"First, I suggest removing ourselves from the stall before Cleopatra relieves herself again." His voice held a smile.

"That is not what I meant, and you know it."

He ducked under Cleopatra's neck and joined Lucinda, settling his hands on each side of her waist. "I believe you know what comes next. I've taken your virginity," he murmured, mindful of the presence of stablehands on the far side of the barn. "For a man and woman in our social circle, more than a simple thank you is required."

He backed her against the wall, his hard frame pressing hers from chest to thigh. He cupped her face in one palm and traced her lower lip with his thumb, his hooded gaze intent on her mouth.

"Then you would marry me out of obligation?" she asked, trying desperately to ease the dread constricting her chest.

He muttered something she couldn't understand and replaced his thumb with his mouth, kissing her tenderly at first, then coaxing her mouth open with the glide of his tongue over the seam of her lips.

Lucinda couldn't stop her response, despite the unanswered question. She slid her arms around his neck and pulled him closer, the tips of her breasts pressed against his chest. The sensation was sweet torture and she shivered, her body quivering with anticipation.

He lifted his head to look at her.

"It would be an honor, my dear Lucinda. Never an obligation," he whispered. "Do not doubt my feelings for you. Ever."

She sighed as he took her mouth again, their mutual need growing hotter by the second.

The rattling of wheels, accompanied by piercing, tuneless whistling, shattered the spell that held them. Will's arms tightened, his head lifted, and then he dropped to the stall floor, taking Lucinda with him. He rolled, putting her against the wall with himself between her and the horses.

The loud noises stopped in front of Cleopatra's stall,

followed by the sound of hay being shifted. "'Ello, my beauty, how we doing today, luv?"

A large forkful of fine grass hay landed in the feeder just above Will's head, bits of dried green leaves and stalks sifting over the two hiding behind the mare and foal. In her enthusiasm to get at the hay, Cleopatra nearly stepped on Will. He didn't move for fear of being seen by the man outside the stall.

"'Ere you go, then," the stablehand whispered, "don't go tellin' the other horses, now. I always save the best for you." The sound of Cleopatra biting and crunching an apple made Lucinda smile despite her perilous position.

The rolling sound started up again, accompanied by the off-key whistling, and signaled the man's movement toward the large stable doors.

The two hiding in the stall waited until they heard the familiar thud of the doors being pushed shut.

Will rose and helped Lucinda to her feet, bending to brush at the hay clinging to her dress. "I can honestly say I've never been in a fix quite like this one," he said, finishing with her dress and turning his attention to her hair.

"Nor I," Lucinda replied, the ridiculousness of her answer causing Will to smile.

With a few quick swipes he knocked the hay from his own attire and shook his head to free his hair of smaller pieces. "Come," he said, taking her hand and leading her around Cleopatra and the colt. He opened the stall door noiselessly and poked his head out to look up and down the aisle.

"It's clear." He pulled her out and gestured for her to follow the stablehand's route. "I'll give you plenty of time to reach the house before I follow."

Lucinda hesitated, torn, wanting desperately for him to pull her back into the stall and continue where they'd left off when the stablehand interrupted them. But she knew how risky such a thing would be.

So instead, she went up on her toes and kissed him, reveling in the heat of his body pressed to hers for just one more moment before leaving him.

15

Lucinda was exhausted, but weariness had been unavoidable. Despite drooping eyelids and tired muscles, she smiled with joy as she gazed out the carriage window at the spring greenery rolling by. She'd awakened early in order to spend as much time as possible with Winnie's foal before leaving.

The little colt had already stolen her heart, his resemblance to Winnie remarkable. He had her color and her kind eye, but more than that, he possessed her sweet and inquisitive nature, making him everything Lucinda had hoped he would be.

"Thinking on the foal?" Charlotte asked from across the carriage.

Lucinda met her gaze. "Indeed. Such a strong little one he is," she replied, leaning back against the squabs. The wheat-colored velvet cushions were soft and comfortable.

Charlotte took up her knitting, the needles clicking as she expertly set stitches in sunshine yellow yarn. "Does he look to be a racer?"

"I can't say for sure at this point, but he certainly has the conformation needed. We'll just have to wait and see what sort of passion for racing he has."

Lucinda glanced out the coach window, where King Solomon's Mine trotted beside the carriage. Will controlled the powerful stallion with ease, despite his injuries. His long-limbed body balanced in the saddle with an athleticism and competence born of long practice.

He wasn't wearing a hat. His thick black hair perfectly suited his untamed nature and was utterly, sinfully sensuous as it lifted and blew back from his brow in the light breeze. He wore a many-caped greatcoat, his shoulders strong and straight. She had a swift, unbidden mental image of candlelight gleaming over his bare shoulders, the muscles flexing as he held himself over her . . .

"Now, that's a different smile altogether."

Distracted, Lucinda frowned in confusion. "I'm sorry, Aunt, what did you ask?"

Charlotte ceased knitting, threaded the long needles into the bright yarn, and tucked them into the basket on the seat next to her. "I didn't ask a thing. I simply made an observation concerning the smile that until quite recently resided on your lovely face."

"Oh," Lucinda continued, still recovering from the vivid image of Will imprinted in her mind. "I'm just so happy about the foal."

"You do not fool me for a moment."

Lucinda's brows furrowed, the likelihood that they would return to their rightful place anytime soon becoming slimmer by the moment. "I'm afraid I've no idea what you're talking about, Aunt Charlotte."

"That," Charlotte leaned forward to point out the window, "is what I am talking about."

"King Solomon's Mine?"

Charlotte rolled her eyes, reminding Lucinda of herself. "My dear girl, I would think after all these years you would realize you cannot hide things from me."

Lucinda flushed under her aunt's knowing gaze, the carriage growing warmer. The coziness of her cashmere shawl, so welcome moments before, now threatened to overheat her. "You're very cryptic." She pulled the shawl from her shoulders and laid it on the seat beside her with meticulous care.

"I concede that cozening your aunt Bessie doesn't take much effort, what with her head being constantly occupied by some drama or another, making it fairly simple to conceal an assortment of truths," Charlotte replied, ticking off on her fingers the points she intended to make clear. "Victoria presents more of a challenge, I suppose, but in the end she admires the sound of her own voice to such a degree that even Prinny himself could convince the woman of his need to gain weight, if given enough of a chance. I love my sisters but there is no point in beating about the bush."

Lucinda peeled off her gloves, since removing her shawl had not provided a sufficiently cooling effect.

Charlotte folded her hands in her lap and pinned Lucinda with a direct, unswerving gaze. "I, on the other hand, listen when spoken to—and, quite honestly, oftentimes when I am not. And you, my dear Lucinda, are in love with the duke."

A fine line of perspiration dotted Lucinda's upper lip, but she resisted the urge to wipe it away. The look in Charlotte's eyes told her that denying her feelings for Will would be pointless. She'd never witnessed her aunt in such form, the usual calmness of her demeanor infused with a blunt, straightforward assurance that surprised her.

Lucinda opened her mouth to reply, then shut it, realizing belatedly that she wasn't sure what she should say. "Aunt Charlotte, you surprise me."

"In what way, dear?"

"Well," Lucinda began somewhat nervously, "I would have expected such a conversation to have been initiated by Aunt Victoria; her abrupt nature seems made for such things. Or even Bessie, whose love of the dramatic you so expertly noted earlier. But you?"

Lucinda paused, not wanting to offend her aunt, though eager to be honest. "I've always assumed that your quiet, calm exterior applied to your character in general. I felt sure any currents running beneath your even demeanor would be anything but fierce. Clearly, I was wrong."

Charlotte leaned forward and patted Lucinda on the knee. "Think nothing of it, my dear. Society's assumption that I am a shy, retiring flower is of great use to me. You've no idea what people venture to say in my presence!"

The two women laughed together, putting Lucinda a bit more at ease.

"But as to your duke—that's very deep play," Charlotte said, returning to her earlier line of conversation without preamble.

"But what of King Solomon's Mine—"

"You would risk your heart for a horse?" her aunt countered, the disbelief in her voice communicating to Lucinda exactly what Charlotte thought of such a thing.

"It is not as if I planned for any of this to happen," she protested.

Charlotte twitched her skirts, straightening the Devonshire traveling dress with precise movements. "Well, of course not. No woman ever does."

"Is it such a bad thing, to fall in love?"

"Then you do admit that you love him?" Charlotte pressed, the concern in her words echoing the worry in her eyes.

Lucinda blinked as tears welled, the relief of unburdening herself nearly overcoming her. "I do."

Charlotte took a deep breath and looked out the window at Will. "And does he return your affection?"

"Yes," Lucinda responded in a resolute tone. There was no need to tell her aunt that he'd yet to say those three words to her. His actions had communicated everything she needed to know regarding his feelings.

Charlotte returned her troubled gaze to Lucinda. "Do you plan to marry him?"

Lucinda squared her shoulders and sat back. "He's given every indication that he intends to propose. It is simply a matter of timing. There are strict social rules to be followed, after all, not to mention a trio of protective aunts to be convinced."

"You know his heart, then, my dear."

"I wonder if any woman has ever known a man's heart more," she answered simply, looking out at Will with a longing she could not bother to deny.

Charlotte reached for Lucinda's hand and took it in her own, squeezing gently. "I cannot say I give you my blessing without some hesitation, my dear. I believe the duke to be an honorable man, and I hope for your sake he is," she said, squeezing Lucinda's hand once more before releasing it and settling back against the cushions. "Now, on to the matter of convincing Bessie and Victoria."

"I'd quite hoped you would puzzle that bit out."

"Impudent girl," Charlotte cried, winking at Lucinda with delight.

The return trip to London had been uneventful, just as Will and his fellow Corinthians had hoped it would be. He'd kept his distance from Lucinda as best he could, riding alongside the carriage. When they'd stopped for the night, he'd convinced the Rosemont Inn's keeper to place Lucinda and her aunt in the same room, in order to keep them safe.

After, he'd seen the two women to their home before returning to Clairemont House, the greeting he received from his mother and brother awkward at best. Lady Charlotte's revelations concerning his parents had sunk in for the most part, no small feat considering the havoc they'd wreaked on his heart, but Will had yet to come to terms with his newfound feelings.

As for Michael, their heated discussion in the ducal bedchamber had been the last they'd spoken before he'd left for Bampton Manor, and the tension returned the moment Will walked into the family residence.

He literally jumped at the chance to leave when news of Lucinda's impending shopping trip reached his ears. Poor Sol hardly had the time for a proper meal before Will pulled him from his stall and urged him on toward New Bond Street.

Will watched, amazed, while Lucinda and her maid walked along the fashionable location. She'd been absent from London less than a week, but somehow the woman apparently found it necessary to empty the shops. The multiple packages Mary carried appeared ready to topple the outspoken maid at any moment.

Gravity being what it was, the round hatbox nestled just beneath Mary's chin wobbled, then fell to the ground, a prim pink bonnet coming to land squarely in the street. The women giggled then made haste to recover the hat along with the remaining boxes that had fallen as well. Two large men appeared out of nowhere, their fine yet ill-fitting clothes causing the hair to stand up on Will's neck. "Bloody hell," he said under his breath, pushing away from the wall he'd been leaning against. He walked swiftly toward the two women.

He quickened his pace, using his size to his advantage as he forced his way through the afternoon crowd. The men approached the two from behind, surprising Mary and causing her to drop several of the packages she'd managed to retrieve. They looked to be making their apologies and offering assistance as the women gestured down the street to where their carriage waited.

Will stepped out into the street and began to jog toward the group, the oncoming coaches easier to dodge than the current flow of shoppers on the walkway. One man abruptly took hold of Lucinda's arm, the other Mary's, and forced the women into an unfamiliar carriage, then disappeared into the crowd.

"Christ," he gasped, breaking into a run and narrowly dodging a curricle as it careened down New Bond Street. The hot breath of a matched pair of horses blew past his cheek as he righted himself and took off again, dread growing in his gut.

He darted toward the carriage. The driver looked up, his eyes widening when he saw Will. He cracked his whip and the bays harnessed to the carriage leapt to life, taking off as if the very fires of hell licked at their hooves.

Despite his strength and speed, Will knew without a doubt that he could not single-handedly stop the oncoming carriage; his options ran out as the horses bore down on him. He lunged out of their way at the last second and went airborne as he launched himself. He grabbed the decorative wooden lip circling the carriage roof with both hands. The conveyance swayed dangerously, rocking under his sudden weight.

He pulled himself up, kicking at the stairs until they fell.

"Get off, damn ye." The driver turned his whip on Will, slashing at the knuckles of one hand until his hold broke. He slammed back against the carriage door, and the sound of Mary's terrified screams reached his ears.

He pulled himself up one-handed, his body hitting the carriage with aggravated force. Ignoring the pain coursing through his wounds, Will stretched to reach the ornamental lip, his right hand closing once more over the carved wood. This time, his feet found the lowered steps before the driver's whip could hammer him. One-handed, he yanked the door open.

A man waited just inside, a knife at the ready. His soulless eyes held no fear when they met Will's.

Will recognized the professional calm of a seasoned criminal and did not waste any time. His balance on the steps was precarious, the swaying of the coach threatening to shake him loose at any moment. He caught the thug off guard, knocking his knife from his hand with one swift blow to his wrist. Before the criminal could recover, Will grabbed a fistful of his hair and yanked, pulling him toward the doorway and out of the carriage. Will saw the man hit the ground, and glimpsed Weston pounding toward them on his gelding, four more riders close on his heels.

Will swung his body through the open carriage door, bracing himself against the rocking, unsteady floor. Lucinda was pressed against the far wall, her hair flowing about her in wild curls, the sleeve of her gown ripped. Mary was clinging to her mistress's side, her eyes wild with fright.

"Lucinda," Will said, gesturing for her to come to him.

The terror on her pale face eased; she slid across the seat, reaching for him. "Who are these men?" she cried.

"I'll explain later," he answered. "We must go at once."

Lucinda looked at Will as if he were mad. "But we're moving."

"Yes." He glanced out the swinging carriage door. Weston raced beside them, keeping pace with the coach. His gaze met Will's and he nodded.

"Surely you're not suggesting that we—"

He didn't have time to explain. Will thought it best to take Lucinda by surprise. He spun her around, her back to his chest, and wrapped his free arm around her waist.

"Weston will catch you," he told her. "Watch out for the carriage door."

Before she had time to protest, he swept her off her feet and moved them outside the coach. He ignored her muffled shriek of terror, balancing on the steps as he passed her to Weston, one-armed, the other anchoring them with his grip on the edge of the carriage roof.

The moment he felt Weston take her weight, he returned for Mary, pulling the now-screaming maid from the carriage and depositing her into the arms of a second mounted Corinthian.

Will yelled an obscenity at the driver, then leapt out and away from the carriage, tucking his body as he hit the ground, rolling across the brick street.

The wheel of an overturned drayman's cart stopped him, his body jolting against the load of spilled vegetables. He braced his hands on the ground and pushed himself upright. The pain he felt all over seemed manageable enough for now, which probably meant he hadn't broken any bones.

He swung his head, searching the street. Several yards away, he found Lucinda, standing near Mary and Weston. Relief that she was in one piece washed over him, making him light-headed for one unsteady moment. Three more agents joined them and Weston left them to set off on a dead run toward Will, the reins of his gelding in his hands. He slowed as he neared but Will waved him on, determined the carriage driver be caught. Weston swung aboard the gelding and quickly disappeared around a corner.

Steadier now, Will walked toward Lucinda. More Corinthians had joined her, clearly unnerving her further. Her expression lightened when Will reached the small group and she stepped closer to him.

"You two." Will gestured to Hopkins and Newell. "Assist Weston and the others." The men climbed aboard their mounts and set off at once, leaving Lucinda and Will with the three remaining Corinthians. "Thomas, I've need of your horse. You three take Lady Lucinda and Mary to the nearest safe house and stay with them until I return." He caught Lucinda's hand in his. "You're safe now. Go with my men and do as they ask. I'll return as soon as I can." He kissed her fingers, the only outward show of affection he was allowed, and leapt aboard Thomas's horse.

She was silent; standing there in the street, covered in dust and bruises, she looked up at him with a face full of confusion and tears.

He could not delay, no matter how much he wanted to comfort her and tell her everything would be all right.

He nodded at the officers, then kicked the horse into a run, urging him on with grim determination.

"Can you tell me . . ." Lucinda paused, unsure precisely what she wanted to ask. The last hour had left her stunned and bewildered. Her mind continued to race, trying to make sense of it all.

"About the men who brought you here?" the woman prompted. She dipped a clean cloth in a bowl of warm water and gently, carefully, washed the dirt from Lucinda's cheek.

Lucinda grimaced as she sat still on the settee, the sting telling her that a scrape existed beneath the grime. "Yes. To begin with anyway."

"Unfortunately, no, I cannot. But I can tell you that you're perfectly safe. There's not a man among them who would harm you."

Dressed in a silk wrapper and matching night rail of deep emerald green, the woman's lush form was voluptuously curved. Her thick sable hair was piled atop her head, held in place by emerald ribbons woven artfully through the loose curls. There was no denying she was attractive, her full rouged lips, almond-shaped eyes, and milky complexion only adding to her appeal. But even distracted as Lucinda was, she sensed something faintly sad in her demeanor.

"May I speak freely?" Lucinda asked the woman as she eased the damp cloth over her scraped cheek once more.

"I know no other way, my lady," she replied. "I am Minerva."

The woman stroked the cloth over Lucinda's forehead, frowning in apology when Lucinda winced. "I'm sorry." She turned away to rinse the cloth in the basin of water. "Now, what would you like to know? I will answer as much as I can."

"Is this . . ." Lucinda peered around the room, searching for the best way to phrase her question. "That is to say, are you . . ."

"A kept woman?" Minerva interrupted, amused. "What gave it away?" She looked about her. "The garish colors, perhaps? An overabundance of pillows, lace, and ribbons?" She paused, looking down at her ample bosom in the seductive silk. "Did my clothing tell you this isn't Mayfair?"

Lucinda swept the room with an assessing gaze before treating Minerva to the same considering look. "All of the above, actually."

Minerva laughed, setting the bowl aside and handing Lucinda a fresh linen cloth. "He said you were a smart one. He never mentioned that you were funny as well."

"He?" Lucinda queried, though intuition and the queasy roll of her stomach told her she already knew the answer.

"You are correct in your assumption," Minerva answered, ignoring Lucinda's second query, and instead addressing her surroundings. "This," she said, standing and turning with a graceful flourish of one slim hand and arm, "belongs to a very wealthy and powerful gentleman, though I often wonder at the power of a man who would give me all of this for what I give him in return."

Lucinda decided against pressing for an answer regarding the man who had spoken of her intelligence.

Instead, she smiled at the woman, quietly applauding her performance, and followed her lead. "Well, he sounds very much like all of the wealthy and powerful men of my acquaintance, I'm afraid."

Minerva's eyes widened in surprise, then lit with amusement. She rejoined Lucinda at the settee, next to a folded green gown and shawl. "You'll want to change out of your gown, I imagine."

Lucinda looked down, surprised by the damage she saw. The once lovely yellow muslin was stained and smeared with mud, the diminutive ivy-print background of the fabric scarcely visible beneath the grime. One sleeve was completely gone, the other holding on by mere threads, and the stocking on her right leg was torn below the knee.

Disconcerted, she felt she really should be embarrassed by her appearance, but given the events of the afternoon, she simply couldn't muster the energy.

"Would you like some help?" Minerva asked matter-of-factly, making it clear she thought none the less of Lucinda for her current state of disarray.

"Thank you, but I can manage."

Minerva ignored Lucinda and instead pulled her to rise and spun her around. "I've seen worse," she said, loosening the gown down the back with nimble fingers. "Remember where you are; there's no need for you to feel anything but superior. It's simply the way of the world."

Minerva urged Lucinda to raise her arms, then gently guided the torn material over her head. She left Lucinda to remove soft half boots, garters, and torn stockings.

Lucinda dropped the ruined silk stockings atop her boots on the floor next to the settee.

"Lift your arms," Minerva commanded, and when Lucinda complied, the other woman slipped the simple green gown over her head.

Lucinda's view of Minerva was briefly interrupted by the gown. She pushed her arms into the sleeves and the fabric fell down her body, covering her to her toes. She twitched it into place, surprised by the simple cut of the soft cotton gown. There was nothing overtly seductive about it; in fact, it reminded her of her own gowns. She glanced up and found Minerva watching her.

"We do not always dress to seduce," she explained, reaching for a shawl and offering it to Lucinda. While she adjusted the length of cashmere around her shoulders, Minerva stood back and surveyed her work. A quick satisfied nod of her head said she was pleased with the results. "Much better."

A firm knock rattled the door.

"That will be *him*," Minerva said knowingly. "Take care, my lady." She crossed the room and pulled open the door.

"Your Grace," Minerva said, moving aside to allow him entrance. She gestured for him to come closer and went up on tiptoe to whisper in his ear before stepping into the hall, closing the door firmly behind her.

Will stalked toward Lucinda, the grim set of his features frightening her. "Will?" Relief that he was here, his body whole and safe from harm, flooded her, and tears threatened.

Will reached her and wrapped his arms around her. "Are you all right?" he asked, his voice hoarse with emotion.

She breathed in the scent of his skin and was instantly comforted. "Yes, I am now." She brought her arms around his waist and pressed closer. "Are you?"

He kissed the top of her head. "Of course. Am I not Iron Will?"

"Don't tease, Will," Lucinda said, leaning back to look up at him. "What happened in the carriage? Who were those men? Where is Mary?"

"Mary is safe. Weston saw to that himself."

"What is going on?" she pressed, her heart beating faster. The hard planes of his face were unreadable.

"Did Minerva tell you anything?" His voice was desperate, demanding she answer.

"No, nothing of consequence," Lucinda got out. "What, exactly, happened in that carriage? Why am I here, and what does all of this have to do with you?"

His eyes darkened but he didn't speak.

"I have a right to know," she insisted. "Please," she begged.

Will's arms slipped from her and he pulled her down to sit next to him on the settee. He took her hands in his. "First, you must promise me that you'll tell no one what I'm about to share."

Lucinda felt the room begin to spin. What was going on? Could Will's legendary indiscretions have left him and those close to him vulnerable to such attacks?

"Will—"

"Do you agree?" Will interrupted firmly, though it clearly pained him to do so.

"Yes, of course," Lucinda replied anxiously.

"Your life is in danger."

The words hung in the air between them, Lucinda unable to take them in.

"A man by the name of Garenne has been hired to kidnap you. He is the man behind today's attempt," Will continued, his grip on her hands tightening.

"I . . . But . . ." Lucinda tried in vain to speak, but could not absorb what he'd said. "This can't possibly be true."

"I would never lie about such things," he replied, rubbing the pads of his thumbs over her trembling hands.

She pulled away and stared at him. "It cannot be. Why would anyone want to kidnap me?"

"I know that this is hard for you to hear," he began gently. "The particulars are not important now, but in short, it's your money they're after."

Lucinda looked away from Will, the pieces of this unfathomable puzzle slowly coming together. "Who are you?" she asked quietly, not entirely sure she wanted a reply, but knowing that she needed one.

He reached to reclaim her hands, swearing under his breath when she resisted. "Please, Lucinda. This is difficult enough."

"Who are you?" she repeated, turning to look him in the eye.

"I am a member of the Young Corinthians, a select group sworn to serve England in matters here and abroad."

"What sort of matters?" Lucinda interrupted as she attempted to make sense of his words.

Will scrubbed at his jaw with one hand. "The details are of no consequence. Lucinda—"

"You're a spy, then?" she asked hesitantly.

"Yes," he answered simply.

More pieces fell into place. Their meeting at the Mansfield ball had been so deliciously unexpected. The interlude in the park an awakening, their lovemaking in the library a rebirth.

And all of it was a lie, done out of duty—out of obligation.

"You're wrong, you know," Lucinda began, her eyes

lowering to fix on her folded hands in her lap. "Details have everything to do with you and me."

She could hear it, the sound of her heart breaking. But she would not let herself cry. And slowly, the numbness of realization and regret settled into her, until she could feel nothing.

"Lucinda, please, let me explain," Will begged, dropping to his knees and covering her hands with his in her lap.

"Do you love me?" she asked, her voice sounding eerily detached, even to her.

"Do not demand this of me, Lucinda," he answered, his voice barely above a whisper.

A pounding at the door was followed immediately by the sound of it opening. "Sir, beg your pardon, but we need to take Lady Lucinda home now."

Lucinda looked across the room. The man standing in the open doorway was the one who had escorted her here earlier in the day. He'd been so kind, so comforting as he'd concealed her in a heavy, hooded cloak and hastened her through the city streets. But it made no difference to her, all that had come before this moment now meaningless.

"Of course," she answered. On some level, she was vaguely surprised that her legs supported her as she stood.

"We aren't through, Lucinda." Will's voice was a harsh murmur beside her and she realized he'd stood, looming next to her. For the first time since they met, her body didn't sing with awareness. She felt frozen.

"Oh, but we are," she said. "I have my answer—and you, your duty."

She bent to retrieve her boots, not bothering to put them back on. "I am ready," she replied to the waiting Corinthian, and turned to go, not once looking back.

*   *   *

Lucinda refused Will's arm as they made their way down the stairs and outside to the waiting carriage. She awkwardly climbed inside, gently tossing her boots and torn stockings to land on the cushioned bench, then delicately sitting down.

Will climbed in after her and slammed the door behind him, taking a seat on the bench opposite Lucinda's.

The carriage rolled to a slow start, the clip-clop of the horse's hooves on the bricks marking each second that passed.

Lucinda reached to part the curtains that hung in the window, a sliver of the setting sun appearing before Will brusquely slid the material back into place.

She looked as if she would argue, then dropped her hands into her lap, her gaze following suit.

"It's for your own safety," he tried to explain, becoming irritated when she failed to look up.

"Lucinda. Please, say something. Say *anything*," Will pleaded, sitting forward on the bench. "Curse me. Tell me to go to hell. Swear that you'll never love me again— I just need a starting place. When you hear what I have to say—"

"I'll forgive you, is that it?" she asked quietly, her face tipping up to meet his gaze.

He reached across for her hands but she hastily folded her arms across her chest.

"I need a chance. Please, give me a chance, Lucinda."

"The Mansfield ball. Hyde Park. The Rosemont Inn— the library . . ." She paused, her face crumpling with distress. "All an elaborate ruse," she finished, shakily inhaling a breath with care.

Will grabbed at the bench on either side of Lucinda's hips, his hands digging into the velvet cushion. "No, you do not understand," he began, the disappointment in her eyes more than he could take.

"Have I misunderstood, then? Has it not been your duty to protect me these last weeks?" she pressed, bitterness lacing her words.

He dropped to his knees in front of her, roughly laying his head in her lap. "Yes, in the beginning, but you have to know that what I feel now has so little to do with duty and so much to do with you."

She pushed him to the floor and slid to the corner of the carriage. "That's not enough, Will," she said through her tears. "And you know it as well as I."

He savagely punched the cushioned back before reclaiming his seat on the opposite bench. "You do not know what you ask of me, Lucinda."

"Are you unable to give to me what I so freely and foolishly gave to you?" she whispered.

"Goddammit, Lucinda, do not do this," he pleaded, sensing defeat. "Ask for my protection, for my loyalty— hell, for my horse. But do not ask for my heart."

"The rest is of no use to me without it."

"Lucinda," he begged, hating himself for denying her.

"Stop!" she screamed, her hands flying to cover her ears. "Not another word. You've no right."

He reached across the space between them and attempted to pull her in.

"You've broken my heart," she cried out, her arms unfolding to strike at Will, landing a stinging smack on his cheek.

Will dropped his elbows to his knees, his fingers coming to angrily thread through his hair. He couldn't move. Couldn't feel anything beyond the shame that threatened to eat him alive.

The carriage came to an abrupt stop, throwing Lucinda backward. "Where are we?" she asked, her voice hoarse with emotion as she righted herself.

"Your town house," Will replied hollowly, lifting his head to meet her gaze.

He watched her as she determinedly altered her countenance, straightening her dress, then her hair, and her face, wiping at her eyes with the back of her hand. She set to work on the ruined boots with deftness, forgoing the stockings altogether.

She was slipping away from him, right before his eyes, and there was nothing he could do.

The driver opened the carriage door and reached for Lucinda's hand. "My lady."

"Thank you," she replied graciously, taking his hand and stepping down, leaving Will all alone, with nothing but regrets for comfort.

16

Will's formal attire was bloody uncomfortable. The neckcloth chafed his throat, and the fine wool of his dark blue coat was too warm.

He surveyed the drawing room of Landsdowne House, noting with irritation that every other male in attendance looked perfectly comfortable. He, however, wished for nothing more than to strip down to his shirtsleeves and forgo the formal dinner in favor of billiards and an endless supply of brandy.

But duty demanded him entirely tonight. Lucinda had agreed reluctantly to continue on with the fictitious courtship, the need to keep Garenne in the dark as much as was possible a top priority at this point in the game.

A portly baron whose name Will could not remember bowed with polite civility as he passed by, an equally portly, horse-faced woman on his arm.

Will returned the greeting and forced himself to start counting backward from ten. God knew he had a perfectly good excuse for being in such a foul mood. He'd broken Lucinda's heart, and in turn, his own. The consequences of his actions were more painful than all of the disappointment and heartache up to this point in his life put together and multiplied a thousandfold.

"William?"

He looked to see his mother at his side, her eyes filled with concern. "Yes?"

"Are you quite all right?"

For the first time that he could recall, he wanted to answer her honestly, but knew he could not. To confess even a small piece of the truth might put her in danger. "Of course. Why do you ask?"

"Well . . ." She touched her nape, smoothing the tendrils there with a gloved hand, "Lady Lucinda and her aunts arrived some time ago and you've yet to join them."

His gaze followed Her Grace's and found the four women in question standing together—conversing with Lady Swindon.

"Bloody hell," Will growled, his neckcloth growing tighter with each breath.

He looked apologetically at the duchess. "Forgive me, Mother."

"No need, William. Though I spend my days in the country, I am as aware of Lady Swindon as anyone else. Do you plan on rescuing Lucinda?" she queried, her gaze returning to the group. "Or shall I?"

Will gave his mother an appreciative look then made his way across the large room. Though no crystal had been thrown, nor did any of the Furies appear to be threatening to pummel Lady Swindon within an inch of her life, Will knew immediate action was necessary.

"Ladies," he drawled, joining the group and standing next to Lucinda. His arm brushed hers and he felt the swift tensing of her slim body.

There was an awkward pause, the Furies acknowledging his presence with notable discomfort, while Lady Swindon simply smiled, clearly enjoying the entire episode.

"Your Grace," Lucinda replied in a clear, controlled tone, laying her hand on Will's arm. "You just missed Lady Swindon's nearly encyclopedic recounting of Iron Will's adventures."

Will looked at Lady Swindon. Perhaps he should have

left her to the Furies. "You cannot believe everything you hear," he commented.

"Oh, Your Grace, modesty does not become you." Lady Swindon's voice was a sultry innuendo, her gaze blatantly traveling the length of him.

The audacity and inappropriateness of her appraisal wasn't lost on the Furies. Their eyes collectively widened before narrowing with affront.

The Duchess of Highbury stepped toward Lady Swindon, her demeanor taking on a decidedly terrier menace. "Lady Swindon, let me tell you exactly—"

"Dinner is served."

Never in his life had Will been more thankful for the readiness of a meal. "Let us adjourn to the dining room," he interrupted Lucinda's aunt before she had an opportunity to elaborate.

The group split up, Will leading the way with Lucinda on his arm.

He bent toward her, the tantalizing citrus scent of her hair teasing his nostrils. "I apologize."

"I'm afraid you'll need to be more specific, Your Grace," she murmured, the placid nature of her smile in direct contrast to her biting tone. "There are so many things for which you should feel remorse."

Will had expected her to reject his apology, though he'd underestimated the strength of the stab of pain her icy tone inflicted.

"Understand this," she continued, lowering her voice further as they neared the dining room. "You've taken nearly everything from me. But you'll not steal my reputation." She released his arm and demurely clasped her hands at her waist. "I'll continue this charade, but in the end it is you who will bear the blame. Not I."

"Of course." Somehow, he managed to keep his tone light and his expression mild as the room filled with chattering dinner guests.

Lucinda took note of those around her with a gracious smile, then turned back to Will. "The stage is yours, Your Grace."

"I will carve him up and put him in a stew."

Lucinda, Charlotte, and Bessie all looked up from their open books and eyed Victoria, their expressions reflecting equal parts surprise and horror at such a statement.

"I beg your pardon?" Charlotte said.

Victoria closed her book and drummed her fingers on the table. "Clairemont. I believe he'd do best in a stew, though I suppose it's possible that he'd suit a shepherd's pie as well."

They were gathered, as they frequently were, in the library, all four of them seated around the large, square table they'd brought with them from the country. It had been built according to the women's specifications; thus, its width and length was more than large enough to accommodate all four of them as well as any number of books and—more often than not—various and assorted tea cups and china plates.

It was their favorite spot, and this afternoon should have seemed like any other afternoon, and indeed it would have were it not for the stony-faced Young Corinthian standing just to the right of the entryway.

Lucinda could not help but glance his way before turning back to her aunt. "Aunt Victoria, do lower your voice. Please."

"Pish-posh." Victoria glared at the agent. "I am quite sure worse has been said of the man—and in much more colorful language, to boot!"

"Yes, let us all be thankful that you've shown a modicum of restraint," Bessie said sarcastically. "After all, you just as easily could have suggested we fillet the man or stuff an apple in his mouth and roast him whole."

"Excellent idea!" Victoria countered, her expression brightening.

"Really?" Bessie said with interest. "I thought the pig suggestion to be slightly de trop."

"Ladies," Charlotte interrupted, sipping her tea before setting the delicate Wedgwood cup down. "Can we all agree that the carving up and cooking of the duke would hardly be productive—or polite?"

Her two sisters pondered Charlotte's request, then begrudgingly nodded their agreement.

"Thank you," Lucinda said with relief, turning her attention back to Gerald Hobson's dry but comprehensive *Timing and Rate of Skeletal Maturation in Horses*. While Lucinda normally approached such topics with unabashed interest, she had to admit that she was having difficulty mustering the enthusiasm for equine anatomy today.

Of course, it didn't help matters that nearly all of Lucinda's energy had been tapped for more personal reasons, chief among them keeping herself from collapsing in tears in front of her aunts.

She'd known this would be hard. From the moment Will had told her the truth, she'd known. But somehow she'd thought it would just be when she saw him, that when she was not in the same room with him, it would be different. She'd thought . . . She didn't know what she'd thought, just that if she was going to cry, it wouldn't be in public. It wouldn't be anywhere but in her own room, with her own pillow muffling the sound.

But now, every time one of her aunts looked at her, her insides began to shake, and she had to look away, or claim she was about to sneeze.

It was awful. It was exhausting. She'd half expected to not wake this morning.

And the night before—dear God, that had been the worst. Why she ever thought she could manage the dinner party at Landsdowne House, she would never know. Lucinda and her aunts had barely entered the drawing room before Lady Swindon swooped down on them like a perfectly groomed vulture. It had been an astounding violation of polite rules, and nearly enough to undo Lucinda.

And then there was Will. Lucinda had not been so hen-witted as to think she could avoid him the entire evening, but when he'd come to her rescue, it had somehow made everything even worse.

He wasn't supposed to be her hero. Dammit, he wasn't *allowed* to be her hero, not after what he'd done to her.

It had been a harrowing few days. Learning her life was in danger was terrifying enough on its own, but when paired with Will's betrayal? It was more than any woman could be expected to bear. Her heart absolutely ached with fear and sorrow.

And now she had to pretend that nothing had happened. She'd had no choice in the matter; the Corinthians had made it clear that her cooperation was vital to the successful completion of the mission. Her aunts, too. Until this Frenchman—Garenne was his name—was captured, none of them could safely go on with their lives.

Lucinda had agreed that her courtship with Will would continue on, exactly as it had prior to the kidnapping attempt. All of their social engagements and outings would remain on the calendar. From the outside, everything would look precisely the same.

But Lucinda could not have been more aware that her life had changed completely, the army of Corinthians assigned to her safety hardly allowing for privacy of any kind.

And through it all, she could not stop blaming herself. It was easier, and far more satisfying, to insist that this was all Will's fault, that he had used her and lied to her, and that she had been an innocent victim.

But she knew that she too was culpable. Despite everything her aunts had taught her, she had made the mistake of listening to her untried heart. She had trusted too soon, been far too quick to believe her own day-dreams. She never should have entertained such roman-tic notions, let alone acted on them. And though it was cold comfort that she was hardly the first woman to fall for Iron Will, the knowledge did provide some small measure of relief.

"Lucinda?"

She looked up, blinking. Victoria was regarding her with a quizzical expression, and Lucinda did not want to guess at how many times her aunt had called out her name.

"Did you find the answer?" Victoria asked.

Lucinda shook her head. "I'm still looking," she mumbled. On the same page. She'd been on the same page for forty minutes. She looked back down and tried to read.

Special care must be given to syndromes of the patella. She was pretty sure she'd read that already.

Bloody . . . stupid . . . If one of her horses had to be put down because of a knee injury, she was blaming Will. It was his fault she couldn't concentrate on the text.

Will.

He was an awful man.

Truly, truly awful.

And he'd never said that he loved her.

Should she have suspected something sooner? Had she been a fool to believe he simply could not put into words what he felt for her?

Well, yes, obviously.

She'd been a complete fool, but worse than that, she'd expressed her love for him, a man who was simply doing his job and nothing more.

It would be so easy to lose herself in anger, to blame him for taking advantage of her. To hate him for the emotions she'd believed he'd shared with her, when all the while he was aware he was only playing a role.

But Lucinda was never one for taking the easy route. She preferred to do something right or not at all.

Years from now, she would look back on this as a lesson learned, she vowed. And for now, she would do what was necessary to keep herself and her family safe, even if it meant pretending that she was the woman she'd been before.

"Lucinda, dear," Charlotte said sweetly. "Are you well this morning?"

Her question pulled Lucinda from her thoughts and she looked up. All three of her aunts watched her with varying expressions of concern, the expanse of the cluttered library table separating them.

Lucinda forced a smile. She and Charlotte had decided to keep the truth of Lucinda's feelings for Will a secret from both Victoria and Bessie. The two had been so angry over being kept in the dark by the Corinthians that the revelation of Lucinda's broken heart would surely have forced them over the edge.

"Yes," Lucinda said, giving the beloved trio a reassuring smile. "Of course."

It was not so hard, after all, to lie, Lucinda realized, turning back to her book.

Garenne would not leave anything to chance this time. The extreme discomfort he found in failure was a new and unappealing sensation and one not easily quelled. Even slitting the throat of a street urchin who had dared to cross his path that evening had done little to abate the viselike grip that the pain currently held on his skull.

"Do you have any questions?" he asked the petite blonde sitting across from him, her cold green eyes taking in their surroundings with catlike precision.

"No," she said simply, her beautiful face devoid of emotion.

He drained his tankard of ale and gestured for the serving girl. "Good." He preferred to keep their conversation minimal. "You will succeed," he told her. "Or you will die."

She didn't flinch, only reached across the table and picked up the soft leather pouch, tucking it into a hidden pocket in her cape, then nodding. "You've no need for concern."

And with that she was gone, silently making her way to the tavern's door and disappearing into the night.

Garenne felt the pressure of the note in his breast pocket. Fouché was growing impatient, even going so far as to question Garenne's abilities. The imbecile was lucky he was safely in France, with the width of the English Channel between him and death.

The woman came highly recommended.

She would succeed, or he would kill her himself.

17

A horse race of some importance, the Queen's Cup took place in late April of every year. The ton made their way annually along the King's Road to Camden, only a few miles outside London. The queen in question had been Anne, who had, upon delightedly discovering a large parcel of flat land during one of her riding expeditions, purchased the hundred acres in order to establish the yearly event.

The popularity of the race had grown over the years, and now the crowds nearly overflowed the grounds.

Will surveyed the noisy gathering from his station near the starting post and grimaced. He'd protested until he was hoarse with the effort, but Lucinda would not yield: She would attend the Queen's Cup with or without him. Her love of horses, once endearing, was becoming downright irritating.

"You really must work on a less ferocious facial expression," Northrop drawled, reining his bay gelding next to Sol and Will.

"But this one works so well in keeping *most* away," Will said sarcastically to his friend.

The two observed the scene in silence. Excited Thoroughbreds pranced and snorted in anticipation, their owners preening over the prized equines while jockeys prepared themselves mentally for the race. The crowd milled about, enjoying the sun and festive frivolity.

"Utter chaos," Northrop remarked.

Will nodded in agreement.

"You should have told me."

Will gave him a quizzical look. "You've attended the Queen's Cup before, surely."

"Not about the race, Clairemont," his friend replied, "about Lady Lucinda."

Will scowled. Carmichael had enlisted Northrop's help despite Will's protests, making the already complicated situation even more so.

"You didn't really believe I'd reformed, did you?" Will kept his tone light, careless.

"You should have told me."

"You know very well I couldn't, so there's no point in belaboring the point, is there?" Will shot back, but he could hear his voice changing, his carelessness unraveling to reveal a darker emotion.

Northrop heeded the warning and broke their stare, turning to look over his shoulder at his wife, who stood chatting with Lucinda and her aunts. "Amelia fears that Lady Lucinda has a tendre for you."

Will kept his eyes fixed on a spot in the distance. "What good does it do to discuss this?"

"And you? Do you love her?"

Will stiffened, hands tightening on the reins. Sol shifted uneasily; he tossed his head and whinnied. "I have a duty to perform, and it doesn't include love."

A chorus of horns signaled the imminent beginning of the race.

Northrop turned his mount toward the women, pausing to look once more at Will. "I wasn't aware that with one you couldn't have the other."

Will reined in Sol and they fell into step next to Northrop and his gelding, the two picking their way across the flattened grass and churned-up ground to join the ladies.

Amelia greeted Northrop with such love in her eyes that Will felt a sudden stab of jealousy slice mercilessly through his already fractured heart.

Lucinda's look was pleasant enough, but the stark contrast between the two left Will cold.

The Furies, however, quickly brought him back to reality. The duchess pinned him with a vengeful glare, while the marchioness haughtily turned away with a huff. Lady Charlotte maintained an air of politeness, acknowledging him with a nod of her head. "Your Grace, a lovely day for a race, wouldn't you agree?"

Will dismounted, Sol's reins held loosely in his hand. "Indeed, Lady Charlotte, it is."

"One might wonder how you could possibly enjoy the race, burdened with what must surely be an unbearably heavy conscience," the sour duchess interjected, walking around to face Sol.

The entire group turned to stare at her, their eyes wide with shock.

She returned their stares with composure.

"Surely I'm not the only one to question the sanity of a man who would keep a horse such as King Solomon's Mine from his destiny?" the woman queried, stroking Sol's silky mane.

"Why would one assume Sol wants to race simply because he is fast?" Will countered, barely maintaining his composure.

"He is a Thoroughbred, Your Grace." She shot Will a look of utter disgust. "And not just any Thoroughbred, but the son of Triton's Tyranny. Racing is in his blood. It is what he was bred and born to do."

Will had to admit that Sol's quickness had everything to do with why Will found him invaluable. The stallion's speed was absolutely essential to Will's success as a Corinthian. Still, he could hardly point out such a thing, not with Lady Northrop present.

"He appears perfectly happy to me," Will answered, standing back to eye Sol critically.

Lucinda joined her aunt, her affection and admiration for the horse obvious as she reached out to caress his velvety nose. "Look in his eyes, Your Grace."

Will walked forward and stared directly into the large, black eyes. They flickered with curiosity and excitement. He'd heard tell of a horse having a kind eye, the relaxed, open nature of the expression speaking to the horse's state of mind. But this was something different. Sol exhibited an eagerness that was nearly palpable as he looked away from Will and chose instead to watch the ebb and flow of the noisy crowd and the horses.

"Do you see it?" Lucinda asked quietly.

"Bloody hell," Will said under his breath, stepping back. Did Sol have the same fire in his eyes when racing through the streets of London on Corinthian business?

"Never fear, Your Grace," the sour duchess said, lovingly patting Sol on the neck. "You may have denied him his first love, but I would bet my carriage and matching grays that he'll take to his new job with even greater enthusiasm."

His new job? What the devil was she talking about? Will opened his mouth to ask her what she meant, but just then, the crowd around them roared to life as the racehorses lined up at the starting post. The Furies joined the crush of humans, pushing their way through with well-aimed pokes of parasols. Northrop took his wife's arm and guided her safely on toward a spot midway down the circular track.

Sol pawed at the ground with his front hooves, his nicker of excitement growing louder. Head up, hooves dancing, ears pricked forward.

"He's too excitable," Will told Lucinda as he tightened his grip on the reins. "I can't allow him any closer to the crowd. If you like, Weston or Talbot would happily escort you to a more suitable viewing spot."

Lucinda didn't answer. Instead, she reached up and clasped the saddle. "Lift me up," she demanded.

"I'm sorry?"

"I've not come all this way to miss the race," she answered, irritation growing in her voice. "The ideal spot for viewing is on the back of this horse. Now, assist me or I shall be forced to ask one of your men."

Will reluctantly placed his hands about Lucinda's waist and lifted her into the saddle. He waited to release her until she found her balance in the seat, sitting sideways in a man's saddle no easy feat. She straightened her pelisse and held out her hand for the reins, silently demanding he give them to her.

"Absolutely not," Will said in no uncertain terms.

Lucinda stared at him with a stony gaze before she shrugged, conceding. "Very well."

Horns trumpeted and the race began. The ground rumbled beneath the pounding of fifteen sets of thundering hooves. Will felt the rhythm reverberating through his boots and on up through his body. He looked at Lucinda atop Sol and found her focused on the race, shading her eyes with one gloved hand to take in the progress.

"Do you have a favorite?" he called to her over the shouts from the crowd.

"Number four, Braveheart," she replied, her head turning as she followed the horses.

Will surveyed the pack of five horses that led the way and located Braveheart, a giant chestnut with amazing speed. "He's fast." He watched as Braveheart broke from the pack, his long, powerful stride eating up the dirt track. "And if I'm not mistaken, it looks as though he's about to win."

Lucinda let out an unladylike shriek of approval. "Run, Braveheart, run!" she yelled, belatedly checking her unabashed enthusiasm with a palm over her mouth.

Will was riveted by Lucinda as she followed the race, her breath quickening with each stride the giant chestnut took, her arms rising in the air, her hands clenched into fists. Her enthusiasm was infectious, and he found himself smiling despite the realization that this time with her, when he was allowed to see her for who she truly was, would be short indeed.

He longed to place his hands around Garenne's neck and put an end to his threat. But Will knew that day would be the last he'd spend in Lucinda's company. There would be censure following their broken courtship. But he could bear that. Being blackened in polite society was nothing new to him.

But to be denied the pleasure of Lucinda's company? That he did not know how he would survive.

Will stared at Lucinda's profile as she braced her hands on the saddle leather and stretched taller, her head turning to follow the horses as they rounded the last turn. Will watched the final furlong, Braveheart crossing the finish line some three strides in front of the other horses. The crowd erupted with cheers, men slapping one another on the back and women hopping up and down with joy.

"My first Queen's Cup win!" Lucinda exclaimed, sliding down from her perch atop Sol.

"I'm sorry?" Will queried. He couldn't have heard her correctly. His lips tightened as he looked down at her, annoyed that she hadn't waited for his assistance.

Lucinda straightened her pelisse and gown, brushing Sol's black hairs off her skirt. "There is a certain confidentiality between agents and their assigned protectees, is there not?"

"Of course," he replied, still not entirely sure what Lucinda was getting at.

"Excellent. Then there is no danger in sharing our plans with you." She finished brushing her gown and turned to await the arrival of the rest of their party. "For some time now, my aunts and I have been building a breeding stable. Braveheart is the sire of Winnie's foal." She looked up, smiling brilliantly at the approaching party. "And now that he's won the right to race in the Ascot, that foal is substantially more valuable."

Will began to piece together tidbits of conversations he'd overheard while in Bampton. The odd comment by Lucinda's aunt concerning Sol's impending enthusiasm for an unnamed employment put everything into focus.

"You see, Your Grace," Lucinda said, her voice crisp and clear, "my heart may have momentarily gotten in the way of my goal, but this was always about King Solomon's Mine."

She smiled as her aunts' "huzzah!" reached her ears. "And in the end, I'll have gotten what I wanted all along," she added.

Will struggled to reply. "You cannot mean—"

"Your Grace, I do not think even your King Solomon's Mine could have outrun Braveheart today," Victoria interrupted, exuberant as the group came to stand next to Lucinda and Will.

He nodded, the weight of not being able to address Lucinda's painful revelation leaving him speechless.

The inner parlor at the rear of Madame Beaufont's salon was small, to be sure, but the amenities and comfort of the surroundings more than made up for what it lacked in size. Divided from the front of the store by a luxurious length of the palest of pink velvets, the exclusive enclave was reserved for Madame's best clients.

Those ensconced within its fashionably papered walls were treated to a dish of Twinings best pekoe tea, the most delicate of patisseries, and the melodious efforts of a single female harpist tucked neatly into one corner of the cozy room.

Madame Beaufont, whose colorful history rivaled that of any member of the royal family, stood before Lucinda and Amelia, scrutinizing the sleeve of the deep purple taffeta gown being held up by one of her assistants.

Her lips pursed as she fingered a rosette. "*Non*, this will not do."

She waved the girl away and turned to gather up a stack of illustrations. "Why a woman of her age insists on such frivolous touches, I will never know."

Amelia leaned forward. "Yes, that would be Lady . . . er, her name escapes me . . ."

Lucinda shot her friend a look. Her attempt at ferreting out the owner of the purple creation was hardly subtle.

Madame Beaufont sat in the chair facing Amelia and Lucinda, fluffing the pink and cream striped pillow to accommodate her petite size. "Lady Northrop, such tricks will not work with me." She sighed dramatically. "Though, if one were to take note of a gown just that shade on Lady Swindon at the Foster masquerade ball, well . . ." Her shoulders lifted in a very Gallic shrug as she shuffled through her lapful of drawings. "It would hardly be my fault."

Amelia bit into an almond biscuit, the smile on her lips bringing to mind a cat who had just swallowed a parakeet. "I knew it," she said smugly after finishing her bite.

"Tsk, tsk," Madame Beaufont remonstrated, while clearly enjoying the gossip as much as Amelia. "Now, ladies, we must choose a design for your masquerade gowns immediately or I fear they will not be completed in time."

Lucinda nibbled at her petit four. Conversations between Madame Beaufont and Amelia always followed the same pattern, Amelia drawing out as much information as she could manage, while Madame Beaufont groaned over the impossibility of finishing her unique creations within the allotted time. Week in, week out, Amelia walked away from the shop with five to seven new tidbits of gossip, and Madame Beaufont always finished the gowns on time.

Their lively interaction was predictable, something that, Lucinda suddenly realized, was truly comforting. With all that had happened—all that continued to swirl around her—Lucinda was more than content to sit comfortably in Madame Beaufont's parlor and watch a scenario play out that she'd witnessed countless times before.

The petite Frenchwoman dramatically whisked an illustration from the stack in her hands and held it aloft. "Lady Northrop, the design for this gown came to me in a dream."

Amelia's mouth formed a delicate O of delight as she took in the drawing of the evening gown, a frothy confection of pomona green. "It is truly exquisite, Madame Beaufont," she exclaimed, poring over the lovely illustration.

"Yes," Madame agreed as she happily eyed the creation. "One of my best, I believe."

The mousy shopgirl returned, bending to whisper in Madame Beaufont's ear.

The designer scowled, then furiously nodded at the girl. "Ladies, I will return in a moment," she said apologetically, setting the illustration down and gracefully rising in a rustle and swirl of skirts. She disappeared through the pink curtain, leaving Lucinda and Amelia alone with the harpist.

Amelia peered after her and the moment the curtain settled, she reached for the drawings, only to have her hand rapped with Lucinda's fan.

"Ouch!" Amelia squeaked, quickly rubbing her knuckles. "Was that entirely necessary?"

Lucinda arched her eyebrows. "It was either that or allow you to bear the brunt of Madame Beaufont's wrath when she discovered you'd had the audacity to peek," she answered with a smile.

Amelia returned the expression. "You are a true friend."

"The truest," Lucinda agreed, taking a sip of her tea and contemplating eating an almond biscuit.

"Do you love him?"

Startled, Lucinda gasped and choked, nearly dropping the delicate bone china cup into her lap. "I'm sorry," she sputtered, allowing Amelia to take the cup and dabbing at the few drops on her skirt.

"Am I to take that as a yes?" Amelia teased, pouring a fresh cup of tea for Lucinda.

Lucinda accepted it and sipped, the hot, sweet liquid soothing her throat, though it could do little for her nerves. She had agreed not to tell Amelia about Garenne or the Corinthians. And there was no way to explain how she felt about Will without divulging this information.

But she *longed* to talk to Amelia.

"You're referring to the duke," Lucinda said, maintaining her composure by carefully not looking directly at Amelia.

Amelia huffed and sat back. "Well, of course I'm speaking of the duke, unless there is another suitor of whom I am not aware."

Lucinda answered with a shrug and set the fragile

china cup and saucer on the table, next to Madame Beaufont's illustrations. "What do you think?"

Amelia didn't say anything for several seconds. "Is he aware of your feelings?" she finally asked, her voice gentle.

"Yes," Lucinda answered simply. "He knows." She swallowed, afraid of how Amelia would respond.

She was immediately enveloped in her friend's arms. "And does he return your feelings?" Amelia asked, releasing Lucinda to sit back, the better to see her face.

The relief Lucinda felt at telling Amelia about Will was overwhelming. She shook her head, tears joining the three tiny tea stains that marred her peach gown.

Amelia produced a lace-edged handkerchief from her reticule and wiped the dampness from Lucinda's cheeks. "Shhhh," she soothed.

"You warned me," Lucinda murmured, her words nearly lost beneath the dulcet tones of the harp.

"It does not matter now," Amelia assured her, taking Lucinda's hands in her own. "I have watched Clairemont in your presence, and he clearly feels affection for you," she said earnestly, pausing to tuck the now damp scrap of fabric into her reticule. "Where there is affection, there is always the possibility that love will grow in time."

Lucinda tried to smile, but Amelia did not know the whole truth. If she had, her dear friend would never have suggested such a thing.

"You are right, of course," Lucinda said, squeezing Amelia's hand, "and I am a behaving like, well, very much as one who has more hair than wit."

"You are a woman in love," Amelia stated matter-of-factly, "and therefore have no need to apologize for your behavior."

"Is this what you wanted for me? All of those suitors you encouraged in the hopes that I would choose one, fall desperately in love, and lose all hope of retaining any semblance of the intelligent, eminently reasonable individual I once was?"

Amelia reached for an almond biscuit, gave it to Lucinda, then selected a second one for herself. "Er, well . . . yes."

The two looked at each other as they nibbled the biscuits, then laughed.

"Lucinda," Amelia said, once their laughter had subsided, "love embellishes your soul, it does not detract. Do you understand?"

Oh, how she wanted to see the sense in Amelia's statement. The idea of love's ability to open up her world rather than destroy all she'd carefully built was nearly irresistible. But it was too late for such flights of fancy.

"Am I to understand you approve of my feelings for the duke?" she teased, hoping to move the conversation toward a lighter tone.

"He is handsome enough, I'll give the man that," Amelia countered.

Lucinda mindlessly bit into the biscuit and chewed slowly. "Yes, well, he's not the only attractive man in London. There will be others."

"Oh no there won't."

Lucinda stopped, a sudden sense of unease settling into her stomach. "Come now, your list of eligible bachelors rivals any of the most determined of matchmaking mamas. You'll find another one soon enough for me."

Amelia bit into the biscuit and crunched, her eyes taking on the look of a seasoned general. "The duke simply needs the right opportunity to apprise you of his true feelings," she began, squinting her eyes as she visually laid out her plan. "And we shall give him that opportunity."

Lucinda's mind raced to catch up with what had just transpired. "I don't think that such a plan is—"

"Vauxhall!" Amelia nearly screamed, the harpist tripping over her note in response.

"Amelia, I—"

"It's perfect!" her friend interrupted excitedly. "In fact, that is where John and I first . . ." She paused, checking herself. "Well, that is another story for another time."

Madame Beaufont's distinctive voice called to one of her clerks, just beyond the doorway.

Amelia placed the remainder of the biscuit in her mouth and chewed quickly.

Lucinda did the same, swallowing just before Madame pulled back the curtain and announced, "Now, ladies, where were we?"

"Are you all right?" Will asked, bending down to look at his opponent. The man was sprawled awkwardly on the floor of the ring, one eye swollen shut. A crimson trickle ran from his nose toward his mouth.

"I'll live, but I'm going to need some help here."

Will stood to the side while two attendants picked the man up, one taking him at the shoulders and the other holding tight to his feet.

"I hope it helped."

Will tensed at Carmichael's voice but awkwardly patted the battered man once on his shoulder and wished him better luck next time, before turning. "You'll have to be more specific."

"Pounding a succession of opponents," Carmichael clarified. "I hope it helped."

Will joined his superior. "Immensely," Will said sarcastically, then motioned for Carmichael to follow.

The two made their way in silence across the club to an anteroom just off the entrance. The room was sparsely but comfortably furnished. Will doubted the proprietor would approve of his sweat-soaked body coming in contact with the elegant furniture, but he hardly cared. The room was empty and would afford the privacy the two men needed.

He pulled a chair out for Carmichael and dropped into the one opposite, mopping at his face with a rough linen towel.

"We've run out of time."

Will stopped and looked at Carmichael, his body tightening at the older man's grim expression. "Time for what?"

"Simply put," Carmichael began, crossing his legs and assuming a casual appearance should anyone happen in, "we can no longer afford to wait for Garenne to make his move. We must lure him out of hiding."

Will gripped the arms of his chair. "What do you mean we can no longer afford to wait? I don't see how we can afford not to."

Carmichael fingered his signet ring, turning it once, twice, as he pondered his response. "We have limited resources, Will. And much as I would prefer to tell you our assistance is not needed elsewhere, it is. Nearly half of our agents are working this case. It cannot continue."

Will ran his hands through his hair before propping his elbows on his knees. "What do you propose?"

"You won't like it," Carmichael replied, "but we've no choice."

"You know I have no qualms about putting myself in harm's way."

Carmichael stared at Will, his face unreadable.

"Bloody hell, man, out with it already," Will said impatiently.

"It's not you we need to use, Will. It's Lady Lucinda."

Will's vision turned hazy as he absorbed Carmichael's words. "You cannot be serious."

"Deadly so," Carmichael responded, the lines at each side of his mouth deepening as he grimaced.

"This is Garenne we're speaking of, not some pickpocket from London's stews." Will's voice remained level, but anger swelled and grew within him. "Lady Lucinda cannot be expected to hold her own against such a man."

"We have no other options—"

"He's a bloody monster, you fool," Will roared, shoving out of his chair to stalk a handful of steps toward the door, then returning, coming to stand in front of the man.

Carmichael's eyes flared, betraying his surprise at Will's outburst. "You forget yourself, Clairemont." The admonition was given in the same calm, cool voice he always used, but a thread of steely warning underlay the words and cut through Will's rage as nothing else could have.

"I apologize," he bit out. He turned abruptly away and reached for the first object he could find. The small side table broke as though it were kindling when Will threw it against the wall.

"I warned you not to get involved with Lady Lucinda," Carmichael said quietly. "You cannot do what we must—see what we see—and expect to maintain any sort of normalcy in your life, especially not with someone so intimately involved in Corinthian business."

Will wiped his arm across his forehead, removing the beads of sweat, and leaned his back against the wall. He knew Carmichael was right, a realization that only added to his pain. Nothing was as it should be, every last relationship in his life was turned upside down. So much so that Will hardly knew how to go about righting them—or if repair was even possible at this point.

"Give me more time," he growled, unable to look Carmichael in the eye.

"I can hold off for three days. No more."

"Fair enough," Will replied, then stalked from the room.

18

"Are there to be fireworks?" Amelia asked Lord Northrop, nearly bouncing with excitement as the group's boat floated along the Thames. Lucinda smiled at her dear friend, whose enthusiasm for fireworks was second only to her love of Cook's strawberry tarts.

Amelia sighed contentedly as she rested her head on her husband's shoulder. Seeing her expression of utter happiness, Lucinda had to admit that perhaps something else had surpassed both fireworks and strawberries in Amelia's heart.

Lucinda found herself sighing as well, though for a vastly different reason than Amelia's. An evening at Vauxhall Gardens was never a restful affair, the sheer magnitude of the spectacle enough to overwhelm the most enthusiastic of attendees. But for Lucinda, tonight presented special challenges.

Although, she thought, glancing down at her dress, she could not have been any better outfitted for the evening.

The dress itself, a fetching gown in the Grecian style, was truly lovely, the golden silk warming Lucinda's skin, while the cut and drape accentuated her curves. The trouble was, there was far too little of the gown for Lucinda's taste. The neckline dipped low in the front, revealing and displaying Lucinda's cleavage, while the sleeves were practically nonexistent.

Madame Beaufont insisted that in light of Lucinda's

involvement with the duke, it behooved her to dress more daringly.

Lucinda sighed again, recalling Madame's air of conspiracy when she carefully placed the wrapped package containing the finished gown in her hands. "Forgive me," she whispered. "But I made a few alterations to the gown." The woman's eyes had positively flashed with delight.

"You should have known better," Lucinda said under her breath, then shivered in response to the light breeze coming off the river. She pulled her shawl higher over her shoulders in a vain attempt at warmth.

"Would you like my coat?" Will asked, his brows furrowing with concern.

No matter how long Lucinda lived she would never forget his voice and the troubling sensations it sent pulsing throughout her body. The deep, husky tone ignited a fire in her belly, little flames licking their way toward every limb until she wondered if she would simply burst. She fought the urge to lean into his warmth, then felt his breath on her bare nape and closed her eyes. She opened them a moment later to see the cool, icy stares from all three of her aunts. The sight immediately strengthened her resolve.

"No, thank you," she said coolly, bracing herself as the boat came to a slow stop, bumping against the landing. Northrop and Will stepped out first, then aided the ladies in debarking, the entire party making their way finally to the Vauxhall Stairs. After showing their season tickets, they were escorted through the crowd toward the Grove, where revelers gathered in groups or inside supper boxes, mingling and enjoying the music wafting from the Orchestra building.

"Much could be said of Vauxhall," Northrop commented over his shoulder, as he led Amelia up the steps toward their supper box, followed by the Furies, Lucinda, and Will. "Though I doubt that the word 'subtle' could be used."

Lucinda saw Amelia playfully swat her husband's sleeve with her fan.

She allowed Will to accompany her into the box and took a seat on a deep red cushioned bench, avoiding his gaze by pretending to be absorbed in the scene below them.

It would be tempting to forget Will's betrayal. So easy to allow herself to be caught up in the spirit of the evening, the knowing glances, intimate whispers—the romance that Vauxhall's proprietors inspired with the heady mixture of sights and sounds all wrapped up with a gaily colorful bow.

Lucinda tried unsuccessfully to cover her expanse of skin with the silk shawl. She glanced up as Will sat down, his worried gaze causing her breath to catch.

He looked away, responding to a question from Northrop.

The dull ache in her heart that she'd grown accustomed to over the last few days only increased when Will was near.

She had been blind with anger, his betrayal cutting to her very core. The intimacy she'd believed to be an expression of their love had suddenly been made cheap and meaningless by the revelation of his ties to the Young Corinthians. But one thought niggled at the back of her mind night and day: There had been more to their lovemaking. She'd seen it in his eyes, heard it in his voice. Felt it in his touch.

She was sure he felt more than duty toward her. She was sure of it, but how could she convince him to admit such a thing?

Lucinda prayed that Amelia had been correct when she suggested that the duke would be more inclined to reveal such close-held feelings if given proper physical inducements.

Will turned his attention back to her. "Have you need of anything, Lady Lucinda?" he inquired, his eagerness threatening her resolve.

"No, thank you," she responded politely, though her nerves were now dancing.

Amelia had promised she would secure a certain amount of privacy for the two to be alone. Her dear friend had assured Lucinda that their plan would work.

Half of her wanted desperately to prove Amelia right. And the other? The other was afraid that even with the dress and the practiced seduction, Lucinda would only succeed in proving her wrong.

The group listened to the music for some time, sipping wine and dining on Vauxhall ham. They visited with friends who strolled by or stopped to visit and enjoyed the antics of the crowd.

The orchestra ceased playing and polite applause filled the air as the musicians left the stand. Amelia stood and gestured for Lord Northrop to do the same. "I suggest we take a stroll before dinner is served," she said to the group.

"I cannot see from down there," Victoria protested. "And Lord Humphrey is about to make a complete fool of himself. I don't want to miss it."

Bessie leaned in toward Victoria and focused her opera glasses on the crowd. "Where?"

"There," Victoria answered impatiently, discreetly pointing toward a tall bald man in evening dress waving his hands wildly as he addressed his wife. "Near the statue of Handel."

"Oh," Bessie began, only to follow with a scandalized gasp when the man in question managed to slosh Madeira down the front of poor Lady Humphrey's gown.

Charlotte adopted a look of disinterest, though she slyly moved nearer to the railing, where the view of Lord Humphrey's antics could be more easily seen. "You go ahead," she said, "do take care not to dally, though." Her gaze rested briefly, meaningfully, on Lucinda, her point made clear.

"Oh, look!" Bessie squeaked, causing Charlotte to turn toward the crowd.

Amelia quickly took Lucinda's hand in hers and pulled her to the stairs, the men following behind. "All right, then," she said over her shoulder as they descended the steps.

The men escorted them into the crowd.

"I haven't walked the Downs for some time," Amelia said to the others. "Lucinda?"

Lucinda hesitated, nervously fingering her shawl. If she agreed with her friend, the four would walk among shrubs and trees that allowed for more intimate conversations. And if she declined, they would take the Grand Walk, the more populated of the two, with nary a private spot in sight. One direction took courage, the other offered safety. Lucinda had been taught by the Furies to never refuse a challenge.

"Yes, the Downs it is."

"Bloody hell," Will growled under his breath as he escorted Lucinda toward the shadowy paths of the Downs. Lady Northrop had suggested the ramble and his friend had heartily agreed, leaving Will and Lucinda to follow.

Will tugged at his neckcloth as they walked, his fingers itching to rip the cursed material free. Lucinda had politely allowed him to escort her to the gardens for the evening. And she had politely smiled at his conversation. She'd politely declined his coat when the wind had picked up. And she had politely taken his arm as they set off after Northrop and his wife.

Will had just about had it with all of the bloody politeness.

The rage Will felt at Carmichael's threat of using her for bait continued to burn in his chest. Allowing Lucinda to act as a decoy would be tantamount to signing her death sentence, plain and simple. After far too much brandy and far too little sleep, Will's heart had given in and surrendered the hopes and dreams that Lucinda's love had offered. Her life was far more important than his happiness.

But dammit all, did the woman have to test him on every front? He discreetly looked out the corner of his eye and assessed her dress. The bodice was cut so low that he could, from his considerable height, peer down at the creamy, white expanse of her breasts, the pink-hued nipples barely hidden from him.

His groin tightened. The scrap of fabric that clung so artfully to Lucinda's luscious curves tortured him. Surely God Himself was testing Will, the Downs yet another obstacle in his elaborate plan.

If it were not for the army of Corinthian agents fanned out about the grounds, Will would have objected to the route. But as it was, not a single suspect individual would be allowed within two yards of Lucinda. All agents had been instructed to attack first, ask questions later.

Lucinda edged closer to Will, pressing the curve of her breast against his arm. "I fear the chill is getting the better of me this evening."

Will flicked a glance over the path ahead of them, noting with displeasure that Northrop and his wife had stopped to admire the life-sized lead statue of Milton. "Here," he offered, slipping his arm around her shoulders, sheltering her next to his body. "Though the Furies would faint from the scandal of it, I fear your freezing to death would be equally distressing."

Will could just make out Lucinda's hesitant smile in the fading light.

"Well, we do, after all, need to keep up appearances if we've any hope of succeeding at this game."

Will nodded in agreement. "And what would mean success to you?" he asked, his voice low and rough.

"I suppose continuing to exist would be rather nice," Lucinda began, steering Will toward a small turnout in the path where a fountain quietly gurgled. "And securing your heart for myself would be most welcome."

Will froze for a moment, certain he'd misheard her.

Lucinda slipped out from under his arm and stood in front of him, bare inches separating them. She let her shawl fall from her shoulders and took his hand in both of hers, pressing it against the thin silk bodice of her gown. His palm cupped the lush upper curve of her breast. "My heart is yours, Will. All you have to do is take it."

He could feel it beating, pounding fast beneath his palm, the increased speed belying her calm.

She stepped closer, rising on her toes to his face. "Take it," she whispered. "Take me."

Her mouth met his, the lush lower lip and curved upper parting.

Will instinctively returned the kiss, pulling her against him, her soft curves accommodating the harder angles of his body.

"Say you love me, Will."

Her fervent plea pulled Will from the mindless fog of lust and desire that held him. She offered him everything. What could he possibly give in return?

He forced his arms to release her and his unwilling legs to step back. "Lucinda, I'm sorry."

She faced him proudly, hands clenched, her chin lifted

bravely. "I love you, but I'll not allow you to have such a hold on me if my feelings are not returned."

"You've no idea how sorry I am—"

"Do you love me?" she asked plainly, her eyes welling with tears.

He would not lie to her, and so Will said nothing, though it killed him inside to remain silent.

"Very well," she said in a hushed tone, retrieving her shawl and wrapping it about her shoulders. "I wish to return to the supper box."

"What can I say?" Will asked, his voice betraying his anguish.

"Nothing." She moved to step around him, wincing when Will grabbed for her wrist and held tight. "You've my heart already, do you really need my dignity as well?" she choked out.

"Lucinda," he pressed, the shock of her words taking his breath.

"Let me go," she pleaded, pulling away.

He dropped his hand from her wrist and followed her onto the path, keeping a safe distance behind her as she retraced their steps back to the crowd.

"But I can't," he whispered to himself, "and therein lies the problem."

It had been easy enough to satisfy Amelia's need for details. Lucinda's vague answers had supplied her hopeful friend with enough encouragement to ensure that she assumed the courtship was continuing on a decidedly more romantic path.

Lucinda was determined to sever her connection with Will, however, and that meant she had to find a way to end her need for protection by the Corinthians.

Securing an audience with Will's superior had been far more complicated than convincing Amelia that her plan had worked. Lucinda had seen little of the duke for the past two days, the time they were forced to spend in each other's company proving both awkward and draining.

"Come with me." Lord Weston held out his arm to steady Lucinda as she alighted from the coach in front of a stone town house, its details hardly distinguishable in the darkness of night. Lucinda spied mullioned windows and a row of tidy hedges before Lord Weston instructed her to watch her step as they entered the building.

She held tight to his arm and allowed him to lead her in, the interior of the building hardly more revealing than the outside had been.

Sparse candlelight illuminated a long hall at the end of which stood two large men—Corinthian agents, Lucinda was sure, though none she had ever seen.

Lord Weston gestured for Lucinda to follow him.

She took a deep breath, then walked quickly, casting brief glances at the landscape paintings and portraits that occupied the walls.

"Gents," Lord Weston said with a brief nod, though neither of the two acknowledged his presence. "Social interaction is not their forte," he whispered to Lucinda, then rapped his knuckles on the door.

"Come in," a man's voice called from within.

Lord Weston nodded for Lucinda to proceed. "I'll wait out here with the opera dancers," he said, then winked.

Lucinda managed a wary smile in return, then pushed the door open and entered.

She could see the profile of the man as he sat at a large desk, his hands busily rifling through a sheaf of correspondence. He stopped when Lucinda approached, pushing his chair back as he stood.

"Lady Lucinda."

"Lord Carmichael," Lucinda replied with as much confidence as she could.

He gestured for Lucinda to sit, then did the same. "I trust that Lord Weston was a satisfactory escort."

Lucinda took the offered chair, thinking back on Weston's role in tonight's meeting. When she'd threatened to expose the Corinthians if he did not arrange the introduction, he'd agreed, though many colorfully voiced misgivings had accompanied his promise.

"Of course," she answered with conviction.

Lord Carmichael settled back in his chair and propped his elbows on the arms. "Lady Lucinda, please know that we had no other choice but to proceed in such an aggressive fashion."

Lucinda had not come for an apology. While the Corinthians' presence was bothersome, at the moment, they were most comforting as well. All except one.

"Thank you, Lord Carmichael," Lucinda said, pausing to clear her exceedingly parched throat. "But that is not why I'm here. I wish to speak to you about the Duke of Clairemont."

Lord Carmichael fixed his sharp blue eyes on Lucinda. "Clairemont is the best man I have, though his involvement with you beyond a professional level is—"

"With all due respect," she broke in, the heat traveling to her cheeks only humiliating her more. "I do not wish to discuss the personal nature of my relationship with the duke."

Lord Carmichael looked confused at Lucinda's words. "I'm sorry, Lady Lucinda. Then I'm afraid I do not understand the purpose of this conversation," he said gently.

"I would like him to be removed from my situation," Lucinda said plainly.

"That is impossible."

His tone was resolute, his answer immediate.

Lucinda's heart dropped. "Nothing is impossible, Lord Carmichael," she replied desperately. "Surely not for the Young Corinthians."

"Lady Lucinda—"

"Please, my lord," she interrupted, loosening the strings of her cape. "Do not tell me what you cannot do, but rather what you can."

Lord Carmichael rose from his chair and walked to the heavy door, murmuring to the men outside before closing it firmly. "Lady Lucinda," he began, coming to sit on the edge of his desk across from Lucinda. "Your life is in danger. To remove Clairemont from the situation would guarantee your death."

He toyed with the large signet ring on his right hand, the engraved band of gold twisting round and round. "I am sorry for the discomfort that his presence causes you," he paused, his gaze enigmatic as it met hers, "but I cannot endanger you further by making such a tactical error. It is out of the question."

It was clear from Carmichael's tone that he would not change his mind, which meant that there would be no relief from the emotional onslaught that Will brought on with his nearness. His very voice made Lucinda want to weep; his touch when he took her arm in the interest of appearance caused her heart to break all over again.

"I will die either way," she said quietly, hardly aware that she'd uttered the words out loud.

"There is something."

Lucinda looked up slowly at Carmichael, the hesitancy in his eyes giving her pause. "Lord Carmichael?"

He was struggling with how to proceed, that was clear. "May I speak plainly, Lady Lucinda?"

"I insist."

"What I am about to propose to you," he began, pausing to clear his throat. "It will enrage Clairemont.

In all honesty, it might cause him to quit the Corinthians."

"The proposition, Lord Carmichael," Lucinda pressed, her anxiety growing.

"If we were able to draw Garenne out into the open, our considerable forces would most assuredly capture him, bringing what has been an impossible situation for both you and His Grace to an end."

"And how would we go about doing such a thing?" Lucinda asked, her heartbeat quickening.

Carmichael grimly gazed at Lucinda before answering. "With bait, Lady Lucinda."

19

"The kitchen exit?"

"You've already asked after that one, Will," Weston said smoothly, the two surveying the Foster masquerade with expert eyes. "Twice, actually."

"Humor me," Will replied in a barely restrained growl.

Weston winked at a group of giggling young misses in Grecian costumes and golden masks as they strolled past with their mamas in tow. "Four men at the kitchen exit, eight at the main entrance, another four near the doors that—"

"Thank you," Will interrupted, fidgeting with his cuff.

"Try to relax," Weston urged, stopping a servant and taking two flutes of sparkling wine from his tray.

Will accepted a glass and sipped, but his eyes continued to scan the Foster's grand ballroom for signs of danger.

The news that Lucinda had agreed to be used as bait had enraged Will. He'd all but quit the Corinthians, his argument with Carmichael both savage and futile. He'd said such cruel and vicious things to his superior that Will was sure the man would never forgive him. His threats of physical harm had failed to affect the man, Carmichael merely standing his ground and urging Will to do what he felt was needed.

Something in Will had wanted Carmichael to fight

back, a physical encounter preferable to his superior's steady implacability. But Carmichael had coolly refused, choosing instead to recount the reasons why the plan was the only option left. Will's rants had fallen on deaf ears, and eventually he'd stopped yelling long enough to listen.

"Her Grace, the Duchess of Clairemont, and Lord Michael Randall."

The announcement of the arrival of Will's family pulled him from his brooding. The two made their way toward him.

"William," his brother said, briefly nodding in greeting.

Will returned the gesture and turned to the duchess. "Mother, you look lovely this evening."

Her Grace smiled at the words, clearly pleased. "Thank you," she replied, leaning in to offer Will her cheek. She smoothed the skirt of her rose-colored gown, the silver spangles sewn into the bodice shimmering with her movement.

"The Duchess of Highbury, the Marchioness of Mowbray, Lady Charlotte Grey, and Lady Lucinda Grey," the majordomo announced.

"But nowhere near as fetching as Lady Lucinda," the duchess replied, turning to watch Lucinda and the Furies enter the ballroom.

Will had been informed of Lucinda's costume ahead of time, though the description had hardly done the dress justice. She moved gracefully toward him, her head held high and a smile on her face. Her deep blue gown floated about her, the silk shimmering in the candlelight. Rows of beadwork in hues of green, purple, and blue danced about the dress in a fanciful design that echoed the peacock feathers adorning her cleverly designed mask. Her golden hair fell over her shoulders and down her back in a waterfall of soft curls.

Will felt the world stop as she approached.

He loved her. She'd captured him, heart and soul, and now, as he drank in the sight of her, he knew he would never recover.

She swept toward him, coming to stand next to his mother. "Your Grace," she said to the duchess, executing a perfect curtsy, then turning to Will and the rest of the party. "Your Grace, Lord Weston, Lord Michael. How perfectly delightful to see you this evening."

"Lady Lucinda, you look stunning. Is Madame Beaufont the one we must thank for creating such a beautiful costume?" the duchess responded, kissing Lucinda's cheek in a warm greeting.

"Yes," the Duchess of Highbury answered succinctly as the Furies joined the group. "Madame Beaufont's cup of inspiration overflows, as you can see." She gestured to herself and her sisters, whose dresses exactly matched the hues found in Lucinda's mask and gown. Each woman wore a peacock feather neatly tucked into her coiffed hair and a mask that matched her gown.

Will grimaced at the woman's poorly hidden indignation, knowing full well that her ire was aimed at him. The ladies had been instructed to wear the matching gowns so that they were clearly visible among the throng, a precaution that, despite their misgivings, the Furies had not been able to refuse.

"It is quite original, each of you complementing Lucinda's gown," Her Grace reassured the Furies.

"Well, that is one way of looking at things," the sour duchess said acerbically. "Though I have to question whether Madame—"

"Is that a waltz I hear?" Will interrupted, eager to stop her before she continued.

The orchestra had played the opening notes of the next dance and couples moved smoothly to the floor.

"Lady Lucinda," he said, offering her his arm. "I believe this waltz is mine."

"Of course, Your Grace." Her hesitation was so brief as to be barely noticeable by any onlooker. She took his arm and addressed the Furies. "I'll return shortly," she said reassuringly.

Will led Lucinda to the dance floor, a reluctance in her step that belied her agreeable expression. He didn't allow her to tarry for long when stopped by a friend or admirer, a glare from Iron Will proving sufficient to clear the path before them.

They reached the far end of the room. The musicians were situated on a dais at the edge of the polished marble dance floor. Potted palms and tall baskets of flowers were arranged about the perimeter, and a multitude of candelabras added their glow to the chandeliers suspended high over the room.

Will turned to face Lucinda and took her in his arms. The music began, and he expertly swept her into the dance steps, encircling the floor before he spoke.

"Why have you refused me entry into your home this past week?" Will asked simply, the frustration over being kept on duty *outside* the town house—and having to hear of Lucinda's demand from Weston—still lingering in his gut.

Lucinda smiled and nodded at a passing couple before looking at Will. "I did not want to see you."

Her honesty stung. "And your role tonight? Was that an effort to end our acquaintance as well?"

"I certainly have no desire to pit myself against a notorious French assassin, if that is what you are thinking," she replied caustically, turning lightly at his lead.

"You must know that I adamantly opposed your involvement tonight," Will growled, the feel of her in his arms straining his control.

Lucinda stiffened at his words, her mouth thinning to

a firm line. "And you must know that you've no right to feel anything beyond professional concern in this matter, Your Grace."

He wanted to kiss away the anger and hurt that had filled her eyes—tell her he'd been a fool to deny his love for her, and beg her forgiveness. He wanted to forget every last reason that had kept him from following his heart.

"Lucinda, please," he began, his voice harsh and strained with emotion. "You're a woman who deserves much more . . . More than I could ever provide."

She faltered and he caught her, easing her back into the rhythm. "I've no need to hear your excuses," she replied bitterly.

Will knew what she needed to hear.

I love you. God help me, I always will.

"Lucinda . . ." He looked away from her, the pain in her eyes clawing at his heart. His gaze was caught by Weston, who stood propped against the wall just to the left of the orchestra. He gave Will the signal to follow, then started walking.

"Yes?" Lucinda asked, her tone taut.

He stopped abruptly and caught her hand, drawing her with him to the other end of the ballroom. "I'm sorry," he said, his body tightening with grave foreboding. "Something requires my attention at the moment. I'll return you to your aunts."

"Do not touch me," she whispered angrily, tugging her hand from his.

"Lucinda, please—" He reached for her arm.

She recoiled at his touch. Belatedly remembering their audience, she pasted a small smile on her face. "Release me," she said through her teeth.

"I cannot leave you alone."

She glanced behind them to where a hall led to the ladies' retiring room. Two Corinthian agents stood near, pretending to be deep in conversation. "I need a moment to myself, Your Grace," she answered testily, though there was a pleading quality to her tone. "As you can see, I will not be alone."

Will's gaze flicked over the two agents and down the hall. He could not follow her into the retiring room. The need to play this evening perfectly if they were to catch Garenne made it absolutely necessary that everything appear as it should.

"Very well," he agreed reluctantly, but caught Lucinda's elbow as she turned to go. "Do be careful."

"Of course, Your Grace," she said hotly, the fresh tears that showed on her cheeks just below her feathered mask betraying her.

Will watched as she walked down the hall and disappeared into the room, his heart in her hands, though she did not know it.

He vowed then and there that when Garenne had been captured he would tell Lucinda that he loved her. And then he would never let her go.

Lucinda waited until Ladies Turner and Hightower had exited the retiring room before dissolving onto the settee in a puddle of blue silk and hot tears. She yanked off her feathered mask and dropped it into her lap, then savagely tore her gloves off.

She was not a stupid woman. She'd managed to avoid marriage to countless men. She owned a portion of what would surely become the most successful breeding stable in the whole of England. She'd survived despite the deadly threat of a maniacal Frenchman.

No, she was not stupid in the least. Yet she'd bared her heart to Will and asked for his in return—no, begged. And he'd refused.

She breathed deeply in an effort to regain her composure, opening her eyes at the sound of someone in the room.

Hastily, she wiped her tears, embarrassed to be found crying. A woman walked out from behind the curtained area at the end of the room. Lucinda blinked with disbelief at the sight of her.

"Lady Lucinda, I presume," the woman said.

Lucinda had the oddest feeling that she was peering into a mirror. The woman standing before her was the image of herself from head to foot. Same hair, same dress, same voice. It was uncanny, and altogether unsettling.

"Who are you?" Lucinda asked, rising from the settee.

A small malicious smile lifted the woman's lips. She stepped nearer. "That is not important."

"I dare say it is," Lucinda responded with asperity, the hairs rising on the back of her neck.

"There's hardly time to argue, Lady Lucinda." A man emerged from behind the curtain, his tall, wiry form coming to stand directly in front of her. "You've been most uncooperative these past weeks," he said in a low, lethal tone, his black eyes narrowing with cruel, maniacal determination.

"Garenne," Lucinda whispered in grim recognition. She backed away awkwardly, her legs bumping into the settee.

She took him in, her mind trying to reconcile what her eyes saw. He was beautiful—almost too beautiful, his pale complexion, aquiline nose, and full lips more suited to an archangel than the devil she knew him to be.

She looked toward the door, her lungs constricting with fear. "I've only to scream and two Corinthian agents will pounce," she threatened, her voice trembling.

The Frenchman squeezed his eyes shut and dropped

his angular chin, reaching to massage his temples. "Your faith in the duke is really quite heartwarming," he remarked snidely, opening his eyes and smoothing back a lock of his dark brown hair. "But I fear I've reached the end of my patience."

He lunged at Lucinda with such speed she didn't have time to scream. He grabbed her and slapped a rough cotton cloth over her mouth and nose. It smelled awful, the noxious fumes nauseating.

Lucinda lashed out, her arms and legs thrashing as she tried to free herself from Garenne's grasp. She clawed at the devil, her nails cutting into the skin of his hand.

"Stupid chienne!" he uttered, pressing harder on the cloth.

"Delay as long as you can," she heard him say, his thick accent slurring. "Do not let—"

All at once, Lucinda's limbs felt too heavy to move, her arms and legs slowing to a stop. She struggled to speak but her words dissolved into an inaudible whisper.

And then the world went black.

She was taking too long.

"Would you not agree, Your Grace?" Lady Mansfield asked.

"Oh, yes, quite," Will replied, though he had no idea what he'd just agreed to. The woman had accosted him the moment he'd returned to the ballroom afer sending Weston off to investigate a suspicious male, and he'd been trapped ever since.

Lady Mansfield pushed her ridiculous checkered mask back into place and smiled widely at Will. "Excellent."

Bloody hell. Will pinned Weston with an angry stare that told him to hurry along.

Weston smiled, clearly enjoying Will's pain as he joined the two.

"Lady Mansfield," Weston began. "I'm afraid I've need of the duke—quite a serious matter, I assure you," he said smoothly, winking at the woman as he extricated Will from her grasp.

"Oh, well, of course," she replied, somewhat reluctantly.

"Thank you," Weston mouthed at Lady Mansfield, wriggling his eyebrows.

The woman turned to rejoin a group of friends near the refreshments.

"Well?" Will asked expectantly, the sight of Lucinda emerging from the retiring room slightly easing his anxiety.

"A man of interest was found in an upper room. He's been detained in the library," Weston answered, his serious tone belying his lazy demeanor.

Will listened with keen interest to Weston's report, though his eyes remained fixed on Lucinda as she walked down the hall.

She hesitated for a moment when her gaze met Will's, offering him a small smile before threading her way through the crowded ballroom.

"Come with me," he ordered Weston. Instinct had him moving to follow her before he realized what he was doing. As he purposefully made his way through the throngs of revelers, he noticed her hair color, just a shade off from his vivid memory of her lying back in the library, her golden hair fanning out about her beautiful face.

His eyes narrowed, his gaze lowering to the woman's shoulders as she picked up her pace. He'd never forget the exactitude with which Lucinda's slender shoulders fit into his embrace, as if they were made only for each other. This woman's shoulder span was slightly wider than Lucinda's, though Will doubted anyone other than he would have noticed.

He was nearly upon her now, his alert senses all but

confirming what he suspected. He caught hold of her arm just as she turned to leave. Pulling her around to face him, he looked at her mouth. Her lips lacked the lush fullness and unique hue of pink that Lucinda's possessed. Nor was her nose a complete match, though Will mentally congratulated Garenne on finding such a passable double. Dread filled his heart as he pulled the feathered mask from the imposter's face.

He spared but a moment to look at her before gesturing for Weston to take her away. And then he ran, screams of surprise erupting from those he pushed aside as he urgently made his way toward the retiring room. He raced down the hall with two Corinthian agents close behind and kicked in the door.

A swift search verified Will's worst fears—they found no one.

"Your Grace." Agent Chilson drew Will's attention to an open window.

Will strode across the room and peered out, noting the distance to the ground. It would have been risky, but Garenne could have accomplished such a task if he'd lowered Lucinda to someone waiting below.

He gripped the window frame with both hands, his lungs struggling to fill with air. "Chilson, have Weston bring the woman to the library. You," he said to the two other agents, "search the grounds."

He released the frame and stood, willing himself to remain calm. He would find her. There was no other option.

20

Lucinda awoke with a pounding headache, disoriented and terrified. She felt about in the pitch black, reaching blindly for anything that might tell her where she was. Her knuckles suddenly scraped against a cold brass knob. She turned it and pushed gently, but the door would not open.

She put her eye to the keyhole and peered out. The outer room was lit, blinding her for a moment.

She squinted until her vision adjusted, then looked again. The room beyond was dingy, its dirty windows shabbily hung with torn curtains. Sagging furniture was arranged haphazardly. And Garenne bent over a large desk, humming a haunting tune while busily writing.

Lucinda pressed her hand tightly over her mouth to hold back a scream. She had no memory beyond the attack in the retiring room that had ended with the foul-smelling handkerchief over her nose. Clearly he'd managed to spirit her away. But to where?

The musty smell of her prison wasn't that of a salt-encrusted sailing vessel, so she felt sure the Frenchman hadn't brought her aboard a ship. The reassurance that she was still on English soil gave her reason to believe that Will would come for her. But she could hardly sit and wait for his arrival, the little she'd been told of Garenne having indicated that he was not to be underestimated.

She reached for the hem of her dress and lifted it, fingers searching her inner thigh for the small knife that she'd strapped there when dressing for the ball.

The sounds of Garenne's approaching footsteps startled her, nearly causing her to drop the knife. She caught the weapon with her other hand and quickly jammed it into the keyhole.

"Lady Lucinda," Garenne called in a disturbingly calm voice. "It is time to rise and meet your destiny."

Lucinda tightened her grip on the knife and held her breath.

He put the key in the hole and turned the knob, jiggling it forcefully in rapid succession. "Come now, do you really think that a wooden door will keep you safe?" He let go of the knob and threw his body toward the door, the wooden slats absorbing the blows with audible cracks. "You stupid chienne. You've tried my patience for the very last time."

Lucinda bit the inside of her cheek, panic rising in her throat. He rammed the door again and a horrified scream escaped from her lips.

"Come out, Garenne. You're surrounded."

The booming voice from outside the house startled Lucinda, sending her jerking back and away from the door. She landed against the far wall with a thud and dropped the knife. She scrambled forward on her hands and knees, desperately searching for the weapon. Her fingers closed over the haft and she gasped with relief. Clutching the knife, she looked out the keyhole, searching for Garenne. He was back at the desk once again, hastily stuffing documents into a leather satchel.

"Do not be concerned, Lady Lucinda," he said over his shoulder, the malevolence in his voice making Lucinda's blood run cold. "We will be leaving here together. Whether you will be alive or dead, well"—he closed the clasp on the bag and turned to cross the room—"that is up to your duke."

Another shout from outside was followed by a loud crack. Garenne's footsteps stopped and Lucinda held her breath, waiting.

The sound of Garenne's retreating footsteps and the low creak of stairs reached Lucinda's ears. She knelt and peered out the keyhole. He was nowhere to be seen, the dingy room empty once more. Fearing what the French madman planned for those who waited outside, she set to work on the lock and prayed that she would escape in time to warn them.

Carmichael had offered Garenne's decoy passage to Canada if she gave them the Frenchman's location. She'd acquiesced, the loyalty between thieves and murderers evidently as expendable as their consciences.

The late-night ride had been pure torture, images of Garenne with his hands on Lucinda flashing in Will's head. He'd urged Sol on at breakneck speed, the entire contingent of Corinthian agents hard on the stallion's heels. They'd slowed to a walk once the hovel had been spied, Will using hand signals to tell his men where to deploy.

He'd taken the lead position, dropping from Sol's back and picking his way through the heavy brush that surrounded the cottage. He walked the perimeter of the house, crouching down at each window to carefully conceal his presence. When Weston signaled that the men were in place, Will had pounded on the door and demanded that Garenne give himself up.

Silence greeted him. Will was hardly surprised, but what little patience he possessed had been used up long ago. He pounded on the door again and yelled for the Frenchman to come out, punctuating his request with a savage kick that left the door split near the bottom.

He was readying himself to kick it in when one of his men shouted for him to stand clear. Will spun, assuming the threat came from behind, but he found himself pinned to the ground under Garenne, the man's pistol poised at Will's temple.

"Your Grace, we meet again."

It took all of Lucinda's remaining mental fortitude to hold fear at bay while she picked the lock. She grunted with relief as the lock gave and opened the door slowly, not entirely sure what she might find on the other side. She narrowed her eyes and glanced quickly around the room. Male voices shouted just beyond the front door.

Frantically, she peered through the darkness, looking for another door. Finding one at the back of the cottage, she pulled on it, prying it open a crack so she could peer out.

Suddenly, the doorknob was yanked from her grip as someone pushed the door wide. Hands grabbed her and pulled her roughly outside; a man rolled with her onto the ground. The scream building in her throat was stopped by a large hand clapped over her mouth. She kicked and struggled against the heavy weight on top of her. He rolled her onto her back with one swift motion. Lucinda flailed her arms and desperately wished for her knife, but it had been knocked free from her hand in the melee.

"Lady Lucinda?" Lord Chilson whispered gruffly, taking his hand from her mouth and looking at her as if attempting to memorize her face. "Is that you?"

Lucinda nodded her head frantically. "Where is Will?"

Chilson climbed off of Lucinda and stood, offering his hand to her. "Are you all right?" he demanded.

"Garenne is loose, we must find him." Lucinda pushed her tangled hair out of her eyes. "*Now*," she implored, though Chilson only looked to the other Corinthians standing behind her.

"Why are you not moving?" she demanded, her entire body shaking.

Chilson took her by the arm and pulled her toward a grassy outcropping where King Solomon's Mine stood, pushing her down onto a large boulder. "Garenne captured Clairemont near the front of the cottage. You must wait here—where it's safe."

His words froze Lucinda's heart, seizing her breath. She could not lose Will, not now.

She wasn't about to sit idly by and allow him to be killed, even if it meant defying the Corinthians. She scrambled to a standing position on the boulder and grabbed Sol's reins, hoisting herself onto his back in one smooth motion. She kicked her leg over and settled into the large saddle, yanking the voluminous skirts of her gown free to allow her to sit astride.

Too late, Chilson realized what she was doing and lunged for the horse. His hand just missed the Thoroughbred's hindquarters as Lucinda kneed King Solomon into motion. She trotted him to the corner of the house, stopping at the sight of several Corinthian officers.

Garenne and Will stood with their backs to her, the Frenchman's pistol cocked and held at Will's temple while he shouted his demands to Lord Weston.

Fear gripped Lucinda as she took in the sight. She would have only one chance to save Will. She looked to Lord Weston and captured his attention with a wave. Swiftly gesturing with her hands and indicating her plan of attack, she shook off his clear refusal. He looked back to the two men, gesturing to Will to be ready.

Lucinda gripped Sol's reins with one hand and wound her other into his mane. Then she kicked her heels hard into his ribs and the Thoroughbred exploded, moving forward in a blur of speed. Despite the thunder of hooves, Garenne had only just turned when Solomon reached him.

Cursing, he lifted his pistol and aimed at the horse. Will grabbed his arm and the gun went off. King Solomon reared, whinnying with fear at the sound of the shot. Will savagely lashed out at Garenne, landing a blow to his jaw that sent the man to the ground. Sol reared again, this time crushing Garenne beneath the force of his massive, slicing hooves as he came back down to earth.

Lucinda's hold on his reins and mane was jolted loose. She threw her arms around the stallion's neck, hanging on desperately as he bolted toward the edge of the clearing.

It took seconds to catch the reins and pull herself upright, tugging Solomon to a stop. He stood, shuddering and wild-eyed as she slid off his back. She looped the reins around a tree branch then ran back to Will.

She threw herself into his arms, burying her face in his neck.

"What the bloody hell did you think you were doing?" he began, pushing her to stand at arm's length. "You could have been killed!" he yelled, then pulled her back in, crushing her lips with a soul-searing kiss.

He broke the kiss abruptly and stared down into her eyes. "You saved my life," he said, his voice hoarse.

"And you saved mine," Lucinda replied, her hands reaching to cup his face. "You brave, bloody fool!"

"You are the brave one, Lucinda, you," he began, looking at her with such love and devotion. "I was a coward. I couldn't see my way clear—I was afraid of what I felt, afraid of what it would mean to admit such a thing—"

He stopped abruptly and swallowed hard. "I love you, Lucinda. I have all along."

Lucinda's heart felt ready to burst with joy as she pulled his face to hers, their lips nearly touching. "It is about time, Your Grace."

He closed the distance between them and kissed her again, a tender lingering touch that filled Lucinda's heart with hope anew.

"Promise me you will never attempt such a dangerous act again," he said as he gathered her more closely to himself.

All around them was chaos, Corinthians descending on Garenne's body while others tended to the nervously dancing King Solomon's Mine. Carmichael aided Lord Weston, who had been grazed in the leg by Garenne's haphazardly fired bullet.

But here, with Will by her side, all was quiet, the world finally as it should be.

"You'll need to make an honest woman of me to earn such a promise, Your Grace."

"Bloody hell, woman, is that all?"

"Hardly."

"Good," he replied, a crooked smile capturing his mouth. "I would hate to think that love had softened your self-possession."

Lucinda laughed knowingly as she looked up into the dark canopy of trees overhead, the moonlit sky peeking through here and there. "Oh, Your Grace. You've no idea. No idea at all.

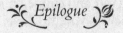# Epilogue

CASTLE CLAIREMONT
DERBYSHIRE
1812

Will rubbed Lucinda's lower back gently, causing his beautiful wife to emit small sighs of relief. "Shall I fetch a chair?" he asked, looking with concern at her sizeable belly where it just skimmed the wood fencing.

Lucinda raised a hand to her brow, shadowing her eyes from the bright sun in order to see the new stallion as he romped in the pasture. "Will, I'm perfectly fine," she answered reassuringly. "Now tell me, what do you think of Thor?"

Will's gaze followed Lucinda's, catching sight of the majestic bay Thoroughbred as he pranced about in the lush green field. The horse had arrived only the day before, yet he'd settled in with ease. "I think my opinion is of no consequence. It's what you see that matters."

"Smart man," Lucinda confirmed, turning to Will and smiling beatifically. "His legs are as straight as they come and his eyes—oh, so kind, yet the sheer, unadulterated pleasure in them when he runs? Yes, I think he'll serve your mares well."

"Better than Sol, then?" Will asked wistfully.

Lucinda reached out and cupped his face in her hands. "I miss him as much as you, my love. But I fear Cleopatra would perish if we were to separate the two—never mind my aunts."

Will knew she was right, of course, the aunts having taken control of the Grey breeding program with iron—and quite expert—fists. In little more than a year the first of Sol's offspring would race, and anyone worth his spurs was sure that it would be *the* moment to see. He would not stir up trouble between Lucinda and her aunts simply because he missed his horse.

He couldn't.

He wouldn't.

Will turned his attention back to his wife, her growing belly making him smile once more. So much had happened in the last year that Will wondered at times if it was all a dream. He'd allowed himself to love and be loved, something he thought was not possible. And surprisingly enough, his world had not ended, but rather expanded in a way that he could have never imagined.

His involvement with the Corinthians had changed drastically, which had surprisingly suited Will perfectly. His life was so full now that he was no longer the angry Iron Will of old, who'd run from his demons while lacking a true path.

He'd found that true path, and blessed peace, at Lucinda's side.

His wife dropped her hands to her hips and breathed deeply.

"Are you quite sure you wouldn't like a chair?" Will pressed.

"Yes," Lucinda replied, turning back to watch Thor. "Your mother and Lord Pinehurst are due to arrive any moment. I hardly want to be found dusty and smelling of horses when they do."

It had taken time. A lot of time, actually, but Will and

his mother were slowly reclaiming the love that had been lost between them. Will could not say that he'd let go of the past entirely, but he'd made a start. They'd made a start, together.

"Will they marry?"

Lucinda eyed Will hesitantly. "Do you want them to?"

"I do, actually," Will replied, rather surprised at his answer. "Do not misunderstand me. All this family needs is another pigheaded male. But they do seem to care for each other. Quite a bit, from what I've seen— though I'm hardly a judge of such things."

"You have the softest of hearts—"

"Speaking of pigheaded men," Will interrupted, sure that his wife would dissolve into a puddle of tears if he did not, "where is that brother of mine?"

"Practicing his proposal on Serendipity."

Will came to stand next to Lucinda at the fence line, capturing her with an unabashedly confused stare. "What could my prized mare have to do with a proposal? And, more important, what could Michael have to do with either?"

"He's intent on asking Lady Mariah for her hand— but not before he's spoken to you first," Lucinda replied, her eyes glistening. "He'll leave for London straightaway after the baby is born, so please, do make yourself available. You've been so caught up in the harvest I fear he hasn't had the opportunity to broach the topic."

"Why on earth would the man want to talk to me? What do I know about proper courtship and proposals?"

Lucinda looked at him full in the face and Will knew they'd not escape the day without one more good cry. "Because you're his brother—a true and proper one, now that you've taken back the ducal responsibilities."

"Don't cry, Lucinda. I'll talk to Mich—"

"It's just that I'm so proud of all you've done. For Michael, and for your mother. But especially for yourself," she said, the tears slowly beginning to slide down her full cheeks.

Lucinda turned to look at Thor, who had stretched his long neck over the fence and was now nudging his nose up against Lucinda's belly. "Tell me that you're as happy as I am."

Will reached out and patted the giant horse softly on the head. "Indeed. And more, my love. So much more."

Acknowledgments

They say that it takes a village to raise a child. Oddly enough, I found the same to be true of writing and producing a book.

Randall. You are mine, and I am yours. I'm pretty sure that I got the better end of the bargain, but I'll take it. Thank you for loving me far better than I could ever love myself.

The Girls. You challenge me to be a better person every single day. No, really. Every. Single. Day. And I love you all the more for it. XO to infinity.

Wallace Dyer Jr. Thank you for Bob Dylan and Diet Sprite, for Christmas trees and deliciously crude humor. You left us too soon.

Michael Dyer. You rolled me down a hill in a box when we were young and told me whatever didn't kill me would make me stronger. You were right.

Julie Pottinger. You picked me up and brushed me off when I needed you to, laughed and cried with me, and convinced me that the impossible *was* possible if tackled one step at a time. Thank you for walking the road with me.

Jennifer Schober. One. Awesome. Agent. Thank you for reminding me that it's all in the journey, not the destination.

Junessa Viloria. Best. Editor. Ever. Your professionalism, editorial skills, and keen reader's eye made this book what it is. Thank you for taking a chance on me.

Jennifer McCord. You shared your expertise and insight at no cost, encouraged me to follow my heart, and became a dear friend. For all of this and more, I thank you. And I promise that we will never again visit *the* spa.

Franzeca Drouin. I've said it before and I'll say it again: Your brain, it is an impressive thing. Thank you for your mad research skills, ability to meet ridiculous deadlines, and coolness in general.

Read on for an enticing extract of

The Angel in My Arms

Stefanie Sloane's second Regency Rogues novel

Available now from Headline Eternal

SUMMER; DORSET
1811

Marcus MacInnes, the Earl of Weston, looked out over Lulworth Cove and chuckled. "Well now, Sully, you've seen it for yourself. Aye, it's my own personal Jericho. Wouldn't you agree?"

The valet's swarthy face remained unreadable, the lines around his eyes deepening as he squinted, his gaze focused on what lay below them. The cove's blue water lapped at the hulls of fishing boats. On the shore, the village dozed sleepily in the warm sunshine.

Exactly the sort of spot a gentleman might just be sent to rusticate after a gunshot wound. Especially if the gentleman happened to be a spy.

Sully turned to look directly at his master. "It looks quiet enough, I'll give you that."

Marcus smiled wryly before turning his horse back onto the leafy path. "Indeed."

Sully followed suit, kneeing his bay gelding next to Marcus's chestnut Thoroughbred. "There *could* be smugglers."

Marcus slowed his mount just long enough to give him a dubious look.

"Or not," Sully admitted somewhat dejectedly.

Marcus ducked his head to dodge a low-hanging limb and the green leaves of one of the massive whitebeam trees that lined the trail. "What a waste of time."

But there was nothing he could do about it. He'd been given an order, and he'd bloody well follow it.

Marcus was a Corinthian, and that meant something. Damn it.

He and Sully continued on in silence. Their horses, Marcus thought absently, seemed thankful for the slower pace after the three-day ride from London to Lulworth.

The shaded lane curved, and ahead of the two riders rose Lulworth Castle, Marcus's home. Originally built as a hunting lodge, the impressive structure had been expanded over the years until it was the largest home in the district.

The unentailed castle belonged to Marcus, due to his mother having been an only child. Yes, it was all his. And it was undeniably magnificent. But it was not where he wanted to be.

Marcus was a member of the Young Corinthians, a clandestine spy organization led by Henry Prescott, Viscount Carmichael. There was an unwritten rule among the Corinthians never to question an assignment. The life of a spy demanded complete loyalty and unswerving belief in your superior's judgment—a fact Marcus found tiresome at the moment.

When a bullet found its way into his leg during a mission this past spring, Marcus had known that his role within the elite organization would change dramatically. Until his injury fully healed, he was more of a liability than an asset in the field.

Nevertheless, when Lord Carmichael suggested that Marcus investigate recent smuggling activity near his ancestral home in Dorset, Marcus nearly abandoned his well-practiced charm and informed his superior just what he thought of the ridiculous assignment.

Finding yourself with a bullet in your leg was one thing. Having your superior send you off on a fool's errand was quite another.

He couldn't deny that in all likelihood he'd made himself something of a nuisance to Carmichael as he impatiently waited for his blasted wound to heal.

And if he admitted that much, then he really could not blame Carmichael for dispatching him to the Dorset countryside when news of a possible connection between radical revolutionaries and local smugglers had the prince Regent's drawers in a twist.

As Carmichael had informed him over plates of roast beef at their club, a string of recent robberies in London was believed to be related to the suspicious activities in Lulworth—and both were somehow tied to Napoleon's supporters.

Marcus had only stared at Carmichael in disbelief, a heavy goblet of brandy poised halfway to his mouth. Really, it was too much to be believed.

But still, Marcus now reluctantly realized, if he was to be completely honest, his irritation with the assignment had as much to do with the location as with the smuggling investigation itself.

During his boyhood, when not in Inverness at his father's estate, the family had split its time between London and Lulworth. At least in London he'd been able to lose himself amid the constant thrum of social and sporting events. But the same could not be said for Lulworth. The hamlet's inhabitants had never gotten over his Scottish father's stealing away the fairest of their English roses. It hadn't helped that the elder Lord Weston embraced his role as the brutish Highlander with particular relish. His habit of donning a tartan and broadsword whenever his family visited the castle had only made things worse.

The locals hadn't liked the father, and as a result, they didn't like the son. And Marcus had known, from a painfully early age, that he simply did not fit in. Not in Lulworth, where everyone from the baker's son to the solicitor's daughter saw him as nothing more than the son of a thief. Not in Inverness either, where the blue English blood in his veins meant he'd never be a true Highlander.

"I've sorely missed Cook's pheasant," Sully said, pulling Marcus from his thoughts.

The stone castle stood before them with all the welcoming warmth of a midwinter snowfall.

"You're an accomplished liar, Sully, I'll give you that." Marcus's amiable tone belied his recent grim thoughts. "But I know you too well. It's Cook that you've been looking forward to, not her creamed peas."

"Pheasant," Sully corrected him. "And it's quite a succulent bird that she cooks," he protested. "Though her creamed peas are quite delicious as well."

Marcus reined in his horse and raised a hand. "Far be it from me to intrude upon the ways of love," he said sardonically, prompting a harrumph from his valet.

With a noticeable lack of his usual ease, Marcus awkwardly swung a leg over the saddle and lowered himself to the ground, an instant stab of pain shooting up from the healing wound in his thigh. He ground his teeth together until the sensation subsided, then drew the soft leather reins over Pokey's head and handed them to Sully. "I'm going to walk off this stiffness. I'll be along shortly."

Sully gave Marcus a considering look then leaned from the saddle to take the reins. "Are you up to it?"

"Awa' an' bile yer heid!" Marcus growled, though the valet's thoughtfulness made him smile.

"Oh," Sully began, turning the two horses toward the stables, "I'll be missing that burr of yours while we're here. Can't be playing Lord of the Manor like one of them Jacobites, now, can we?" he teased. "I'll be in the kitchen, then."

"Oh, that's a given," Marcus shot back, sounding like the perfect London swell. For as long as he could remember, he had made it a habit to hide his burr from everyone but Sully and the Scottish side of his family. There was simply no good reason to remind people of his ancestry.

"I'll send the hounds out if you've not limped your way home by dark."

"That's terribly thoughtful of you, old friend."

"Don't mention it—"

"And I do mean *old*," Marcus added with a gleam in his eye.

He could just make out another harrumph as Sully clucked to his horse and rode on, his pace quickening as he disappeared into the copse of trees that separated the expansive lawn of Lulworth from the rest of the grounds.

Marcus stretched, trying to ease the aches in his travel-weary muscles without irritating his wound. He turned and strolled, limping slightly, toward the wood, his destination undecided. The tension that had gripped his gut when he'd first spied the castle slowly dissipated as he moved farther into the trees. He tugged at his carefully tied cravat, a low sigh escaping his lips as he yanked the length of white linen free of its intricate knot and unwound it from his throat. He mopped his brow with the dust-covered cloth before dropping it into the pocket of his deep brown riding coat.

The shade from the green-leafed canopy of oak trees provided some relief, but Marcus needed more. He stopped to orient himself, looking north, then east. Realizing that he wasn't far from the lake where he'd fished as a child, he set off at a faster clip.

A refreshing swim was precisely what he needed. The water would cool his body, clear his head, and, hopefully, tire him to the point that he no longer cared about where he was.

A high-pitched scream shattered the quiet and stopped Marcus in his tracks. A second scream followed, and Marcus ran, willing his wounded leg to keep pace with the rest of his body as he crashed through a bank of quickthorn bushes.

He fought his way through the thicket, the branches lashing his arms and legs until he broke into the open. The castle lake lay before him, sparkling in the sunlight.

He examined the water's surface, then the shore from left to right, but failed to find the source of the screams. Something moved suddenly in his peripheral vision. He narrowed his eyes and once more searched the lake. Water rippled in a circle too large to have been caused by a jumping trout.

He stripped off his coat and prepared to dive in. Just then two figures broke the surface of the water. A peal of feminine laughter filled the air.

"You promised!" a young male voice whined indignantly.

Marcus squinted against the sun and made out a boy, sodden hair plastered to his skull.

"I never promised, Nigel," a woman's voice answered teasingly, "and it's very poor form of you to lie."

Marcus shielded his eyes with one hand to see the woman better. She bobbed up and down in the water, clearly amused with whatever had transpired between her and the boy.

Suddenly she looked straight at him, her eyes widening in surprise.

And then she smiled. A brilliant, wide smile that

seemed to light up the entire world. She was soaking wet, auburn curls in damp corkscrews atop her head and hanging to her shoulders. Her ivory skin flushed under the hot sun, a trailing frond of green water weed peeking out above the neckline of her dress.

Marcus could not imagine a more bonny sight.

She seemed about to speak to him when her gaze shifted past him and over his shoulder. Shock and dismay filled her expression. "No, Titus!" she cried out. "No!"

Marcus turned his head just in time to make out a massive dog galloping toward him. The fawn-colored animal launched itself into the air, toppling Marcus backward onto the clay earth of the lake bank.

The weight of the beast's body settled on Marcus's chest and it planted a dinner-plate-sized paw on either side of Marcus's head. Then the dog lowered its massive face, the drool from its sharp-fanged mouth threatening to drop at any moment.

Marcus held himself completely still, knowing full well the animal had the upper hand. The dog sniffed carefully, its noxious breath hitting Marcus's nostrils with pungent force.

"Titus, get off that gentleman now. This! Very! Instant!"

The dog offered Marcus a sheepish, apologetic look before swiping its lolling tongue in friendly salute across Marcus's face.

"Now! Get off him. You bad, bad boy!"

Another apologetic look and the dog rose, allowing Marcus to sit up.

The woman leaned down to peer anxiously into Marcus's face.

"I must apologize for my dog's behavior," she said earnestly, now leaning so close that Marcus felt tiny droplets of lake water hit his skin when she moved.

"He is—"

"A menace to society?" the young boy at her side offered, giving Marcus a toothy grin.

"He is an enthusiastic participant in life." The woman rose to her feet to glare at the boy. "Titus is simply in need of proper instruction in manners."

"That is one way of looking at him," the boy countered, pointing at the dog, who was now a few feet away and busily tearing holes in Marcus's castoff coat.

"Titus!" the woman protested, dashing toward the Shetland pony–sized dog. She tripped on a tree root and landed awkwardly on all fours, her nicely rounded derriere sticking up in the air.

Marcus stood with difficulty, wincing, his leg throbbing like the devil. He brushed without much success at the dirt stains on his buff-colored breeches and white linen shirt.

"Who is she?" he asked, failing to hide his stunned reaction.

The boy, whose features exactly matched the young woman's, chuckled. "Oh, no one of consequence, I assure you." He offered his hand to Marcus and shook enthusiastically. "I, on the other hand, am Nigel Edward Tisdale."

She was now engaged in a heated game of tug-of-war with the dog, her petite frame hardly a match for the big dog's superior strength.

"Marcus MacInnes, Earl of Weston," Marcus replied, hiding his burr with practiced ease. His gaze returned to the woman. "I wonder, should we assist Miss—"

"Not *the* Errant Earl?" the boy asked in wonder.

Marcus turned and looked at the lad, assuming that he had misheard. "I'm sorry, what was that you said?"

"Surely you know what people in these parts call you? I'd rather poke myself in the eye with a sharpened stick than listen to my mother and her friends gossip, but even I've heard the talk, and it's—what's the word I'm looking for?" Young Nigel paused and drummed his fingers against his lips as he thought.

"Unfavorable," Marcus offered helpfully.

"Well, I was going to say 'downright nasty,' but yes, 'unfavorable' will do."

Clearly, while the world about it continuously moved forward, the village of Lulworth stalwartly cleaved to unfounded and exaggerated assumptions. Marcus assumed that he should be offended, but honestly, he had neither the energy nor the interest at the moment.

He looked back to the woman, who was desperately attempting to maintain her foothold. "Shouldn't we . . ." he began, gesturing toward the pair.

"Oh, no, that would irritate Sarah to no end," the boy answered, watching the scene with marked delight as he wrung out his sodden shirt. "And trust me, you don't want to irritate my sister."

Marcus couldn't help but picture the woman irritated—enraged, really, as he sensed it would take very little to make her so. Her auburn hair flying about her like a fiery halo, her skin heated to a delicious pink hue.

Marcus shook his head from left to right, wondering if the dog had indeed done some sort of damage to his mental faculties.

The two males watched for a moment more as the woman dug in her heels and seemed to be gaining the upper hand. But then the dog began to drag her forward, pulling her lower and closer to the ground until she collapsed with an audible expulsion of breath, face-down in the dirt.

"Sarah?" the boy queried in a mischievous tone. "Have you rescued Lord Weston's coat?"

The woman froze. Then slowly she released the torn

coat and pulled herself upright, brushing lightly at the front of her wet, mud-stained gown.

"I beg your pardon, Nigel. Did you say 'Lord Weston'?"

The dog galloped to a stop beside her and dropped the coat at her feet.

"Bad dog!" she whispered vehemently, bending to snatch up the torn garment.

The boy elbowed Marcus in the ribs. "Why yes, Sarah," he said, drawing her attention back to her question. "The coat belongs to *Lord Weston*."

The lady's demeanor changed instantly. She leveled a cool glance at her brother, her chin tilting slightly higher. Her diminutive shoulders squared and she attempted to unobtrusively peel the clingy gown from her fair skin.

Marcus stifled a laugh. She was covered from head to toe in dirt and God only knew what else. Any woman in her right mind would have fainted from the embarrassment of the situation. And, he realized, any man would have politely excused himself by now.

Yet, here he was.

"I do apologize for my dog's behavior, Lord Weston," she said agreeably. The trailing bit of bracken at her hemline did little to aid her dignity as she walked toward him. "And I will, of course, pay for the damages to your coat."

She thrust the ruined article of clothing toward him, avoiding his gaze.

"Mother is going to be apoplectic when she hears about this!" Nigel said with glee.

She caught Nigel's arm with some force, if the boy's pained expression was any indication. "Nigel, make yourself useful and properly introduce us, please."

"She'll be abed for days with this one—"

"Nigel!" the young woman remonstrated, maintaining a polite, if strained smile.

"Very well," Nigel begrudgingly agreed. "Sarah Elizabeth Tisdale, may I present Marcus MacInnes, the Earl of Weston."

The bizarre quality of the moment was not lost on Marcus. Here he stood, clothing torn and mauled by what was clearly the result of a misguided romantic encounter between a canine and a large bear. The female standing in front of him was in absolute and, not to put too fine a point on it, scandalous disarray. And a devilish sprite was performing polite introductions in the middle of the wood.

It was of Shakespearean proportions, a farce, to be sure.

He should be appalled. Any man of his standing would be.

But he was delighted.

And he couldn't remember a time that he'd been so thankful for the ache in his leg and the need of a walk.

"Miss Tisdale," he said, offering a respectful bow in her direction.

She offered an awkward curtsy. "Lord Weston, I'm delighted to make your acquaintance."

Marcus found it oddly amusing, their mutual adherence to the proprieties despite the clearly improper circumstances of this encounter. "And I yours."

She looked at him then, a blush settling on her ivory skin. "We were not aware you were in residence at the castle."

"Do you only make use of the lake in my absence?" he asked teasingly, his charm returning.

"I can assure you, sir, that we do not make a habit of trespassing on your—"

"We most certainly do," Nigel interrupted indignantly. "It's the best fishing in the county."

Miss Tisdale looked as if she might spontaneously combust. The flush of heat traveling from her neck upward would most certainly erupt in flames upon reaching her auburn curls.

She took a deep breath, an impish grin coming to rest on her lips. "Oh, all right, then. We do. Now, Nigel," she paused, looking about as if searching for something, and then whistling in a most unladylike fashion, "do secure Titus's leash."

The earth shook as the huge dog ran toward them. Marcus braced himself as Titus came to a sliding stop mere inches from his legs.

Nigel retrieved a leather lead, coiled in a serpentine pile near the bank. "I don't know why we bother with this. It would hardly keep him—"

Miss Tisdale daintily cleared her throat and shot Nigel a murderous look. "The lead, Nigel."

No sooner had the boy obeyed than Titus lifted his massive head and caught the scent of something on the wind. He bounded off with Nigel in tow, leaving Marcus and Miss Tisdale quite alone.

She watched as Titus dragged her brother along, a small smile forming on her mouth. "Serves him right," she said under her breath.

Marcus pretended not to hear her, as it was the polite thing to do. Still, he smiled.

He could not look away. The sun had begun to dry her mass of auburn hair so that it gleamed in the sun, threads of gold catching the light in a dizzying array. He wanted to reach out and touch it, to measure the weight of it in his hands.

Her profile enthralled him. Her pert nose—sprinkled with freckles, no less—was the perfect accompaniment to her high cheekbones and that damnably kissable mouth.

"I apologize, Lord Weston," she offered quietly, without looking at him.

Marcus abruptly ended his cataloging of her features. "For trespassing or for Titus?" he quipped.

"Both, actually," she answered, turning to look at him, a charming smirk lighting up her face. "And the mud. I'm really quite sorry for the mud."

And just like that, she ran from the lake bank and disappeared into the shrubbery, her long auburn hair swaying behind her as she went.

"What in bloody hell just happened?" Marcus said aloud, not sure what to do next.

The Angel in my Arms

**A Regency Rogues novel of lethal spy
games and exhilarating passion.**

Marcus MacInnes, the Earl of Weston: A sinfully handsome
agent tasked with a mission involving a smuggling ring.

Miss Sarah Tisdale: An unconventional beauty
whose family are under suspicion.

Amidst an unlikely case, desires burn and love simmers.
With everything on the line, will passion prevail?

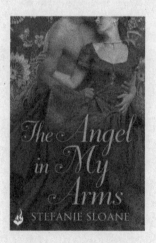

'Utterly delectable and seductive'
Teresa Medeiros

The Sinner Who Seduced Me

**A Regency Rogues novel of daring spy
games and smouldering passion.**

James Marlowe: An agent with the riskiest
of missions to infiltrate a deadly French crime ring.

Lady Clarissa Collins: The exquisitely stunning woman
who broke his heart and is in great peril.

Ex-lovers thrown together in the most lethal of situations.
Can the past be put behind to save one another?

'Powerfully emotional, sexually charged'
Romantic Times

The Saint Who Stole My Heart

A Regency Rogues novel of danger, intrigue and steamy seduction.

Dashiell Matthews, Viscount Carrington: An impossibly handsome spy on the hunt for a notorious London murderer.

Miss Elena Barnes: A voluptuous beauty as intelligent as she is fearless.

As fate causes the crossing of paths, will everything be risked as the two join forces?

'Everything readers of Regency romance crave'
Amanda Quick

The Scoundrel Takes a Bride

A Regency Rogues novel of dangerous spy games and seductive passion.

The Right Honourable Nicholas Bourne: A notorious scoundrel whose help is sought on a dangerous mission.

Lady Sophia Southwell: The secret love of his life promised to his brother, who needs his help exacting revenge.

Together on the darkest of cases, will love overpower vengeance?

'Perfect blend of tender romance and heart stopping adventure'
Fresh Fiction